Second Olympus

K.A. STEWART

Also From K.A. Stewart

The Jesse James Dawson Series
A Devil in the Details
A Shot in the Dark
A Wolf at the Door
A Snake in the Grass

The Arcane West Trilogy
Peacemaker

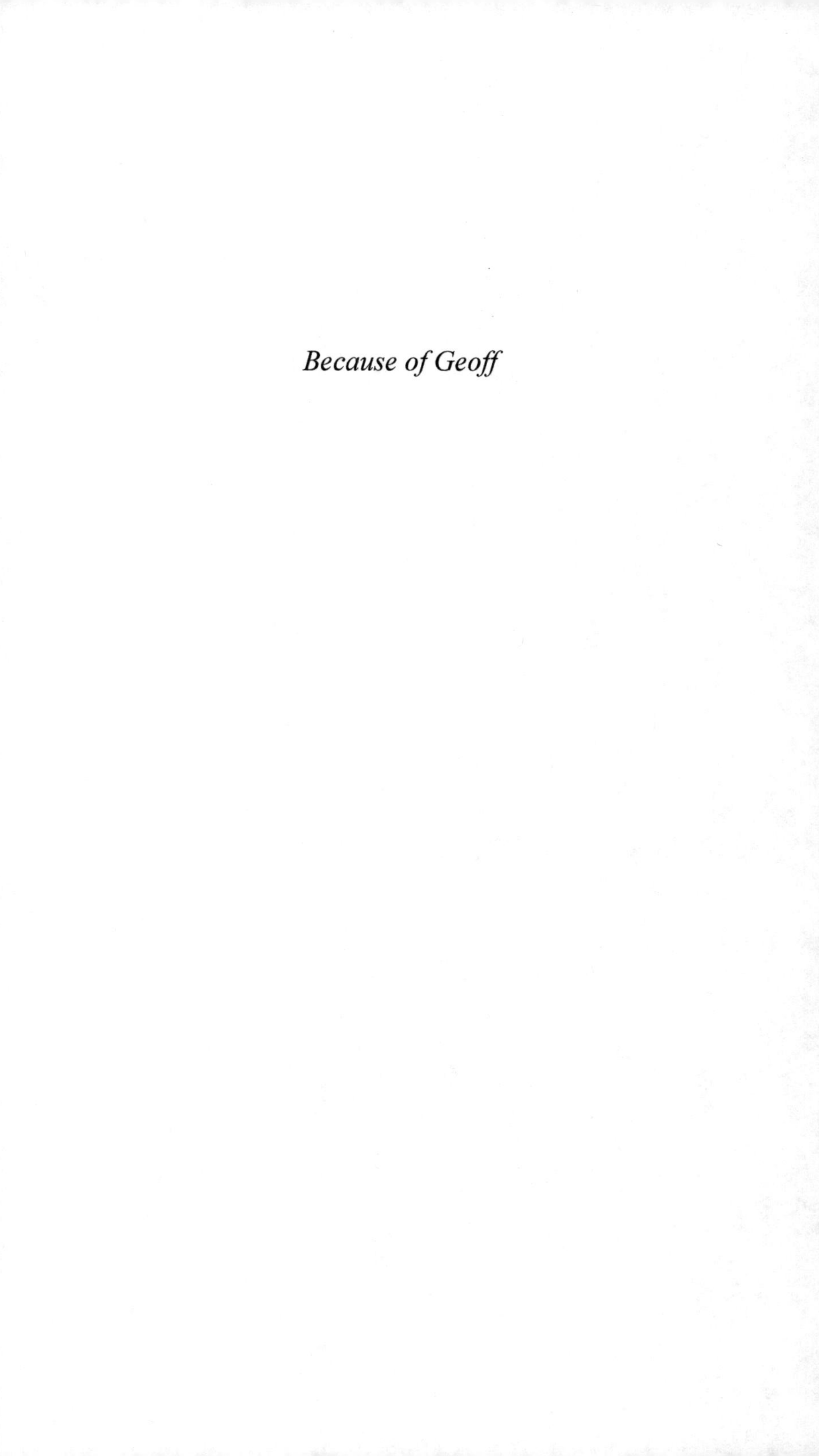

Because of Geoff

ACKNOWLEDGMENTS

This book has been 8 years in the making, and as such, I know there are people I'm going to forget to thank. They're going to be the first beta readers, the ones who slogged through the earliest incarnation of this thing, who did the really dirty, ugly work that has to be done on any story trying to be born. And so for all of those whose names I've forgotten, thank you. For those whose names I do remember… First, my thanks are to Geoff Glover, without whom there would be no story to tell. I also want to thank Lori Diederich, who showed me the music, and Ramsey Hootman for saying just the right words at just the right time. And for the others: Janet, Kelly, Will, Jenn, Caron, Tracey, Gita, Alice, Maryn, and the Purgatorians. You've all either read and offered notes, or simply put up with my whining about this book for literally years, and we're still friends (I think).

And as always, Scott & Aislynn, because without them, I wouldn't bother getting out of bed most days.

The war on Olympus lasted thirty years and fifteen days. Upon the dawning of the sixteenth day, Artemis wept in the darkness, for there were no more gods to conquer.
~Emris Virit, Scholar, Second Olympic Dynasty

CHAPTER 1

The darkness stared at her through the window, turning her pale-haired reflection into a black-eyed, haunted thing, gaunt and accusing. It always stared at her, day or night, reminding her of her sin. She could never forget. The darkness would never forgive.

Dimly, she knew someone was speaking to her, someone who had come here for her express attention. Perhaps she had even summoned him herself. She could not recall. She turned, fixing a cool gaze upon the pudgy, unkempt man seated before her heavy oaken desk. His clothing marked him as part of the laborer class, patched and cut from cloth no doubt decades old. His stringy hair was combed across his balding pate, the strands stuck down by his own bodily oils. His spectacles perched there also, most likely forgotten. He sat up straighter, assuming he had her attention, and his babbling increased in pace.

She didn't even bother to process his speech. His words didn't matter. His crime was evident. She let her gaze travel over him slowly until his voice trailed off into uncertain silence, his sweaty hands twisting at the remnants of a battered felt hat. "The painting. It is yours?"

The artwork in question hung on the wall behind her chair, an impressionist style piece of a girl in a white gown, walking through a field of flowers in the sunlight. The sunlight! To think of it. Its owner had been very proud to put it on display, assuring her that it was an original work, the first in recent human memory. She knew better.

"Yes, ma'am. My lady. My own work, from my very own hands."

"Oh, I have no doubt of that." Her narrow-heeled boots clicked a soft cadence across the marble floor as she moved to stand before the painting. "I am quite certain your hand painted every stroke here."

It was a lovely painting; she had to concede that. The girl was poised on the verge of looking back over her shoulder, as if someone dear had called her name, her blond curls caught in a frisky breeze. Her loose white gown bespoke innocence, an almost childlike naiveté. The wildflowers hovered on the brink of swaying before that same wind, frozen forever in a brilliant spring moment.

It was too perfect. Each brush stroke had been placed with precise calculation, not with the whimsy of true creation. Every layer of pigment had been formulated for one desired effect, to be a perfect replication of the original. It nearly succeeded, save for the signature in the lower right hand corner. The false initials stood out as a glaring obscenity on an otherwise pleasant canvas.

"You are not an artist." The pronouncement hung in the air, marred only by the interminable squeak of the ceiling fans and their intertwined pulleys.

"…My lady?" To his credit, he sounded

genuinely puzzled. She had to give him marks for his persistence.

"You are not an artist." Her brocade coat rustled as she turned to face him again, and she swept the tails aside to seat herself in her own chair. She perched there, high collar framing her face, every bit the queen she knew herself to be. "You are a forger, a rather good one, but you are no artist."

"My lady, I swear to you I—" She held up one manicured hand, and he stammered to a halt.

"I know you are not an artist, because the original painting is currently sitting in my very own vault, three floors below this one. You have copied this from a photograph, perhaps, and done a commendable job considering the source."

The fat, sweaty man paled considerably, knuckles going white on his poor hat. The sour smell of fear made her smile.

"I do not believe you intended to deceive me. I am certain you never meant for this…craft of yours to come to my attention." He grew decidedly greener with every word she spoke. How odd. Was she not being comforting? Her warm smile, her pleasant tone, were these not things they wanted to hear? "But there are no artists. Not anymore. And to insist, to my face, that you are… This is not worthy of one of your skill."

He began blubbering, tears leaking from his eyes even as snot streamed from his bulbous nose. "I am sorry, my lady, I did not mean…I did not wish… Please forgive me, most merciful one…!" For one brief, horrifying moment, she thought he might crawl to her, attempt to touch her.

"SILENCE!" Her voice thundered through the vaulted room and outside, lightning arced through the murky clouds, illuminating how low they hovered over the city. Her stomach churned faintly at the man's grotesque display and bile rose in her throat. Quickly, she stood once more to pace to the black window, gazing out over Elysia. Her Elysia. "Remove him from my sight."

The large man at the door, silent as a statue until this point, moved to collect the hysterical little creature from the chair. The would-be artist whimpered like a craven hound, and the pungent smell of urine tainted the air as her bodyguard dragged-carried him out the double doors. She watched it all in reflection, a dark and shadowy parody of reality.

The heavy doors closed, cutting off all sound and sealing her in solitude, both cursed and blessed for it left her alone with the darkness.

Far below her lofty tower, the city of Elysia sprawled before her, the gaslights marking the lines of narrow streets like dewdrops in a spider's a web. Here and there, an ancient trolley trundled on, marked by lights that moved in awkward jerks and stops. Indistinguishable from this height, the humans scuttled about in those streets, pursuing their tiny lives, surviving day after day, night after night.

High above them, brushing the bottom of the low-hanging smog, two airships ghosted through the sky, the spotlights sweeping the ground below. The perfect circles of white light darted amongst the tenements like living things, quick and curious. Occasionally, they would stop, investigating something thoroughly, but then they would flit on like the butterflies of old.

Out of her view to the right, the Factory smoked and rumbled along in its incessant duties, providing power and light to the populace. Surrounding the base of the tower, the Greenery glowed, a fluorescent beacon behind glass that provided all organic sustenance to the grateful multitudes.

In the center of the tower, the pillar that held the world on its axis turned slowly and inexorably, with nary a vibration to betray its function. Its rotations powered the great clock at the top of the tower, the large hands setting the pace for all life in the city.

And the darkness. It too was a living thing, waiting beyond the high city walls, hungry, devouring all that could not withstand. Only the flickering gaslights held it at bay, and it strained against them. *Long may they burn.*

She, Artemis, stood above it all in her tower, her Olympus. *Long may she reign.* Artemis of the hunt, of the golden curls, the virgin goddess. No more. It was all gone, gone and flown away.

The sound of her fingernail snapping drew her out of her reverie, and she looked at her torn and bleeding finger with faint curiosity. The glass of the window was deeply scratched where she had raked her nails down it. Blood on her hands. She always had blood on her hands.

For one moment, she could see eyes, green as her own but not hers, staring back at her with the one unasked question. *Why?* And his blood coated her hands hot and thick, running down her arms to drip off her elbows. It splattered on the toes of her boots.

A sharp slap to her face got her attention. "Artemis!" The broad-shouldered man had returned, and he shook her once to be certain she was aware of his existence. "I need your attention here."

She blinked, looking around the room. The blood was gone. The face in the glass was gone. So was

the blubbering fat man. When did he leave?
"Heracles…"

He gave a long-suffering sigh, and nodded. "Yes. Focus please. What would you have us do with the forger?"

"I…don't know…" Her eyes drifted toward the black glass again, and his hand darted out to snare her chin, forcing her to meet his eyes.

She was not a small woman. She had a warrior's height, her body toned and muscled by millennia of hunting and combat. Even in her long narrow skirt and cumbersome coat, she was a formidable combatant. Everyone knew this.

And yet this man, this halfbreed, could make a tiny glimmer of fear quiver through her stomach. He towered over her by half a foot, and his shoulders made more than two of her. He could crush her throat, snap her neck, with the one hand that gently held her face captive. His dark eyes, black as the day and night both, searched her face. What was he looking for?

"The forger, Artemis. Focus. I have him held in a cell, but you did not say what you wished done."

Oh yes, the pudgy sweaty man. Her gaze found the painting. "I think… He has skill. There is no need to waste that, artist or no. Put him to copying things from the vault."

There was a tension in Heracles' shoulders that seemed to ease, and he nodded, releasing her chin. "Very well, my lady. Will you be returning to the gala?"

Artemis frowned in puzzlement. "What time is it?"

"Perhaps ten minutes until Dark?" He stood with his massive hands folded before him. Even at ease, his arms strained the seams on his neat white shirt, and the thick leather belt around his waist looked more like armor than decoration. A pistol rested in a worn holster on that belt, next to a short-bladed knife that was more tool than weapon, but still deadly. Once a soldier, always a solider. Even his hair, once gold and now gone dusky in the endless dark, was cropped short in the soldier's fashion, though the war was long behind them. He had refused to dress for the ball they'd attended this night.

"No…no, I think I shall send Persephone to make my farewells." Yes, that was the thing to do. She couldn't bring herself to return to that seething mass of fawning humanity, no matter how pretty the lights, how cheerful the music. The story of the would-be artist had given her a welcome escape, and she felt no need to go back. "Leave me."

"As you will." He bowed slightly from the waist, and turned with a snap of his heels.

Her eyes went again to the window, watching the city. The scurrying little lights were fewer, farther between. Curfew was coming, and the clock high above tolled its mournful warning. Dark was coming. Time to be home with those you loved.

"Heracles."

He paused at the doors. "Yes?"

"Come to my chambers in an hour."

There was a long moment of hesitation before a resigned, "As you will." The doors closed softly behind him.

He would come. He always did. It mattered not if he did so out of obedience or affection.

A skittering noise in the corner drew her attention, and she caught a flash of white fur as one of the ratcatchers went about its deadly work. *Mink. Once, they were called mink.* There was a pained squeak, and the faint scent of blood reached her. A tiny life cut short under the sharp fangs of a predator. It made her smile softly. That was how things should be. The hunter always triumphed over the prey.

As if it felt her gaze, the white ratcatcher scampered out of the shadows, back arched playfully. A spot of bright red marred its fur beneath its black mask. Kneeling, Artemis scooped the animal into her arms where it curled contentedly. She stroked the fur, smelling the pungent musk it emitted. It brought back faded memories that drifted away like smoke when she tried to grasp them.

There was a forest once, the floor dappled with light filtering through the canopy. She remembered running, lithe as the deer she paced, remembered planting her feet and drawing her bow… A hiss of a shaft in the air, the thrum of a string… Blood on her hands… A dark-haired man with swarthy skin smiling down at her, and a blond man with her green eyes full of pain, asking her why… No sooner did she reach for it than it was gone, and try as she might, the lost days would not return to her.

She was not aware of the passing minutes until the clock atop her own tower chimed the final bell. Far below, the Factory groaned and clamored as a team of workers turned the wheel to shut the valves. Beginning at the outer walls, the yellow gaslights dimmed and extinguished, the wave of darkness moving inward. It sped toward the base of the tower, the blackness halted only by the shining Greenery. The greenhouses held the never-ending night at bay, and the tower would gleam throughout the long Dark. Any who might open their eyes would see it, Olympus shining through the night. And within it, their golden goddess, their Lady watching over all.

The ratcatcher was limp in her hands, its tiny neck snapped.

Chapter 2

Geoff was going to be ill. He clung to the arms of his chair, listening to the rusty wheels squeak faster and faster as the chair spun in dizzying circles. "Lia, this isn't funny!" Beyond his coarse blindfold, he heard her musical laughter, and the spinning slowed, then stopped. Her scent, that of clean soap and oil paint, wafted over him, her long hair brushing his cheek.

"Oh, you poop. You're no fun at all." She pushed the chair in a straight line with sudden purpose.

"Where are we going?"

"Can't you tell?"

No, after all the spinning, he was quite disoriented. Which was her aim, after all. "What is this about? I'm supposed to help Ambert at the shop today."

The vibration of the chair's wheels changed when they hit the cobblestones. They were crossing the street then. He could hear the rumble of the elderly trolley blocks away, the steam engine wailing a plaintive lament as it let off pressure. The hiss of the gaslights couldn't quite cover the sound of other people, standing quietly. They still shuffled, breathed, fidgeted with their hands. He could hear them. Lots of them.

"It's a surprise, silly!"

"For what? It's not my birthday or anything." He wracked his brain, trying to recall what special occasion he might have forgotten.

Lia giggled and mussed his hair. "Since when do we need a reason?"

Geoff sighed. Only for Lia would he allow himself to be blindfolded and wheeled around like some kind of invalid. He was a madman, that's what it was.

She halted the chair abruptly, jerking him in his seat a bit. "Are you ready?"

"Oh Gods, yes." The blindfold was yanked from his eyes, and he blinked in the yellow gaslight for a moment, orienting himself.

His own tenement stood behind them, the building swaying precariously in the gentle breeze. Lia had taken him no further than across the street, to stand before Ambert's carpentry shop. Geoff blinked in puzzlement, realizing that most of the denizens of Deeptown had turned out for…whatever this was. Now he wished Lia had given him time to wash his face or at least put on his good shirt.

The twins, Jon and Rik, had come straight from their shift at the Factory obviously, still coated in sweat-streaked coal dust. Ambert was there in his canvas apron, his grizzled cheeks fit to bursting he was grinning so big. The Morrows, all seven children in tow, had lined up in a neat row of white-blond heads from tallest to smallest. Kedrick had stopped stirring his ever-brewing cauldron of stew long enough to drop by, and the baker from three blocks over turned out coated in white flour, a contrast to the blackened twins. Even Raffa, the rat lady, had made an appearance, her cart of dubious delicacies put aside for the moment.

Geoff craned his neck to look at Lia, and she offered him one of her breath-taking smiles, her pale blue eyes almost glowing in her heart-shaped face. "Go on, look. What's different?"

He shook his head and brushed his bangs out of his eyes, observing the scene. "Besides everyone turned out like a Liberation Parade?"

"Oh, Geoff…please look harder!" He got the feeling he was about to disappoint her greatly, and that made his heart clench. Obediently, he looked harder.

Ambert, good sport that he was, pointed one thick finger under his arm, indicating that Geoff should look behind the old carpenter. And Geoff finally noticed the door.

He frowned, gripping his wheels to propel himself closer. The door was in the wall of Ambert's shop, and most definitely had not been there yesterday. It was solid and unadorned, obviously the old man's own work, with a tarnished brass knob.

The knob was, Geoff noticed as he reached for it, just the right height for someone wheelchair bound. "A new door, Ambert?"

"Your door, boy. All yours." The old carpenter was surely going to blow a gasket if he grinned any harder. "Go on, go on, open it up!"

Geoff only blinked in confusion. It was Lia who finally took the lead. "Oh for Gods' sake. Here!"

She reached over him, her slender hand giving the knob a quick twist, and the mysterious door swung open. "It's yours, Geoff. All yours! We all helped!"

Inside was a room. Geoff wheeled himself inside, noting that the door was wide enough for his wheels to clear easily. A pot-bellied coal stove stood in the corner opposite him. There was a worn braid rug in front of it. A small table stood in another corner, one gaslamp hanging over it, flickering cheerfully. The chair beside it was covered in a garish assortment of patchwork blankets, but it looked comfortable. A pair of his crutches leaned against the chair as if they'd always been there.

Directly across from the entrance, another door stood open, and Geoff could see a bed in there, adorned with another of the hectic quilts. A low bed, he realized, low enough that he could lever himself in and out of his chair with ease, and wide enough for two. His face grew warm at the thought.

Half afraid that everyone could see his thoughts written on his face, he looked back to Lia, to find her clasping her hands before her in anticipation. She nibbled her lower lip, a lock of pale blond hair falling in front of her eyes. "Well?"

"This is…for me?"

Lia nodded happily. "Ambert gave up some space from his shop, and Jon and Rik helped build the walls, then knocked out a space for the door last night, and oh you should have seen them trying to be so quiet and not wake up the entire district, what with it being after Dark and all, and—" Ambert placed a meaty hand on her slight shoulder, and she giggled, falling silent.

"Everybody pitched in, boy. You couldn't keep trundling up to your place as it was, not with that damnable lift breaking down every other day. We decided you needed your own place on the ground level. Something comfortable for you."

Geoff gazed at all the grinning faces, and was torn between laughter and tears. Sure, the hovel he squatted in was drafty, and rocked in a stiff breeze, and yes, the lift never worked and he had to use his crutches to walk up the four flights of stairs more often than he liked, but… "I…I can't pay you for the space, Ambert." Ground level space was at a premium, and Ambert was lucky to have the large shop that he did.

"Hmph. Don't recall asking for money." The carpenter looked offended, his salt-and-pepper brows drawing together. "You help out at the shop enough, and on Market days. Don't figure I need more'n that."

"And look, I hung one of my paintings!" Lia pointed to a rather large picture on the wall. It was a fanciful thing, a sunset in purples and pinks, reflected on a vast sea. Lia swore she'd dreamed it up in her very own mind. It was one of Geoff's favorites.

"Oh Lia…You didn't need to do that. That one will bring a good price at Market."

"Nonsense. It's yours now. Don't you dare try to get me to take it back." She crossed her arms over her spare chest and glared at him. Her pique lasted all of five seconds before her eyes lit up again. "Oh, and look what Raffa found in the catacombs!"

She snatched up something from the small table and pressed it into his hands. He brushed his bangs from his eyes again, and turned it over.

It was impossible to tell how old the book was. The gilt title had long since worn off, and the leather cover was cracked and stained. The pages within, though, were in good condition, and his fingers traced the printed words. "A Song for Artemis."

Lia nodded. "Raffa said it was written by one of the last great bards, before the end of the war. She thought you might like it."

"Raffa said all that, did she?" Geoff looked up for the strange reclusive woman only to find her hovering within touching distance. He flinched, only partly in surprise. The aroma was…distinctive.

The old woman reached out a filthy, gnarled hand to pat the book. "For my bitty birdy…yes yes yes.…he likes this, Raffa knows…" The edges of her greasy, sooty rags brushed across Geoff's skin, and he made a conscious effort not to recoil.

"Thank you, Raffa." Whether or not she heard him was open to debate. Raffa only rarely acknowledged being spoken to, and her rheumy eyes always stared straight through a person, rather than at them. Still, she smiled underneath her matted, stringy hair, and babbled quietly to herself as she withdrew. The next time Geoff looked up, she was gone, vanished without a trace.

The day quickly turned into a small party, with the Morrow children scampering up and down the four flights of stairs to bring Geoff's few belongings down and install them in his new home. Kedrick and the baker brought food, and Jon pulled out his tin whistle to provide a bit of music.

Geoff was watching Lia and Ambert dance, when another voice carried across the crowd. "Who started the party without me?" Inwardly, Geoff winced. Keras, while guaranteed to make a party lively, was also guaranteed to take everything entirely too far. They'd be lucky not to have the Hunt down on them for disturbing the peace.

True to form, the spry little man had a woman on each arm when he worked his way to Geoff's side, and he dismissed them both with swats on the fanny. "Go on girls, find yourself something to eat." Keras threw his arm around Geoff's shoulders, never noticing how the younger man cringed away. "Happy day, Geoffroi! A new home, it's a glad thing!" Grinning, he displayed his stained buckteeth. His mop of dark curls was confined beneath the fedora he always wore, and his ratty fur coat, hanging to his knees, matched the color of his scruffy goatee, dangling from the end of his pointed chin. And despite the fact that he looked quite like an overgrown deeprat, somehow he always had female companionship.

"Thank you for coming, Keras." The words were spoken to empty air, the trader literally dancing off to spin Lia out of Ambert's arms. Her laughter, like delicate chimes, rang out, and Geoff did his best not to roll his eyes.

It was always Keras. The weasely little man could sell a candle claiming it was the last ray of sunlight, and was more than capable of talking his own grandmother out of her knickers if so inclined. He was quite happy to regale anyone who would listen (or couldn't get away) with his many conquests and exploits.

Geoff didn't dislike the man, exactly, but there were times when his patience with the scruffy trader wore painfully thin. And there were times, like now, when Keras was leading the children in a dance, cavorting while playing his multi-flute. The little ones were so happy, so carefree, and Geoff couldn't bring himself to be cross.

"Geoff! Isn't it wonderful that Keras was passing by!" Lia flopped next to him on a crate, out of breath, her cheeks flushed and her eyes sparkling.

"Oh, yes, just wonderful." He chuckled a little, then leaned close to speak quietly into her ear. "You looked lovely out there dancing."

She grinned, nuzzling his cheek for a moment before smoothing her hand over her flyaway hair. "Oh, but I'm out of practice. Keras makes me look so clumsy." Fifty-ton weights tied to her ankles could not make her look clumsy, but Geoff didn't have time to convince her of that fact.

Keras scampered over and tugged her to her feet again. "Now now, Geoffroi, no monopolizing the beauties!" In a trill of pipes, they were gone again, leaving Geoff to call good-natured protests after them.

Her seat was quickly occupied by Rik, his twin Jon flopping down near Geoff's feet. "I don't know how he does it, but he does it every time." The trio of men watched Keras frolic with identical shakes of their heads.

Jon nudged Geoff's leg with his elbow. "You should ask her to dance. I could play something slow."

"Maybe in a little bit." Keras spun Lia in a circle, her pale hair flying about her like a golden halo. She gleamed like the Goddess herself, even if it was blasphemy to think so, and every time she turned, her eyes would find him and she would give him one of those smiles that made his heart pound and his head swim.

Rik snorted. "Well, someone has to stop the little rat before his head gets too big and he falls over. Excuse me." The big man pushed himself off the crate, and on the next pass of dancers, smoothly cut in between Lia and Keras. Her laughter rang out above the trader's loud protests.

"Just let me know when you want to dance." Jon lapsed into a comfortable silence, both of them watching the party spin on around them. That was one thing that Geoff appreciated about the big mechanic. He was quieter than his more boisterous twin, and he knew how to just let Geoff...be.

Geoff waited for the moment when the dancers were starting to flag, then nodded to Jon. The big man took up his tin whistle, and the piercingly clear tone cut through the rest of the noise. Geoff pushed himself up out of his chair, pleased to see that the ache in his knees had was negligible. The chair had been more for Lia's whim than necessity today. When he caught Lia's eye, he held out a hand to her, and she darted through the dancing couples to link her fingers with his. Her eyes sparkled as she led him slowly onto the dance floor.

His knees had never been right. That was something they'd known from birth. Oh certainly, he had good days, where it was merely a persistent ache, but he also had bad ones where walking was impossible and the chair was his only option. And the day could switch from one to the other abruptly and without warning, if he exerted himself too much. So dancing, truly dancing, was normally beyond him.

The lithe girl twined her arms around his neck, and he let his hands settle on her narrow hips. Geoff rested his forehead against hers, and together, they swayed to the music. It might not be the most elaborate dance, but this at least he could do.

Other couples paired off, some just barely moving their feet at all, and others waltzing their way across the impromptu dance floor. Geoff paid no attention. His eyes were only for the woman in his arms, and Lia gazed up at him with utter adoration in her blue eyes. How under the long dark sky could he have possibly been so lucky?

Jon played longer than the song warranted, giving the two lovers a chance to linger at their dancing, but in the end, Keras grew restless and broke in with his multi-flute, bringing the tempo up once more. Geoff retreated to his wheeled chair, and Lia settled on his lap, the pair of them content to just watch for a while.

It was more laughter and gaiety than Deeptown had seen in some time, and with Keras in attendance, it lasted until the clock on Olympus Tower gonged the first curfew warning. Jon and Rik departed to catch the trolley three blocks over, for the Dark shift at the Factory, intending to nap on the long ride. The Morrows collected their brood and herded them toward home and bed. Kedrick and the baker wandered off down the street, arguing over the proper consistency of dumplings, and Keras vanished at the first sign of being asked to clean up, much to everyone's annoyance and no one's surprise. The young man was left alone with Lia and Ambert in his new apartment.

Without an audience, he finally allowed himself to relax and truly gaze around in wonder. "How did you do all of this without me knowing?"

"Wasn't easy." Ambert chuckled. "Secrets spread faster in Deeptown than the Lady's legs, and that's the truth." The old man glanced at Lia and blushed. "Begging your pardon."

Lia smirked and plopped herself in Geoff's new armchair, curling her feet up beneath her worn skirt. "I thought for sure you would figure it out when Ambert quit asking you to help out at the shop. That was when Jon and Rik started building the walls."

Geoff hid his small glimmer of pain behind a sheepish smile. "I thought I'd broken one too many things, and he didn't want me to help out anymore." A wheelchair was an ungainly thing, even when the wheels weren't half rusted and creaky.

"Hmph. I'm happier to have you around than any other dozen people I could name, boy. You don't forget that. I always got a place for you at my shop." The carpenter clapped him on the shoulder hard enough to make him wince, then directed a stern glance at Lia. "Curfew's in less than an hour. You be scampering home before Dark."

"I'm going soon, I promise." She gave Ambert

an impish grin as he lumbered out the door and closed it behind him. Her blue eyes came to rest on Geoff in his wheelchair. She lit up the room better than any ten gaslamps. "Do you like it?"

"Oh yes. It's wonderful." What he wouldn't give to see her curled up in that chair every day for the rest of his life. Even the thought made his heart hurt, he wanted it so badly. "And that's my favorite painting."

"I know." She hopped up with a grace he often envied, and gathered her crocheted shawl around her shoulders. "Walk me home?"

"Of course." He abandoned the chair as unnecessary, but took up both crutches, settling his forearms into the cradles.

Lia raised a pale brow at him. "I thought you were having a good day."

He shrugged. "They're handy. Sometimes." The truth was, he felt nearly naked without them, always unsure what he should be doing with his hands.

Lia's home was only five blocks away, past the trolley tracks to the north. Over the years, her family had managed to hold onto a large expanse of ground-level territory in a fairly stable tenement. Taking up almost the entire first floor, there had always been plenty of room to house the whole family. Even Geoff himself had lived there for a time, as a child, before the desire to strike out on his own had driven him to claim a squat across the street from Ambert's shop. But now there was only Lia, her mother taken by illness four winters ago, and the young woman had turned her unexpected luxury into a painting studio.

The double bed in Geoff's new apartment had been a message, he knew. An invitation for her to join him in his home, if he wouldn't join her in hers. Of course, they all knew damn well that if Lia left her studio for even one night, the squatters would swarm the place within days. The only way to keep something was to sleep there. She couldn't leave, and he wasn't ready to make that step. Not quite yet.

The streets of Deeptown were largely empty, this time of night, the residents retiring obediently before the curfew could fall. There were still lights in a few oil-papered windows, silhouettes moving about as people bedded down for the night, but no one lingered out, fearful of drawing the wrath of the Lady's Hunt.

The scuffling in an alley to their left, not two blocks away from their destination, was the first warning. The pungent smell of rotting meat and unwashed flesh that wafted out of the darkness was the second, and Geoff let one crutch dangle off his arm to grab Lia's elbow, pulling her closer to him. "Walk faster."

It was too late, though. They'd been spotted. The creature that crept out of the shadows was human, mostly, but the ravages of disease and starvation had rendered it spindly, and walking fully upright seemed beyond it, scuttling on hands and feet filthy with coal dust. Hairless, gaunt, clad in the remnants of rags, it was impossible to tell if it had been male or female before, and its enormous eyes were bright with fever.

It raised its head, scenting the air, and its gaze went straight to the pair of lovers on the street. "Yesss…oh pretty things, smell so sweet…"

"Go." Geoff tried to urge Lia on, already knowing that she wouldn't leave his side.

"So it can track me home? I think not."

The wretched creature inched closer to them, licking its cracked lips. "Smell so sweet…sweet to eat, sweet to taste…" This one had been at it long enough to have the palsy, Geoff noted, its hands visibly trembling every time it raised one of them to wipe the saliva from its mouth. The teeth had been filed to points, he saw, though most were now black and rotting.

"Be gone, lotus eater. The Hunt will have you soon." Geoff shifted his weight to his better leg, the left one, and freed his arm from the cradle of the other crutch.

"I only see the one," Lia murmured behind him. "If the swarm catches us here…"

"No. It's alone." He couldn't have said how he knew, but there were no more of the half-starved cannibals lying in wait. This one, no doubt weak enough that its own kind would devour it, had fled its pack.

"Sweet…pretty…one taste, just one taste…? Please?" Wheedling, the voice reedy and unpleasant, it tried to creep closer.

"Stay back. I will only warn you once."

It scooted forward once more, and behind him, Geoff felt Lia flinch. Her instinct to recoil from the horror of the lotus eaters was natural, but like so many feral things, it triggered a pursuit response. The skeletal creature lunged, rotting fangs bared, and Geoff flipped the foot of the crutch into his hand and swung all in one fluid motion. The heavy cuff at the top end connected solidly with the cannibal's skull, and the sick thud echoed against the buildings around them.

The waif-like thing went flying across the cobblestones, moaning when it came to a stop against a pile of refuse. It didn't rise, though, and that was the important thing.

"Come on, before it gets up." It might have been a mercy to kill the thing, Geoff knew, but he'd never been able to make himself take a life, not even one so pathetic as that.

The generations of forced confinement within the walls of Elysia did not sit well with all minds, and the lotus eaters were those who had shucked off the bonds of sanity and reason. It began with small things, snatching rats out of the gutters to devour them raw, and it progressed quickly to attacking and eating other humans, the deviants finding a sick sort of bliss in the atrocity of it. The practice of cannibalism spread disease through those that partook, and as their faculties lessened, they often resorted to hunting in swarms to overwhelm their prey. In large numbers, they were viciously lethal. Caught alone, though, lotus eaters were usually cowardly, and it was easy enough to scare them away with a few shouts and the occasional blow.

The couple walked as fast as Geoff's gait would permit, both of them watching and listening for the unmistakable scuttling sound behind them, but they made it to Lia's doorway with no signs of pursuit. Geoff watched the street while Lia got the door open, but when she tried to draw him inside, he resisted.

"I'll be all right going home. Don't worry."

"Geoff…"

"Just bar the door when I'm gone, all right?"

"What if the swarm comes?"

He shook his head. "It's going to rain soon, I can smell it. Even the lotus eaters have to take shelter from that. I'll be fine."

She frowned at him for long moments, before sighing. "You're a stubborn arse."

"Yes I am." She tipped her face up to him, and he leaned in obediently for a soft kiss. "I'll see you tomorrow."

"First thing in the morning. I need you to help

me choose things to take to Market Day next week."

"As you wish." He gave her a half-bow from his crutches, then waited to be sure he heard the bar dropped down across her door before he started the walk back home.

Despite his assurances to Lia, Geoff kept an eye out for the stray cannibal as he rounded the corner of the block. The lotus eater was gone, however, without even a smear of blood to show where it had lain. There was another shape in the shadow of the alley, though, and before Geoff could even raise his crutch, a soft chuckle issued forth.

"Bitty birdy wouldn't hurt Raffa, would he? No no, not my bitty birdy."

"Darkest night, Raffa, you scared the life out of me." He sighed as the odd old woman shuffled her way out into the lamplight. "What are you doing out this time of night? It's nearly Dark."

"Bitty birdy is out…"

"Well, yes, I was walking Lia home. But I'm going home now, and you should be too. It's going to rain soon."

The old woman snorted, her amusement clear despite the fact that her face was mostly hidden under the tangles of her matted hair. "Rain rain, go away, come again another day…"

Geoff sighed and tried not to roll his eyes. Raffa's ramblings took the form of children's rhymes, on her good days, and utter nonsense when her mind was wandering a bit farther afield. "I don't think wishing is going to make it stop. Go home."

"Go to bitty birdy's home. Making sure he gets there. Making sure he doesn't get eaten up, yum yum."

"Saw that, did you?"

"Filthy vermin." She turned her head and spat on the street.

Geoff chose not to comment on the irony of *her* of all people considering someone else filthy. "All right, you can walk me home, but then you *must* find shelter. Please?"

"If bitty birdy wants." She fell into step beside him, not close enough to touch, but near enough that they could be considered walking together.

The drone of the airships hummed overhead as they walked the last three blocks in the yellow gaslight. Spotlights swept the streets and alleys, lingering on the odd duo for a moment before moving on. Geoff knew it'd be back the moment curfew tolled, to see if they were still out, in violation. A recorded announcement played over the tinny loudspeakers above. "All citizens must remain indoors until the lifting of Dark, by order of the Lady Artemis, long may she reign. Sleep safely."

It took a conscious effort not to turn his steps toward his old tenement, his old squat on the very top floor. The new door in Ambert's wall stuck out like a sore thumb, and Geoff had a hard time believing it was real.

"Look, if you want, you can stay here tonight. The chair looked comfortable…" He turned to look for Raffa, only to find that she had vanished. "Or not…"

Still marveling that he had a right to, Geoff turned the brass knob and let himself into his new apartment, shutting the door firmly behind him.

His fingers traced the smooth grain of the wood, feeling the almost invisible seams where Ambert had pieced it together from other sections, other doors. It was fine work. The carpenter had a touch he'd never seen matched.

The new book, Raffa's gift, he placed carefully on the table under the gaslamp. With the clock already clanging its final warning, he wouldn't have time to read anyway. That could wait until tomorrow when the lights would come back on. He bedded the coal stove down to provide warmth throughout the night without burning the place down. That'd be a fine thing to happen, his first night in his new home.

The ache in his knees was more pronounced now, the ten-block walk taking its toll. Still, he pushed his wheeled chair into the corner of the main room, and propped his crutches up against the arm of the chair. His chair. He actually owned a chair. In his old place, he'd only had a narrow cot for a bed, and an upended metal crate to serve as a table for his rusted lamp.

Poking his head into the bedroom, he discovered a tall wardrobe against the far wall, his very sparse collection of clothing hanging from the bar. His shirts and trousers took up perhaps a tenth of the empty space, but it was easy to imagine Lia's dresses hanging next to his things.

In the corner to his right was a simple wash basin, the glaze on the porcelain crackled with time, but still serviceable. A mirror hung above it, mildewed around the edges, but remarkably clear for all that.

The bed he'd been given was a true luxury, and he eased himself down with a contented sigh. The springs beneath the mattress squeaked faintly, but it would be leaps and bounds more comfortable than his old one.

He kicked off his worn boots and nudged them under the bed. Stripping off his trousers, he laid them neatly at the foot of the bed, then added his folded shirt to the pile. The fabric was so old, it was nearly transparent in places, and soon even Lia's skill at patching things was going to do no good.

Movement in the mirror caught his attention, and he flinched, then immediately felt ridiculous. It was only his own face staring at him, after all, but it was something he didn't see that often.

He was a young man still, not yet twenty-three winters. His brown eyes were a touch too wide, like those of a doe he'd seen in a picture once, and his cheekbones were inordinately high for a typical male. His jawline was smooth and unmarred, never needing shaving, and his chestnut hair hung in half-hearted curls around his face. Geoff tucked the wayward locks behind his ears again, making a mental note to get it cut, at the same time knowing that he wouldn't. Lia liked his hair long.

The apartment was glorious. The ground-level space was extravagant in and of itself, but then to furnish it and give him warm quilts and other gifts… It was just more proof that for whatever reason, Geoff led a blessed life.

He should have frozen to death that very first winter, a deformed infant left in the black snow. But the residents of Deeptown found him, cared for him, raised him. In recompense, though he wasn't able to make the trek to the Factory, he found other means of employment, helping out at Ambert's shop, or Lia's studio, or Kedrick's kitchen. Someone always needed help, and they were happy to trade goods or vouchers for his efforts.

Outside, the last warning klaxon sounded, and the constant hiss of the gaslights died away to silence, leaving the city in total darkness. In the walls, the rats scurried and scuttled, fleeing the oncoming rain. After them came the ratcatchers, and the sounds of small furry battles would rattle the tenements throughout the night. It was a soothing sound, familiar and comfortable.

Geoff flopped back onto his new bed, stretching his arms and legs out just for the novelty of reaching for the edges. Room enough for Lia to curl up against his chest on cold winter nights, the pair of them snuggling beneath a pile of cozy quilts. They could read to each other, or play games or…well, of course, or. When the time was right, when he was done making his way on his own, then he would ask her to wed, and she would say yes. She'd already told him so.

The pleasant thought stayed with him as he drifted to sleep, and the last thing he heard was the sizzle and splat as the thick, sooty rain began.

<u>CHAPTER 3</u>

The image in the full-length mirror was one of absolute perfection. Golden curls were piled artfully atop her head. The silken gown draped gracefully from bared shoulders, to golden bracelets at the wrists, to pool at her enameled toes likewise adorned in gold. The style was old, ancient in fact, but fitting the day's ceremony. A tastefully gemmed crown of golden laurel leaves nestled in her hair, reminding any and all of her status. *As if they needed reminding.* Artemis pursed her painted lips thoughtfully as the servant girls finished dressing her, but had to admit that she looked superb.

She felt superb as well. She always felt better on worship days, as if the adoration of her people helped keep the voices and the darkness at bay. It would be nice to step outside for the few moments required. She didn't leave the tower often enough. Hardly ever, come to think of it. Yes, more outings were called for, and soon.

Behind her in the mirror, another blond figure appeared and stood waiting with hands clasped. Her gown was olive drab, with a high collar and a multitude of tarnished brass buttons down the fitted bodice. The skirt itself fell straight to the floor, the slits up the sides revealing the dark brown trousers beneath, tucked into calf-high buttoned boots.

"That color does not become you, my dear," Artemis observed.

"Then I shall endeavor to wear it more often."

Artemis raised one brow, eyeing Persephone's reflection in the mirror. "A bit bold today, are we?"

"No more than always, my lady." The blond woman had no expression on her face, a carefully neutral façade that Artemis longed to shatter into a thousand bloody pieces.

The golden goddess turned from the mirror to face Persephone, the servants around her scrambling to keep up as they slipped jeweled bangles onto her bared arms. "And this is what you choose to wear to worship?"

"It would not do to outshine yourself, my lady." A ghost of a false smile flitted across Persephone's lips and was gone.

"Leave us," Artemis snapped at the servants, and they scattered. She watched Persephone as the door closed, leaving them alone in Artemis' private chambers. There was no hint of fear, not even a tremor. Darkness take the woman! "I could condemn you to the Factory, until you learn the error of your ways."

The blond woman nodded agreement. "You could. But you won't." She turned on her heel and headed for the door. "Heracles says the square has been secured, and it is time. You are to come."

The door leapt from Persephone's grasp and slammed shut again with a boom that echoed against the high ceilings. The woman turned to look at Artemis, a slightly raised brow betraying her annoyance. Not fear, no, but irritation. Damn her to Tartarus, except that was just what she wanted.

"Make no mistake, Persephone. Your continued existence is at my whim. You would do well to remember that."

There was ice in the other woman's blue eyes, a cold fury seeping through her pleasant mask. "And if I die, you will have to contend with my husband. Remember *that*."

Artemis snorted, despite the cold fist that seized her heart. "Your husband is dead."

"If you believed that, I wouldn't still be here." Her skirt swirled around her as she turned and strode out the door, leaving it hanging open.

Her hands clenched, hard enough to draw blood from her palms, and the mirror fractured into a spiderweb of tiny images, all of them showing a seething Artemis. She watched her own eyes, multiplied by millions, staring back at her, and each set told her what she hated to see. There was fear there, fear and helpless anger. And what did she have to be afraid of? Was she not Artemis?

"I am the queen of Olympus!" Her voice mocked her, bouncing off the paneled walls, the vaulted ceiling. "I am the keeper of the world pillar! I do not fear you, Hades!"

He was dead. Or so far fled that it amounted to the same thing. Hades had not been seen since the war. The coward had fled at the end, ahead of the destruction wrought by Artemis' armies. No doubt, he had crawled into a hole to fade away, or perished somewhere outside the wall. To venture beyond the walls of Elysia was a death sentence for god and mortal alike. The land itself waited to poison the unwary.

"I do not fear you." A million tiny mouths aped the words back at her from the shattered mirror, giving lie to her assertion.

And they will come from below, from the depths of no return, and with them, they will bring your death. The seer's voice, the words of a long-dead oracle, burned in her mind. *They will come from below.*

"No they won't." She spoke to the empty room, heedless that she had no audience. "No one will return from there. I saw to it. There will be no return from below."

Are you so certain? That was not the seer's voice, but one that sounded more like... *The dead must go somewhere, sister dear.*

"Stop it," she whimpered, clapping her hands over her ears. "Leave me alone." But it didn't stop. In fact, it called her name several times. "Just leave me alone!"

"Artemis?" Strong hands gripped both wrists, and she caught her breath, looking up. Heracles frowned, drawing her hands away from her face. "Are you well, my lady?"

She blinked, then glanced around the room, finding herself alone with her bodyguard and the creaking ceiling fans above. "I…" The voices were gone, both the long-dead seer and the other. Gone as if they had never been. "Yes. I am fine." Quickly, she smoothed her hands over her dress and gave her curls one last pat to seat her crown firmly. "You, however, are late. Let's go."

She left him standing behind her as she swept out the door and headed for the lift, her long train gathered elegantly over one arm. "I do not fear you," she whispered to herself.

The square below Olympus Tower was a seething teeming mass of humanity divided neatly into two distinct groups. Every person in the city of Elysia, many hundreds of thousands strong, were crammed into that one small acre of property. There was scarcely room to breathe and no room at all to move, but depending on one's level of wealth, one's circumstances might be better.

The social elite, those with homes surrounding the tower proper, managed with little jostling amongst themselves, their space jealously guarded by liveried servants and the Lady's own personal guard. They huddled in their silks and velvets, pretending that their white fur collars were from some exotic beast rather than the ratcatchers that roamed every house in the city. They kept their eyes carefully turned away from the squalor within touching distance.

For everyone else, it was make do as they could, smashed against fifty of their nearest neighbors. Children sat on parents' shoulders, calling and waving to agemates nearby. The adults merely attempted to make space for as many as they could, without being crushed against the glowing glass walls of the Greenery.

There was one horrifying moment when a slight elderly woman fell, disappearing beneath the feet of her fellow citizens, but a helpful neighbor in the crowd, a burly Factory worker, picked her up and sheltered her with his own large body until she could get her balance again. It could have been worse. She would not have been the first to be trampled to death on a worship day.

The guards surrounding the perimeter of the square seemed not to notice the danger inherent in packing so many people so close together. Beyond protecting the swaying poles of the gaslights, keeping them from toppling into the crowd, they made no effort to interfere. Their orders were to keep everyone there for the entire service, and to make sure that no one, no matter how sickly or frail, had shirked their duty to the goddess and remained at home. Door-to-door searches had been going on since the lifting of Dark, and would continue until the moment of the Lady's appearance.

As the guardsmen passed, each man armed with pistol and baton and accompanied by a large speckled hound, the crowd pressed tighter to give them room. No one wanted to draw the attention of the Lady's Hunt. There were worse things than arrest, if they got their fangs into a man.

Conversations amongst the populace were hushed, but the sheer number created a low roar, ebbing and flowing like the tide of the now-mythical sea. Only when the door of the tower opened did the voices cease, dying away in a wave rippling outward from the raised dais where the Lady would appear.

The Lady's bodyguard appeared first, the demigod Heracles. His dark eyes scanned the crowd, and each person there felt certain that his gaze found them and only them, and they were secretly relieved when his attention passed on. When all had been deemed satisfactory to him, he stepped aside and allowed the Lady to emerge from her shining tower.

To Artemis, the upturned faces glowed with adulation and the deep silence was one of hushed anticipation. She paid no mind to Persephone as the woman took a place near the door, in no danger of drawing attention away from the golden goddess. Artemis paused, gaze roaming the crowd, letting the tension build for long moments. It was nearly palpable, an invisible haze above the thousands of living, breathing creatures. She wondered, briefly, how long she could get them to hold their breaths. The moment stretched out until she could no longer stand it, then she raised both hands, palms out, bestowing her blessing upon the populace.

On cue, the crowd roared, and she closed her eyes to bask in the adoration. So many voices from so many throats, all proclaiming their love for her, their goddess. They would scream themselves hoarse if she did not lower her arms, shout until their throats simple refused to obey them any longer. But she was a benevolent goddess, and she lowered her arms after only a few moments, the sound dying away to the breathless silence once more.

The wizened priestess stepped up next to her then, her old bones creaking audibly as she knelt to press dry kisses to the goddess' feet. Artemis watched with detached curiosity. How much longer could the ancient creature survive? It took a woman at each elbow to lower the decrepit priestess to her knees, and neither of those women were what one would call young. The entire order of priestesses was crumbling before the goddess' very eyes. It was vaguely revolting, and Artemis did her best not to flinch away from the desiccated fingers that clutched her ankles.

Again with aid, the elderly priestess regained her feet, and shuffled to the antiquated microphone at the edge of the dais. A young woman knelt at its base, holding tight, mindful that the heavy apparatus had toppled into the audience before, striking and killing an unlucky onlooker who'd been unable to dodge in the press of the crowd.

"And lo, She did look upon the world, ravaged by

war and famine." The priestess's voice croaked out over the speakers surrounding the square, only half the crackles and snaps the fault of the electrical system. "And She swept those survivors to her bosom, and bade them take shelter with her."

Artemis watched the crowd, their rapt faces upturned, hanging on every word though they'd heard it all of their lives. Every man, woman and child in Elysia was present, their worship feeding her, sustaining her. It was all she had ever asked for all she had given them.

"And She erected the Great Wall—"

"Long may it stand," murmured the crowd.

"—to protect us from the dangers of Outside. And She lit the Great Tower—"

"Long may it burn."

"—to hold back the long Dark, to give us a beacon in the endless night." There was a long pause then, and the old priestess stared blankly into the crowd as if she'd forgotten the words she had repeated every day of her life. One of her none-too-young acolytes finally whispered the next phrase to her, careful to keep it from the microphone, and the priestess nodded in response. "And she forged the Great Pillar—"

"May it stand for eternity."

"—and on it our world spins steadfast. And so to Her we give our thanks and our love, our eternal devotion and our very lives. Hail, the Lady Artemis."

"Long may she reign."

Long may she reign.

That last refrain always stayed with her the longest, the genuine plea from her people to stay with them and guide them through the darkness. She could recall very little of the day's worship service after that.

The tolling of the curfew bell had come and gone

an hour before, leaving only Olympus Tower shining in the dark. The man in her bed sat up, gathering his clothing to depart. So many scars marred his smooth skin, received in both in battle and toil, his immortal blood doing nothing to erase the marks of shame and bravery both.

"You're leaving?" She ran a hand over Heracles' bare back, and he tensed beneath her touch but didn't stop dressing.

"I need to check in with the men, make sure the building is secure." The Hunt, Artemis' personal army, was Heracles' responsibility. One she thought he often took too seriously, usually when it was most inconvenient for her.

"Dark has fallen, curfew is set…the building is secure." She stretched, allowing the sheets to fall away from her nakedness. He never once glanced at her, and she frowned. "I am a goddess, Heracles. Who could hurt me?"

That at least earned her a slight turn of his head and a frown. "Gods have died before."

A chill settled over her, and she tugged the sheets back around her bare arms. *They died by the hundreds, any and all with immortal blood. Their fingers turned black, their eyes milky, their lips split and bled black pus. They held hands out to her, begging for mercy, begging for her to end the pain she had inflicted.* Oh yes, she knew gods had died. Her hands were covered in blood.

"No one knows the way. They will never know. I am safe." Still, she hugged her knees to her chest and glanced around at the dark corners of her bedroom. The darkness was there, seeping in from the outside it seemed. It watched her always. Or perhaps it was merely the gleaming eyes of the ratcatchers, the tiny hunters patrolling through the nooks and crannies of the tower.

Heracles only snorted in response and stood up, buckling his belt. "I have no faith in 'never', my lady." He turned to give her a slight bow. "If you will excuse me."

The room was jarringly empty after he left, the hollow echo of silence grating on her nerves. The whisper of her own breath seemed loud, as if it drew all attention to her. Even the walls had fallen silent, the vermin and their predators taking their battles elsewhere.

You are never alone, sister dear. Artemis whimpered and pressed her hands to her ears. Dammit, she should know better than to curse the silence, because he would always be there to fill it. *The dead must go somewhere.*

"You're dead," she mumbled, and cursed herself for acknowledging him. It would only make him louder.

Oh yes, no doubt about that. Very dead, dear sister. You saw to that.

Above the tower, above the low-hanging smog and ever-present clouds, thunder rumbled quietly. In the black glass, Artemis' face stared back at her, eyes as wide as a startled doe. Only somehow, it was not her face, but someone else's, someone she once knew… Transfixed, she rose from the bed and padded naked to the window.

Thick rivulets of sooty water ran down the panes in grooves carved by decades of acid rain. Beyond that, the lights of the Greenery glowed in the night, and further out still, the dark waited, holding Elysia in its grip until morning. Like two glowing eyes, her airships shown in the blackness, silently prowling the sky through the acid drizzle.

Eyes… It was the eyes that caught her. Green

eyes in the glass, like her own. Golden hair in curls to broad shoulders. Chiseled features, sculpted and refined. She raised a hand to trace the sharp cheek bones, and the reflection did the same, fingertips meeting against the cool window. "Apollo?"

Nothing. He was gone, save for the reflection in the black glass. Thunder boomed overhead, and she flinched. When she looked back again, the face was her own, wide-eyed and staring. Only the darkness looked back from outside, seeing into her soul and judging her flawed.

They will come from below… The old seer cackled madly in her memory. *From the depths of no return.* "I killed you too quickly. You should have suffered for your impudence." The dead woman tittered in the back of her mind.

Artemis rested her forehead against the cool glass. They never left her in peace. Even in her sleep they whispered to her, all those who were dead at her hands. They never let her escape. But they'd been louder, lately, harder to banish. Somewhere, something was stirring, and the spirits of the dead were restless.

And in the dark, they waited.

CHAPTER 4

On his good days, Geoff didn't mind going to the mandatory worship so much. It always felt like a small adventure, dashing to catch the rickety trolleys that never really stopped, leaving Deeptown to pass through the other wards, calling out to folk you hadn't seen since the last worship, a month ago. Deeptown was the farthest ward from the Tower, pressed tightly against the looming wall, and so the residents always had a place farthest from the dais, the last to arrive and the first to leave, avoiding the dangerous press of bodies in the square proper.

On his bad days, however, when his knees were so inflamed that the pain brought tears to his eyes and even his wheeled chair was an agony, those days he hid himself away in Lia's studio. As the Hunt swept the districts, searching for shirkers, Geoff would pass the time concealed in a tiny room at the back of the shop, his scent masked by the potent aromas of Lia's paints and oils.

He didn't know what the small room had been built for originally, but it came in most handy. He had enough room for his chair and a small table, an oil lamp giving him enough light to read by while he waited out his temporary confinement. The cupboard smelled like Lia, her art so much a part of her that the scent of linseed oil and pigment had simply become *her*.

He flipped carefully through his new book, the

one Raffa had rescued from the depths of the catacombs beneath the city. The old woman was always finding interesting things in those caverns, apparently oblivious to the dangers posed in the weakened tunnels and mined out shafts. And quite often, she was delivering them to her "bitty birdy". Geoff never knew why she chose that particular moniker for him, but Raffa's well-known lunacy saved him any embarrassment from it. Raffa was just Raffa, and if she wished to call Geoff a bitty birdy, then so be it.

The world's treasures waited down there in the catacombs to be found, or so the story went, the Elysia they knew only built on top of the corpse of the Elysia of old. While Geoff wasn't certain there was treasure, the book itself was precious enough.

"And in her hand she bore the arrows of wrath, and with them, she smote her kin and all those who opposed her. The first to fall was Zeus, father of Artemis, Lord of Olympus, with a poisoned arrow in his breast. And when the opposing armies saw their leader struck down there was wailing in terror, for surely the end times were upon them."

Geoff paused in his reading and glanced around the small closet, as if someone might hear him speak the forbidden name and call him to account for it. It was rumored that the Lady Artemis could hear her father's name whispered leagues away, and would wreak terrible vengeance upon the speaker. But long moments passed, and nothing happened.

Encouraged, he settled in to read. The story itself was one everyone knew from the time they were old enough to sit on an elder's knee and hear it told. The gods themselves began to war on Olympus, so long ago that no one could number the generations. Immortal clashed with immortal for three decades, and the humans paid the price in blood and catastrophe. Just when it was certain they would be destroyed by the very beings they worshipped, the goddess Artemis devised a way to kill the unkillable, to slay a god. In the chaos that ensued, the god Apollo was slain, and the light of the sun was snuffed from the sky in an eyeblink. The survivors sued for peace, and when the dust settled, Artemis was the queen of Olympus, and by her hand the walls of Elysia were raised and the humans found shelter there from the ravaged world outside.

Everyone knew that story.

This one was better, Geoff decided, because it was written by someone who had been there, who had seen it with his own eyes.

So engrossed was he that the time slipped away before he knew it.

"Geoff?" Lia's voice was muffled, through the hidden door, and he nearly didn't hear her. "Are you still here?"

The door creaked open, bathing Geoff in yellow gaslight. He blinked a bit until he could focus on Lia's slender form. "Oh…are you done already?"

"Already?" She chuckled and reached for his chair to pull him out of the closet. "It went nearly an hour late. The high priestess forgot her lines again."

Placing his book in his lap, page carefully marked, he swatted her hands away from his chair. "I can do that…"

"Hush, you." She dismissed his protests with a muss of his hair, and flitted over to her work table. "I brought meat rolls from Kedrick's. I thought you might be hungry."

"I could eat a little." The insistent growl of his

stomach indicated he could eat an entire shanty. "You know, at the first Liberation Day celebration, they served lamb and goat and beef. Not just meat." The dingy gray substance provided from the Greenery's stables was edible. And that was really all one could say about it.

"Was that in your book?" She handed him a roll of baked dough, stuffed with meat and whatever else Kedrick could get on market day, then settled in to eat her own, her legs swinging carelessly above the floor as she perched on the table.

"Mmf." He mumbled confirmation through a mouthful of food.

"Do you know what I was thinking of, today?" Lia nibbled daintily at her food. "The tasting game. Remember that?"

Geoff laughed lightly. "It's been years, Lia. We were children."

She pouted. "Oh you remember, I know you do. What do you think lamb tasted like?"

Because he could see her genuine desire to resurrect childhood games, he thought carefully. "I think it was like...deeprat, without the grease."

Lia made a face, giggling. "Oh that sounds awful."

"All right then. What do you think goat tasted like?"

She thought, chewing her meatroll thoughtfully, then grinned. "Deeprat *with* the grease."

He chuckled. It was an old game, something they'd played for hours on end when they were small, spinning all sorts of possibilities out of their imaginations. The most outlandish suggestion usually won the day. "What about thyme?"

"Hey, it's my turn! But I think it tasted like that

green potion of Keras', the one that's supposed to grow hair on the head. Pungent and sharp."

Geoff frowned. "You tasted one of those potions?"

"Just a little, a long time ago. It didn't do anything to my hair." She snickered, her nose wrinkling pertly. "What about marjoram?"

"No, wait, I want to talk about this potion." Geoff grinned a little, seeing the pink blush steal across her pale cheeks. "When was this, and where was I?"

Lia sniffed and tossed her hair over her shoulder, but her blue eyes sparkled with merriment. "I don't spend *all* my time with you, Geoffroi."

Leaning forward, he caught her hand, and tugged her from her seat on the table. "Oh really?"

"Yes, really. I have friends. And things to do. And such." With a giggle, she allowed herself to be pulled into his lap, twining her arms around his neck.

"Not sure how I feel about you having *other* friends," he teased, then tilted his head to steal a kiss. That was how they occupied themselves for the next few minutes, until Lia squirmed uncomfortably, and retrieved the book she'd inadvertently sat upon.

"So, are you enjoying your book?" She idly flipped through a few pages until Geoff took it from her, saving himself from losing his place.

"I'm not very far into it. Some of the verse is pretty archaic."

"You can read to me later. Find me a pretty passage."

Geoff chuckled. "It's about war and its aftermath, Lia. There's not much beauty there."

"You'll find it." She nodded, planted one more kiss on his lips, and hopped to her feet. "Come on, I've got seven paintings that are wanting frames for market next week, and I can't do it without your eye."

Not one to let a meal pass him by, Geoff stuffed the rest of the meat roll into his mouth and wheeled along behind her, gingerly maneuvering around her easels and canvases.

"Oh, and I have a new one to show you too!" Lia grinned back over her shoulder at him, and he nearly choked, trying to swallow his food so she wouldn't mistake him for a deeprat with full cheeks.

She moved so lightly, even in the cramped confines of her shop, nearly flowing around the piles of wood she used to stretch her canvases. Her pale hair, caught back from her delicate face with two tiny clips, provided a perfect frame for those heart-shaped lips and her beautiful eyes. A man could get lost in those eyes and be quite happy for it, Geoff thought.

His vision of those deep eyes was interrupted as an oil painting was shoved in front of his face. He had to lean back to get it into focus, then blinked. "Is that…me?"

Lia moved to kneel at the arm of his chair, nodding happily. "I used your face and hair…it's actually from that legend you read me, the one in that old book… Icarus?"

Geoff could only nod, stunned. He'd found the tale in one of Raffa's old musty tomes, and read it to Lia one day when the acidic rain kept them indoors. Oh, how he wished he could be that boy, flying up to touch the sun, even for a moment. And Lia had made it happen, after a fashion. The strong back and shoulders he'd earned from a years in the chair or on crutches. The soft waves of chestnut hair, the line of the jaw as the subject was just about to look back over his shoulder…yes, that was Geoff. Geoff, with wings of whitest feathers, soaring against the brilliant sun that no mortal in living memory had ever seen.

"It's…amazing, Lia. Truly amazing." He knew his cheeks were red; he could feel the heat creeping up from his neck. It was an odd combination of pride and embarrassment that warred within him.

"This one's not for sale. It's for me to keep." She rose, carefully extracting the canvas from his grip. "But I'll frame it anyway, if you find one that will work."

With her back turned, Geoff allowed himself to truly examine the painting, noting how exquisitely she'd defined the muscles in his back, the strong biceps in his arms. Vanity wasn't something he indulged in often, but damn if the painting didn't make him look handsome. Such a gift she had, and to think she would spend it on painting him. "You should charge more for your work at market, Lia. You could make enough to find a better place, out of Deeptown."

The look she gave him was one of puzzlement. "Why would I want to do that?"

"I don't know. Maybe find a building that doesn't sway in the high wind? Somewhere on ground that isn't dug out? Somewhere that you'd be invited to parties with wine and pretty dresses?"

Lia snorted. "You stop trying to get rid of me, Geoffroi. Deeptown is my home. I'd miss you, and Jon and Rik, and Ambert wouldn't be able to lug these frames on the trolley at his age…"

Geoff barked a laugh. "Immortal spirits preserve you if he hears you call him old."

Before Lia could answer that, the very building shook around them, and soot sifted through new cracks in the walls. A heartbeat later, the sound reached them, a tremendous boom that rattled their teeth in their heads. Lia threw her arms over her head to protect herself from falling debris, and Geoff felt his chair vibrate across the wooden floor. Then all was silence. The pair stared at each other with wide eyes for long moments, bracing to see if it would come again.

"That was nearby." Geoff finally broke the silence.

"Come on, they'll need help." Lia grabbed a pile of blankets from the corner, things she'd intended to tear into painting rags, and tossed them into Geoff's lap.

He nodded and together they bolted toward the door, his chair easily keeping pace with her as she ran. He wondered briefly how they would know which way to go, until they reached the street and gazed in horror at the distant orange glow of flames, reflected on the low-hanging smog. Somewhere, a gas line had burst.

"Lost Lord of Tartarus, have mercy on them," Geoff whispered, and put his wheels in motion.

There were two certain hazards of life in the lower wards of Elysia. The first was building collapse. The only room to grow was up, and when building supplies were scarce, most dwellings were cobbled together in a most haphazard fashion. They waved in the wind like the tall grasses of old, and at least once a month, one of them gave up the fight against gravity and collapsed in on itself.

The second danger stemmed from the over-mining of resources beneath the city. The gas, oil and ore had to come from somewhere, and Elysia perched on a precarious crust over tunnels and caverns that could swallow entire districts. It had happened before.

The cobblestone streets were treacherous at best for the wheeled chair, but Geoff powered himself over them with his arms, following the sounds of yelling and the crackling of hungry flame. The raging inferno, visible above the rooftops, was not in Deeptown, but in the next district over, called Worryville. Even blocks away, he could feel the heat radiating on his face, and the timbers on some of the shanty roofs were smoldering as he passed. They'd lose blocks at best, districts at worst, if the flames weren't controlled.

Arriving at the scene, Lia darted toward a large group of women who were already tearing up old clothing and sheets, preparing the bandages that would surely be needed. Too many times, the lower ward residents had performed the same tasks, for the same reasons.

A sinkhole had indeed opened up, swallowing one building entire. Its nearest neighbor lay sprawled drunkenly across the hole, the middle of the five story building sagging as its structure slowly succumbed to the inexorable downward pull.

The broken gas line roared flames into the sky, the heat melting and withering anything that could not retreat to a safe distance. Horrified onlookers gathered where they could, unable to get close enough to check for anyone trapped in the teetering building.

Tiny voices, pitched high in terror, filtered through the roaring fire to reach the helpless crowd. Merciful spirits, there were children in the downed building. Through the smoke, Geoff could see the pale faces in the windows, waving tiny hands from their topsy-turvy prison.

"There are children in there!" He yelled, in case somehow, no one else had noticed. Wide eyes in soot-stained faces only turned to gaze at him, each gaze telling a tale of hopeless certainty. No one could get to them,

not against the flames. "Someone has to do something!"
The eyes turned away, watching the tragedy in the
making. Geoff gripped the wheels of his chair until the
metal cut into his palms, wanting to scream at his own
uselessness. Someone had to help!

Nearby, a water pipe fell to the blistering heat and
burst, sending an arc of water into the air in contrast to
the column of flame. Most of it hissed away into
scalding steam, but some splattered to the street,
dampening the growing crowd. Geoff never noticed, his
eyes fixed on those pale faces in the broken window.
The building gave a lurch, sagging further into the
sinkhole, and the tiny voices screamed.

"You must help, you must *do* something…"
Geoff mumbled the words to himself, feeling the futility
of it even as the words passed his lips. He could not
help. He knew that.

Even knowing that his legs would betray him, he
pushed his chair forward, all the while muttering to
himself his new mantra. "Do something, do *some*thing,
do something!" They couldn't just sit and watch those
children plunge into the catacombs below. Between one
push and the next, a sudden tightness made him gasp
and grab for his chest and his vision swam drunkenly.

A man standing next to him blinked and stood
stick straight for a moment, then his head snapped to
look at Geoff. "Those blankets. Give them to me!"

Geoff handed over the blankets from his lap, the
pressure in his chest abating just as quickly as it had
come. He watched as the man went into action, running
across the street to soak them in the burst water pipe.
Three more men joined him as they saw what he was
doing, and draped in wet blankets, the quartet made to
brave the heat and flames, working their way slowly

toward the toppled building.

"Here, divert the water, keep it on them!" Someone else yelled, a voice in the crowd, and suddenly they were all moving, working in concert to angle the spray toward the would-be rescuers.

Steam rolled off of Lia's discarded blankets, but the men pressed forward under their protective canopy of wet cloth. Geoff held his breath as one by one they crawled onto the side of the building, the man in the lead urging the children to climb out the window and come to him. The sound of groaning timbers sent a lance of cold through Geoff's chest, and he leaned forward as far as he could, as if his very will could hold the building where it was for a few more precious moments.

Hand to hand, the three children were passed back to safety, then each of the four rescuers retreated, sacrificing their precious blankets to shelter the children in their arms. The moment the last man reached the dubious safety of cobblestone, the building gave one last sigh and folded in half, tumbling down into the caverns below the street. The crowd roared with one voice, surrounding both heroes and victims, ushering them away from the flames, taking them to shelter.

And Geoff remembered to breathe. The strange pressure in his chest was gone.

"Geoff! We have to go!" Lia was suddenly there, soaked and sooty like everyone else, her pale hair hanging limply around her face. She tugged at his chair, pulling him away from the scene. "The Hunt is coming with the pipers, they can't see you!"

Dimly, he knew she was right and he allowed her to drag him away, back toward Deeptown, even as the sounds of booted feet, of marching huntsmen, came down another street. Over that, the incessant drone of the approaching airship, no doubt armed with more water to pour upon the flames from high above.

Though the Hunt served as the Lady's personal guard, and the only law Elysia knew, they were at their very core nearly feral hounds, and their handlers not much better. More than once, the sight of a weak or infirm person had triggered their prey instinct, and they would leap upon the unfortunate victim, tearing them to bloody shreds with their powerful jaws. The sick and the elderly knew to make themselves scarce, when the Hunt was coursing.

Though he was more than capable of propelling himself, Lia pushed him through the rough streets until they reached her shop. There they huddled together in her doorway, the girl seated in his lap, their arms around each other for comfort. Geoff petted her pale hair, and Lia tucked her head under his chin, both of them silently thanking the Gods that it hadn't been their ward, their home, their friends. They watched until the orange glow against the clouds died, the gas cut off perhaps by the industrious pipers who spent their lives tending the city's only source of fuel. If Lia noticed that Geoff was shaking, she never said.

CHAPTER 5

The lift clattered noisily, despite the thick fabrics hanging on the walls to dampen the sound. It was a familiar rhythm, soothing, and Heracles could count the passing floors just by the change in tone as the gears and chains ratcheted the small car upwards.

It finally creaked to a halt at the twenty-second level, and he turned the winch to crank the doors open. He had only a split second to see something rocketing toward his head, and he ducked just enough to let the vase fly by and shatter against the wall behind him. With a sigh, he picked a shard of porcelain out of his cheek and stepped into the room.

Two maids, long skirts hiked up in their efforts to flee, brushed past him and took refuge in the elevator. The two women cowered together, watching fearfully until the door cranked shut and the lift began its descent.

"Artemis?" The Lady's chambers were largely open, only a few pieces of artfully placed furniture between him and the dark, unadorned windows. There were limited places for the increasingly erratic goddess to hide.

"I said get out!" He heard her shriek and ducked again on instinct, shaking his head as the fireplace poker embedded itself, quivering, in the wall to his left.

"That's not lady-like, Artemis." He stood, turning to find her armed with another of the fireplace implements, green eyes glittering with whatever mad rage had taken her this time. She stood there nude, crouched in a fighting stance, the long-handled shovel held before her like a sword. Her golden hair hung in tangles around her bare shoulders, her maids apparently driven off in the process of dressing her. "Give me the shovel, my lady."

"I'll take your head off too, you ungrateful cur!" She ran at him, swinging, only to find her arm caught in his steel grip, the sound of her skin slapping his palm loud against the vaulted ceilings. She blinked in confusion. He squeezed her wrist until her numb fingers gave up the shovel, and it clanged as he kicked it across the floor, spinning away under the antique piano in the corner.

It was a dangerous game he played, Heracles knew. Mad or not, Artemis was a goddess, and he was merely a half-blood bastard. But it seemed when her mind wandered far from this place and time, so too did her knowledge of her own strength and skill. He could usually get away with physically overpowering her.

"Now, what has upset you, my lady?" Feeling her muscles relax in his grip, he slowly released his hold on her arm.

Artemis looked around the room as if she had never seen it before, then wrapped her arms around herself. "I'm cold, and it's so dark, and they will not let me rest..."

Another man, a kinder man, might have reached for her then, drawn her into his arms, comforted her. Heracles was not that man. Not anymore. He walked to the divan and picked up her robe, handing it to her at arm's length. "Cover yourself."

She slipped the silk around her shoulders, seeming smaller somehow now that her rage had drained away. "Could you…turn up the fire?"

With a nod, Heracles went to open the valve on the fireplace, the gas jets flaring brighter as they burned. "Now. What was this little incident about?" He'd lay equal odds it had been something or nothing. Those seemed to be the two choices of late.

The goddess gazed around her apartment, perhaps trying to find the object or person at fault. "The painting…"

"Which painting?" She had thousands, locked carefully away in the vaults, alongside other ancient works of art and literature. Impossible to tell which one had triggered some memory that sent her reeling.

"That one." With a trembling hand, she pointed toward a pile of rubble in the corner.

Upon investigating, Heracles found a shattered frame, the painted canvas barely clinging to it in an effort to remain whole. With a sigh, he spread the wreckage out on top of the piano, doing his best to lay the shreds of fabric in their appropriate places.

It was – had been – beautiful. The setting sun cast pink and lavender rays over a long-forgotten sea, a wind-twisted tree atop a high cliff the only witness. He wanted to feel that breeze, tossing his hair, wanted to feel the last rays of that sunlight sting his eyes. "What did this beautiful work do to so offend you?"

"It wasn't me, it was them. This is what had them so riled up, they knew it was here…" She moved to hover at his shoulder, as if the painting might spring at her in retaliation for its own destruction. "I've never seen it before."

Heracles frowned at her babbling, but examined the artwork with renewed attention. Whatever demons and past sins plagued Artemis' mind, she had a mental catalogue of every original work of art left from before the war. There were copies made as she permitted it, to be sure, but there had been no new creations since… Well, since Artemis had done what was necessary to win. "That's impossible. There are no more muses, Artemis, and therefore no more inspiration for new works."

"And yet here it is, all the same. They knew it was coming." She gathered the courage to reach out and touch it, tracing the letters of the tiny signature in the corner. It said, simply, "Lia".

"Where did you get it?"

"It was delivered…a gift from Lord…somebody."

"Who is the artist?"

"A young woman in the lower wards. They say she sells her works at the little market they have every so often." She seemed to be shaking off the fugue of her madness, and her eyes narrowed sharply. "I want this girl, Heracles. I have to know. Her very presence amongst them could be a risk, if she is…"

"She's not." As firm as he made the words sound, and as much as he wracked his brain, he could not find any memory of this particular painting. And for a human to produce such an image, such a tribute to the sun she had obviously never seen… "She's…found a book or something in the catacombs." The look she gave him was venomous, and he sighed inwardly. "Very well. I'll fetch her for you."

"No. I'll do it myself." He looked at her in surprise, and she smirked, holding herself tall as a queen should, even dressed in the slightest of robes. "It has been too long since I've walked amongst my people."

Trying to ignore the overwhelming sense of impending disaster, Heracles excused himself to go ready the car for the next day's excursion. The clatter and clank of the lift did little to soothe him, the image of the brightly colored painting etched into his mind. Surely, it was a replication of something. The girl could not be a muse, not again after so long.

"Dead and gone," he murmured as he stepped off the lift. "Unlike those of us who are dead and remain."

"Speaking to yourself, Heracles? A sure sign that your mind has turned."

The demigod turned to find Persephone lingering in the tower lobby. "Lady Persephone. Good evening." He bowed from the waist, a gesture of an age gone by.

She gave him a smile, her heels barely making a sound on the marble floor as she approached. Her hair was gathered at the crown of her head in a loose bun, tendrils escaping around her face. There was a smudge of ink on her chin. "Haven't I told you to dispense with all the formality, old friend?"

"And it appears I've forgotten once again." He did try to smile for her, but the expression seemed so alien anymore. Lacking a mirror, he couldn't be sure if he was smiling or grimacing. Perhaps they were not so different in the end. "You've ink on your face."

She chuckled, and slipped a handkerchief out of her sleeve. "It's a wonder I'm not speckled black like one of her hounds."

"You've been working in the library, then?" He offered his arm, and she slipped her hand into it. How strange that she seemed so slight, so delicate, next to

Artemis' strength, and yet she seemed more solid too, like something bound her to the world where it threatened to throw Artemis off at every turn.

"Returning to it, actually. I've just come from visiting Mother."

"And how fares the Lady Demeter?"

"She is still here. Like all of us." The abrupt bitterness in her voice was erased in a soft sigh. "Forgive me. I don't mean to take my irritation out on you."

"That's what I am here for, my lady."

Persephone snorted. "You do enough duty as her whipping boy. I won't mistreat you so."

There was really nothing to say in response to that. He was what he was. They walked in silence toward the library, accompanied only by the hum of the gaslights.

"I understand she's chasing muses again." The comment came from nowhere, and Heracles gave Persephone a questioning look. She shrugged her slender shoulders. "She sent two maids to the servants' quarters in hysterics. Word travels."

"She…wishes me to investigate. I am certain it will be nothing. She's chasing ghosts, not muses."

"And if she's not?" Her hold on his arm brought him to a stop, and she faced him seriously. "What if, after all this time, a muse is reborn? What then?"

Heracles shrugged his broad shoulders indifferently. "Then there will be a blood bath for anyone who came in contact with her. Whether it's needed or not."

"So you agree that Artemis' methods are not always correct?"

"She's stark raving mad, Persephone. We knew it

the day the war began, and it's only getting worse." It had been many long years, watching the once-proud goddess descend into madness.

The blond woman tilted her head to look up at him. "Then why do you serve her?"

"What else am I going to do?" The growl in his voice had cowed braver men, but she never flinched. She had heard it before, of course. "She won't let me *die*, Persephone. She won't let me go, and the only hope that I might find a way to end all this is if I stay here, and you find something in those crumbling old tomes."

"Hsst!" She pressed her fingers to his lips and darted looks up and down the empty hallway. "She may hear."

"Let her. What can she take from me that she hasn't already?" He did take a moment to listen to the silence, warrior's senses straining for eavesdroppers. "Have you? Found anything?"

Her gaze dropped to the floor. "I'm starting to believe I'll never find it. There are…snippets. Rumors of hints of mysteries. It's infuriating."

"Someone had to have known. And what they knew, they wrote down. She can't have destroyed all trace." He frowned in thought. "Maybe another section of the catacombs, somewhere that hasn't been mined out, or…"

"The city is sitting on a soap bubble, Heracles. It's mined out, and all artifacts have to go through her."

"Then ask Hephaestus again. He forged the damned things, he must know what they were made of."

"I have. Again and again, I ask. And he always gives me the same answer."

"That he will never forge another." Heracles sighed. He could respect the other god's morals, but…they were inconvenient.

"I think he only sees me still because he's lonely." The beautiful woman ground her teeth in frustration. "There are times I wish I could just walk out the door and be done with it all."

"You could." That, he said in a whisper. "The guards wouldn't stop you."

"And then what would she do to Mother? And without Mother, all of these people would starve." She cast her hand out toward the darkened city. "As long as she has Mother, she has me. And as long as I am here, Hades doesn't dare intervene."

A patrol rounded the corner at the end of the hallway, and Heracles tugged Persephone into motion, tucking her hand into the crook of his arm again. He nodded to the uniformed guard as they passed, and received a salute in return. He was, after all, their captain. The booted footsteps receded down the corridor and out of earshot.

He glanced back once, to make sure they were alone again, before he spoke. "You believe he is still alive, then?"

"Of course. I would know if he wasn't. She believes it too, else she wouldn't keep such a tight hold on me."

They reached the door of the library, and made to part ways. Heracles paused before the door could close. "If he is still alive, what is he doing all these centuries?"

"Waiting," came the firm answer.

"For what?"

Persephone smiled, a secretive curve of the lips. "Inspiration."

That single word plagued him the rest of the night. Hades had a long wait ahead of him indeed if he was holding out for some sudden flash of insight to show him the way.

There was no inspiration. There was no innovation, invention, or creation. The muses were dead, slain by Artemis' hand lest they reveal the secret only she knew. And the power to kill a god would remain hers and hers alone. *Damn her to Tartarus.*

Damn him to Tartarus too, while he was handing out curses. At least there he would be that much closer to his family and friends. To be sure, the Elysian Fields – the real one, not the bleak mockery in which he now lived – had been walled off long ago, again at Artemis' will. But perhaps he could sit there, against the wall, and feel their presence on the other side. Perhaps someday, they would forgive him for all he had done.

This girl he would fetch on the morrow…would she forgive him, one day? Most likely not. Even when they proved the painting a forgery, Artemis would not let this one go. She lived in a world of shadowy threats and ghostly assailants. Whoever this girl was, she would suffer for Artemis' madness, and Heracles would be the one to hand her over.

As he lay in bed through the long dark – blessedly alone since Artemis had not demanded his services for the evening – he dreamed. Or rather, remembered, because the death of the muses had also stolen dreams from the living. They had only memories through their sleeping hours now, often cruel in their truth.

They walked hand in hand along a beaten dirt path, the boys scampering ahead of them. Megara looked up at him with an adoring smile, squeezing his arm. The sunlight glinted off her hair, and he paused to bring a lock to his face, inhaling her sweet scent.

"Are you happy?" She asked him that question often. She just liked to hear his answer.

"I could not be happier, my love. I am the wealthiest man in the world."

Even knowing what was coming next, Heracles let the memory-dream unwind, savoring those few precious moments of bliss with his family. The laughter of his children, the touch of his wife, pleasures long since gone and forgotten in the waking world.

His first recollection was something sticky on his hands, and he wondered which son had played a prank on him. They were known for their mischievous ways. As he opened his eyes, the smell assaulted him, that of drying blood. He was a warrior of many battles, he knew it well.

Heart hammering in his chest, he rose from the bed. "Megara? Wife? Answer me!" There was no sound in the small house, a structure always filled with the stirrings of life and family. The silence pressed in on his ears, and his head ached fiercely with it.

He stepped to the doorway of his bedchamber, staring out into the common room and—

Heracles forced his eyes open before he could see them again, their bodies sprawled negligently over the floor in pools of blood. That memory he would keep from his mind's eye, if he could. *Damn Hera, too.*

Was she there with his family, he wondered? Cruel irony if the woman who took them from him could see them every day, and he could not. Did dead gods go to the Elysian Fields? He'd probably never know. The walls were there, just like the walls of the city, keeping the heroes of old confined and helpless. All for some mad oracle's garbled prophecy.

And they will come from below, from the depths of no return, and with them, they will bring your death. Artemis built the walls to keep anyone from returning, and not even Heracles, who had once stormed the gates of Tartarus single-handedly, could bring them down.

"We are all damned." The only answer was the emptiness of his room.

CHAPTER 6

"How exactly was I chosen to be the tug-drone here?" Geoff aimed his complaint behind him as he cranked the wheels of his chair, which had somehow become tethered to a small cart of framed paintings.

"Because you're the one with the strapping, manly arms. Now quit complaining, we're almost there." Lia shot him a breathtaking smile and he rolled his eyes with a chuckle. As if he could refuse her anything. She leaned her shoulder against the cart and added her slight weight to the pushing, and slowly they made their way over the uneven streets toward the market. "Next time I'll ask Jon or Rik to help, all right?"

"Don't you dare." Buckling down, his biceps bulged, straining the seams of his threadbare shirt. He made a mental note to see if Lia could let it out again, later. Or, if he could haggle well today, perhaps he could just buy himself a new one outright. It had been forever since he'd purchased new garments.

With a few more powerful heaves of his arms, he propelled them past the last looming tenement, and the wide open square finally came into view. Or rather, normally wide open, but now littered with ramshackle booths and huts, set up to display the wares of the lower wards.

If worship days were days to be quiet and introspective, then market days were the polar opposite, a festival of colored lights and tantalizing foods. Long strings of oil lanterns crisscrossed the square, the waxed paper lamps glowing in cheerful colors. They were no doubt filled with rendered deeprat fat, an energy source they could use without incurring the wrath of the Factory, and the air smelled like sizzling food, making Geoff's mouth water. Somewhere, someone had already started the music, the high tones of a tin whistle threading through the crowd. As the day wore on, there would be more musicians, adding harmonicas, multi-flutes and washtub percussion and perhaps even an ancient fiddle or two, and no one would mind the missing strings. Geoff loved the music. He loved to watch Lia dance.

Several people saw the struggling pair and called greetings, but Geoff couldn't take his hands off his wheels long enough to wave back. Children and ratcatchers already scampered through the crowds, getting underfoot and causing general havoc when someone stepped on a stray urchin or predator. Nearby, raised voices spoke of some very enthusiastic bartering.

"There's Ambert, come on!" With one last burst of combined energy, they managed to get Lia's cart of finished and framed paintings to the large booth Lia shared with the old woodworker.

"There you are! Here I was thinking I'd have to eat these all myself." The grizzled man grinned and tossed them each a hot roll, the waxed paper wrapper just dripping with sticky syrup. Lia squealed her thanks and Geoff juggled his from hand to hand, the warmth of the bun a bit much on his stinging palms. Stinging and now sticky palms, he corrected himself. Nothing to do but scarf the sweet as fast as he could then wash his hands at a nearby hydrant. The rare sweet was worth it, though. So worth it.

While Geoff was about that, Ambert did most of the unloading, lost spirits bless him. At Geoff's insistence, the Icarus painting had made the trip, but when he turned to find it holding a position of prominence on the back wall, he wondered what he'd been thinking. He felt his face grow warm, and half feared someone would realize it was supposed to be him. It was then he made the solemn vow to remain in the back of the booth for the day, unless Lia or Ambert desperately needed him.

It was a plan easier formulated than carried out. With no rain falling, it seemed everyone in the lower wards had turned out for market day. The booths directly across from them were selling clothing and blankets, some new, some secondhand. Down the constructed lane, one could find everything from small motorized windup toys, to the latest in protective eye goggles, to Raffa, selling her dubious roasted rats on sticks. No doubt, Keras was there as well, plying his wares to the crowd.

Everything from potions to make one beautiful, to powders that would cure everything from lice, to deeprot, to black lung. You name it, Keras had it, or could find it. And if it didn't always work as advertised, well…that was someone else's problem. It was next to impossible to pin the shady trader down when his concoctions went awry.

Ambert's work was always popular, and he would be guaranteed to part with everything from platters, to door hinges, to hair combs. But his skills at repair were even more in demand, people bringing wooden items from many districts around to see if he could patch up their ancient treasures. And while the customers kept him hopping, it was up to Geoff to manage the cashbox and negotiate trades. Occasionally, he would look over at the gruff carpenter and get a small nod or shake of the head on a barter, but for the most part, Ambert trusted him to deal fairly. Before noon, he had acquired a small collection of coins in various states of agedness, and several service vouchers that would stand Ambert in good stead, come colder weather.

At the other end of their small counter, Lia's customers were often quite a different ilk than Ambert's. Servant drawn rickshaws came and went in regular fashion, the passengers dressed in finer clothes than Geoff could ever hope to wear. Every now and again, he would catch a whiff of some scent as they milled about, evidence that they were at least wealthy enough to visit a perfumery.

People like that only came from the upper wards, those districts nearest the Tower and the Greenery. They were the ones with the coifed hair and oiled mustaches, the ones in velvets and brocades polished wooden buttons instead of tarnished brass toggles on their coats. Even the servants themselves were dressed impeccably in their matched and tailored uniforms, with gold and silver cording at the shoulders and cuffs. Their polished boots gleamed in the yellow gaslight. No worn out, second-hand footwear there.

If they took any notice of the chair-bound man only a few feet from them, they never made any remark. Perhaps, as Ambert had once told Geoff, they simply refused to see anything that was not to their liking.

There was a small lull in the crowd near midafternoon, and Geoff took that opportunity to escape from the booth altogether, exploring the richness of the market on his own. Children darted around his chair as he maneuvered through the crowds, and folk that he knew called greetings to him over the din. Twice, he caught sight of Raffa, peddling her cheap street snacks, and once Keras passed him at a full run, followed closely by a handful of Factory workers who were clearly bent on doing the shyster harm. There was nothing to do but laugh and watch the chase vanish down the lanes. They weren't likely to catch Keras, and whatever slight he'd offered would be forgotten before the end of the day.

Geoff's own hard-earned wages he spent on a delicate metal hair comb for Lia, and he splurged on a new shirt for himself, the fabric tightly woven with decorative embroidery around the collar and cuffs. With his packages in his lap, he propelled himself back toward Lia and Ambert's shared booth when a low, throbbing sound emanated through the throng. All conversation died, and heads turned to see where it was coming from. Layered on top of the mechanical hum was the tramping of many booted feet. That sound, at least, he knew.

"It's the Hunt," someone whispered, and it was taken up and passed through the crowd. The mass parted, and Geoff wheeled himself backwards to stay within the protective screen of bodies.

The marching unit came out of the street to the north, and in the midst of it, a sleek black vehicle nosed its way around the corner, looking rather like a stalking cat in the pack of hounds. The engine purred menacingly, the dynamos within spinning to keep the auto powered. The crowded square had just enough room between the lines of stalls to allow the car to pass with its escort of uniformed Hunstmen on either side, and the silent onlookers cleared the path in mute obedience. The vehicle's iron-rimmed wheels crunched over the uneven cobblestones, the metal chiming faintly at every rotation.

No one drove a car into the lower wards. Less than a handful of the wealthy still had an auto that was operational. Even in the uppermost districts, society's elite made do with human labor and servant-drawn rickshaws.

"The Lady Artemis…" That whisper too was taken up and bounced through the crowd, and Geoff felt an inexplicable cold chill run down his spine. Why would she be here? She hadn't left the tower in years, and to come to market day of all things? Glancing around to be certain he wasn't going to roll over anyone's toes, he edged his way closer.

The prowling car came to a halt a few stalls down, and the guards stepped back to make room as the driver climbed out. He was a mountain of a man, broad-shouldered and muscled, his hair cut short in a soldier's crop. He would have dwarfed Jon and Rik, and the twins were the largest men Geoff knew. Even Ambert in his prime would hot have been a match for the auto-driver's physique.

The large man's eyes swept the throng of people, and more than one shrank back as his gaze passed over them. Hand resting on the pistol at his belt, he finally nodded, finding things to his satisfaction.

Heracles. Geoff felt a small thrill of excitement at seeing the actual legend so close. The distant view they got on worship days was nothing compared to this. *I've read about you.*

Heracles, the son of Zeus. Heracles, the champion of champions. He had even stormed the gates of Tartarus once, and walked away victorious. Geoff knew him, through the tales told at his childhood bedside, and the books Raffa had pilfered from the catacombs.

Deeming the street safe, Heracles walked to the rear door of the car and opened it. A vision stepped out. Dimly, Geoff knew it was the goddess Artemis, but it took him some moments to get past gaping openly. On worship days, he'd seen her across the span of the great square, and she commanded attention even then, but here, up close… *Within touching distance, if I moved just a little…*

Nearly as tall as Heracles herself, she moved with the grace of a trained fighter, and the long copper-colored coat she wore over her gown did little to conceal the muscles in her arms and shoulders. Her hair, gleaming in the colored lights, was piled high in a tumble of artful curls, and there was an ethereal beauty about her face that spoke at once of her separation from the hordes she ruled over. Her green eyes swept the faces around her, and Geoff felt the urge to physically flinch, clamping down on it ruthlessly. No, Artemis was not, could never have been, human.

The goddess moved away from her car, her cadre of guards surrounding her and forcing the civilians to give way. Her steps never wavered, as if her destination had never been in question. She stopped in front of Lia's booth.

"You there. Girl." The terse words rang out through the unnatural stillness, edges of ice coating what could have been a pleasantly melodic voice. "These are your paintings?"

He couldn't see Lia, lost behind the bodies of Artemis and her guards, but he could hear her clearly. "Yes, mum. Is there one that catches your eye?" Lost spirits bless her, she was trying to make a sale to the goddess herself. Geoff couldn't help but grin for a heartbeat, proud of his brave girl.

Artemis didn't seem to hear Lia's question at all, her attention on the framed works that leaned against the cloth covered wall. "And you painted them all yourself."

"Yes, mum. I've just said so." Geoff could hear the faintest hint of puzzlement in Lia's voice.

Again, Artemis seemed deaf to the girl's words. She ran her hand over one of Ambert's lovingly carved frames, gazing in what appeared to be rapt adoration at a painting of Olympus Tower silhouetted against the mythical sun. She stood silently for so long, stroking the picture frame over and over, that Heracles cleared his throat. "My lady?"

His voice snapped the goddess out of her reverie. Spinning on her high-heeled boots, she stalked back toward the car, tossing "Take her" over her shoulder. "The paintings, too."

No one in the crowd understood what she'd said until Heracles stepped around the counter and reached for Lia. Visible now, Geoff watched as she froze, her blue eyes wide in disbelief. "Please don't resist. I promise you I won't hurt you if I do not have to." The demigod could have snapped Lia's arm with one hand and no effort at all, but instead he took her elbow gently, escorting her out of the booth.

The blond girl was halfway to the car, and a few Hunstmen were gathering up her precious paintings, before Geoff truly realized what was happening.

"No! Li-mmmmmmfff!" A rough hand, calloused and dry, clamped over his mouth, and the arm around his throat held him like a length of steel.

"No no no, bitty birdy… Can't have you singing, no no no…" Raffa's parched and cracked voice whispered in his ear in her singsong way. "Can't be letting them see you, no no no…"

Geoff grabbed the old woman's wrist in both hands, trying to pry it away from his face, but she may as well have been solid marble beneath her sooty rags for all the good it did. Her wasted, emaciated form would not be budged. The crowd around them seemed oblivious to the struggle, all eyes on the spectacle in front of them rather than the drama in their midst.

Raffa's fetid breath was hot on his cheek as she kept up her one-sided conversation, watching as Heracles put Lia in the car and prepared to depart. "Oh, himself won't be happy about this, no no no… Too close, too soon… But they won't find my bitty birdy, no no no… No singing for the bitty birdy…"

Only when the black auto growled its way out of sight did Raffa release him, and Geoff whirled the chair about, not caring if he ran over her toes. She only took one step back, tugging on one lock of matted, dirty hair and grinning. "Why did you do that? They took her, and you just let them! Why didn't someone *do* something?"

"Wasn't time yet, no no no…always about time… Time for this, time for that…time for what was, and what will be…but not now, no no no…"

For the first time, Geoff felt within himself the capability of doing another person harm, and he spun the chair away from her forcefully. She cackled softly behind him as he wheeled himself out into the lane, joining the others who were gazing after the Lady's car in shock.

Lia… A large hand came to rest on his shoulder. "Why, Ambert? Why did they take her?" He looked up at the grizzled old man, feeling the world drop out from under his wheels. Lia was gone.

"Dunno, boy. Maybe just 'cause the Lady said so." The old carpenter squeezed Geoff's shoulder lightly. "She'll be back. With amazing tales of what the inside of the tower looks like, no doubt. It'll be fine."

But it wasn't fine, and it wasn't going to be fine. People who went to the tower didn't come back. The taken ones stayed taken.

Hissing filled the air as thick, sooty rain began to fall, and the merchants dashed to put their wares under shelter. Tendrils of smoke and steam wafted up where the acidic liquid touched something not tempered against it. Geoff didn't even notice until a heavy drop splattered on the back of his hand and started to burn.

"Come on boy, let's get you home. Market day's over, I think." Ambert wheeled him back under the awning, but Geoff's eyes never left the glowing beacon to the north. The tower would shine on, always. And now his Lia would shine within it.

*For she so loved human kind that she gave herself to their survival.
Alone and silent, she governs the seasons without aid of the sun,
and all reap benefit from her.*
                    ~a fragment of a book, found beneath Deeptown

CHAPTER 7

"This is absolutely ludicrous," Persephone hissed, her eyes flashing. "You're torturing that child."

Heracles drew himself up stiffly, frowning. "I can assure you, she hasn't been harmed in any way. And I don't appreciate the accusation."

"Look at her, Heracles! You can't tell me this isn't torture." The pair turned to look through the window, watching the blond slip of a girl sob her heart out even as she tried to put brush to canvas.

The young woman's hand wavered, the quivery lines and hesitant colors showing none of the talent her earlier works had proven her to possess. A blob of ochre paint splattered to the canvas, obviously not where she'd intended it to be, but she didn't seem to care. Stacks of similarly marred works leaned forlornly against the walls surrounding her, a colorful prison smelling of oil paints and linseed oil.

In the week she had been at the tower, the girl, Lia, had done nothing but sit with tears rolling silently down her face on her best days, and on her worst, she had flung canvases and easels about the room until even

Heracles had been forced to retreat. It seemed not to matter that she had been clothed in fine gowns, or fed sumptuous foods, or that for the first time in her life, she experienced a hot shower in pure, clean water. No, she adamantly resisted her confinement, refusing to produce the evidence Artemis had demanded.

At first, Heracles had taken the onset of constant rain outside to be a good sign. Muses were, at the core, water nymphs, and perhaps the girl was conjuring water from the very clouds in her distress. But surely, the pure water she had been bathed in would have done something for her disposition, had she truly been a water nymph. The shower had no effect, and the girl, like the weather beyond the tower, continued to drizzle all over herself.

This was not the muse.

It did not mean, however, that there wasn't one, a fact Heracles would take to his grave if he must. Something had happened there, in that squalid market. Like the brushing of a butterfly's wing across his skin.

"You're not even listening to me anymore." Persephone turned away from him in disgust, letting herself into the distraught artist's lovely little cell.

The girl's voice carried out through the door as it closed. "Please…I just want to go home."

The former warrior pressed his fingers against his aching temples with a weary sigh. There wasn't a single female in the tower that was pleased with him at the moment. Artemis was furious with the captured artist's inability to perform miracles on command. Persephone blamed him for the girl's unjust imprisonment. And lost spirits knew, the girl herself had every right to hate him. He hated himself.

After all, they had the wrong person and he knew

it.

Within the small room, Persephone gathered the girl close, petting her hair and murmuring soothing nonsense. Her gaze, however, was fixed on the mirror the window became on that side, glaring daggers at Heracles.

He sighed again, and turned away. *What would you have me do, Persephone? Reveal to Artemis that a muse exists? That I am actually dreaming for the first time in centuries?* And oh, what dreams. Hand in hand, he and his wife had walked along a cliffside he had never seen, to watch a sunset that had never happened. Only upon waking did he realize the setting had come straight from one of the blond girl's paintings. He clung to that dream, hoarding it jealously. If Artemis knew, she would find a way to take it from him, deprive him of even that small comfort.

But where did it come from? That was the thought that had plagued Heracles' mind for days. And as he walked the lower halls of the tower in a half-hearted patrol, he pondered it still.

It had to have been in the market. It had to have been close. But try as he might, he could picture no other female that he had passed close to. Only the willowy child, Lia, and it was a certain thing that the girl had been exposed to the muse as well. Her paintings proved that, by their very existence. Perhaps hidden in the back of a booth? Or someone the car merely passed by in the street?

His wanderings found himself in the Greenery, and he grimaced as he realized his location. No sooner had he stepped through the first steam-clouded door than four be-goggled heads poked out of various nooks and crannies, looking him over and dismissing him just as quickly. The Greenery drones were always more interested in their own incessant tasks than any visitors. One of them went scuttling past him in its once-white coat, gender impossible to tell behind the goggles and the faint greenish tinge of mold on all exposed skin.

Cockroaches, he thought, taking care not to get too close to the mildewed forms. Once they had been human, he knew, but decades of dampness and darkness and artificial lights had turned them into something else. Occasionally, he could pick out one that was newer than the rest, one that had not lost their identity, whose skin was still pinkish and whose goggles hadn't become a part of their face yet. The rest of the drones typically kept those well away from the rest of the tower denizens until they were well indoctrinated. Heracles didn't know the process, and didn't want to.

The big man threaded his way through low work-tables, ducking the complicated piping system that hung over each to dispense the warm mist that was a water source to the unidentifiable plants being cultivated. He jostled one table and three drones converged to shoo him away, muttering disapproval in the strange shorthand they had developed. He gladly moved away, feeling the dampness already condensing in his hair, trickling down his neck and under his shirt. Even a few moments in the Greenery could leave one feeling waterlogged.

The door he'd entered by was evidently in the heart of the new growth section. The Greenery surrounded the base of the tower, and was divided into wedges, each one containing foodstuffs in different stages of growth and production. They cycled like the seasons of old, one being replanted as soon as its fruit was harvested, a never-ending circle of artificial life and death progressing around the nucleus that was the tower.

He passed through another door between sections, and found himself in a room where the plants were larger, though not yet mature. The drones there peered at him momentarily, then scurried away on their chores, no doubt pollinating something in replication of the industrious insects of lost times.

One table was filled with what he thought were tomato plants, though the tiny orbs he saw dangling from the vines were sad imitations of the fruits he remembered from his youth. There was only so much that false light and recycled water could do, and the resulting crops were bland, colorless, and nearly indistinguishable from each other. And the meat… He just shuddered to think of it. Gray, formless, almost entirely synthetic. Herdbeasts had died along with the sun and their grazing grounds. The protein now was produced near the hub of the Greenery, and Heracles was careful not to investigate too thoroughly. There were just things he was happier not knowing.

Pure chance brought him through one more door, where he was confronted by a dozen agitated drones who refused to let him pass further. Their impudence annoyed him, and he finally barked "Move!", scattering them with terrified little chitters. The drones didn't go far, hovering at the edges of his perception, bleating amongst themselves.

Seeing the silent figure seated in a large chair against the wall, he realized why they'd been so reluctant to make way. They'd been protecting their queen.

"I won't harm her, you know." Whether or not the drones understood him, or cared, he couldn't tell.

The Lady Demeter sat in her makeshift throne, silent and immobile as she had been for…longer than any mortal's current memory. The rich velvet of her gown had long ago become indistinguishable from the layer of soft moss growing upon it, and her ebony hair, hanging straight past her shoulders, was threaded with dark vines, the leaves a faint purple against her raven tresses. Veins of green stood out against her pale face, like living lace. Her hands, visible at the ends of her sleeves, were likewise tinged green, taking on the damp growth like the flesh of every other living creature that spent more than fleeting moments in the humid Greenery. Her eyes stared sightlessly straight ahead, the surfaces gone milky at some time in the past.

"Lady Demeter." He gave her a bow anyway, out of respect for Persephone if nothing else. The younger goddess paid visits to her mother nearly every day, insisting that Demeter was aware of all that took place around her. "Your crops look good, this day." He received no response, of course. She hadn't spoken a word, that he knew of, in ages.

Persephone claimed that it took all of Demeter's concentration to keep the Greenery running as smoothly as it did, imposing her will to keep every mouth in the city fed despite the less-than-ideal circumstances. It was the duty she had taken on after the war, trading her freedom to save the mortals that had looked to the gods for guidance all along.

Still, Heracles could easily believe that the goddess knew he was there, and it made him uncomfortable. Did she blame him, he wondered, for what he had become? "Um… Your daughter will no doubt be along to see you soon. She tells me often how she enjoys your visits."

"Not answer. Know this." Heracles flinched, looking down to find one of the drones looking up at him. The genderless creature barely came up to mid-chest on the big man, and it offered a small smile, displaying brownish rotting teeth. "Forgive startle. Lady not answer. Help you?"

It was nearly impossible to follow along with the abbreviated language the drones used to communicate. Heracles wondered if Persephone had mastered it. "No, I don't need any help. I just stopped to greet the lady, and I'll be going now."

"Happy is. Like visit." The drone reached out to stroke Demeter's still hand with a look of rapt adoration on its face. Or, what little of its face was visible around the enormous goggles. "Wish good fortune, you."

Heracles tilted his head. "How do you know she is happy, if she does not speak?"

A beetle appeared out of the drone's hair, ran down its neck and disappeared into the dingy white coat. Heracles' stomach rolled. "Happy is. Say we. Know."

Heracles' brain ached from trying to fill in the missing components to the sentences, and he desired nothing more than to end the odd conversation entirely. "Then I am pleased to have brought happiness to her."

The drone gave a happy little caper, much to the warrior's amazement. "Happy she, happy we!" The sentiment was echoed from other drones, unseen behind the numerous tables of flora and fauna. Many voices chorused "Happy she, happy we!" over and over.

Unnerved, Heracles made his bow to Demeter, and headed for the door. The talkative little drone followed him, and he started to wonder if it was going to trail him all the way to the exit. "Did you need something else?"

The short creature paused, tilting its head thoughtfully. Male, Heracles decided. At one time, this one had been a male. Something about the voice. "Need little. Desire more."

"Is that your sentiment, or hers?"

He earned a brown-toothed grin again. "Happy she, happy we."

"And what would make her happy, besides visits?"

The drone's smile faded, and it seemed even the green mold on its skin lost some of its color. "Free she, free we."

Heracles sighed. "I can't. She knows that."

The drone nodded sadly. "Sorrow she, sorrow we."

A mournful refrain of "sorrow she, sorrow we" followed Heracles out the door, through multiple sections of the Greenery, and he swore he could feel the beetles crawling on his skin until he escaped to the relative sanity of the tower proper.

And oh, sanity was relative. For example, Artemis at the moment seemed in full possession of her faculties, and was rather pleased with herself for it. Even her clothing seemed to reflect her jubilation, her overcoat a color of sky blue that had not been seen overhead in centuries, and the trousers beneath a buttery yellow. She had even gone so far as to scatter sapphires through her shining curls, caught in a fine net of gold mesh.

"Look at this. Just look at it! Olympus help me, I've been blind!" She jabbed a finger at one of the confiscated paintings. "Right here in front of us, all along. I wonder at my addled wits, sometimes."

Heracles wondered too, as he watched her exclaim and coo over the artwork, but Artemis in a good mood wasn't something to be questioned. "And just what is it that we have missed, my lady?"

"What do muses do, my ardent warrior?" She gave him a smile, obviously delighted to be instructing the unenlightened. For his part, Heracles bit back a grimace at the endearment. "They inspire. Nothing more. Never, ever in their history, do they create." She turned back to the painting, stroking the frame like a beloved pet. "And what do artists do? They write songs about their muse. They compose odes to their muse. And…they paint their muse."

For the first time, Heracles paid attention to the artwork. It was a bold composition in bright colors, a winged man silhouetted against a vibrant sun. The light shone through the delicate feathers, and settled in the subject's chestnut hair, picking out highlights of copper and gold. He seemed just about to look over his shoulder, and the smooth line of his jaw was beautiful, in an almost androgynous way. The muscles of his back, though cast in shadow, were well-defined, obviously someone who had labored.

"This is our muse, Heracles. Find her."

"That is a man, my lady." She gave him a scathing look, and inwardly he sighed. He had hoped to distract her from the obvious, and had failed.

"Look at the line of the jaw, the soft waves of hair. This could easily be a feminine form, adapted in the imagination to fit an old legend. Icarus, if I remember correctly." The goddess nodded, smirking to herself. "No, this is our muse, and she must be in that filthy little borough. You will find her."

Heracles didn't want to find her. At least, not for Artemis. Not when he had his first flickering of hope in centuries. "And how do you propose I do that? I doubt she'll just walk out and present herself to me."

"The girl, of course." Simply oozing self-satisfaction, Artemis turned to run her fingers over his chest. "Release the girl, and follow her. She'll lead you right to her muse." Her arms slid around his neck, and she pressed herself against him, murmuring against his lips. "You'll do this for me, my warrior, won't you?"

As Artemis claimed his mouth in a possessive kiss, Heracles imagined the feel of her slender neck, crushed to jelly in his powerful grip. It would do nothing of course, save make her angry, but the idea itself had come out of sheer imagination, and he savored it. Even as she ordered him to her bed to service her, the newborn idea was his and his alone, like his dream, and she couldn't take that away.

CHAPTER 8

There were more faces in Deeptown these days. Refugees from Worryville's most recent disaster had moved into any vacant tenements they could find and were busy trying to rebuild their lives. Once, such a population influx would have meant a different kind of disaster for Geoff, who would have had to fight to keep the small space he had claimed for his own. With his new apartment adjacent to Ambert's, he no longer had that worry. And his good fortune totally escaped him.

It had rained every day since they took Lia away. No one in Deeptown, or its neighboring districts, could remember such a long downpour. Even those buildings that were tempered and inured against the acid rain were starting to succumb, eaves and staircases sagging precariously where the bolts holding them had simply been eaten to nothing. And in the rain, no one could get out to make repairs, so there was nothing to do but huddle indoors and wait for the inevitable collapse.

Geoff didn't care if the buildings fell down around him and everyone else. The wheels of his chair became pitted and rusty from his daily trips to Lia's home, and the only acknowledgement he made of the inclement weather was to switch to his crutches and make the five-block trudge on foot. He kept an oiled canvas over his head and shoulders to protect him from the dismal precipitation, but as the sooty streams in the streets swelled daily, his shoes were slowly being eaten away. At night, he tried to pretend that his tortured knees weren't swollen and hot to the touch. He cut a rather pathetic figure, hobbling his way to and fro at least twice a day, but he didn't have it in him to worry about such inconsequential things. It was either get out and move, or sit alone in his room with his heart in ruins.

At Lia's, he went about cleaning up her small studio, stacking canvases by size, organizing her paints by color, making plans to frame the few remaining pieces for the next market day. He patched up the new leaks brought on by seven days of rain, struggling to balance on the short ladder with his aching legs. And when those tasks finally ran out, he simply sit and read, surrounded by her scent, his mind wandering to grim what-ifs and maybes more than the text on the page.

And the oracle looked upon the goddess with blind eyes, and spoke the words "And they will come from below, from the depths of no return, and with them, they will bring your death." And Artemis struck her down in one blow, and cursed her.

Geoff was certain he had read that same passage more than once. As he looked over the page, he realized he'd been staring at the same one for hours. With a sigh, he closed the book and rubbed his head with one hand. Seven days. She'd been gone for seven days. He couldn't remember going that long without seeing her beautiful face ever in his life. It seemed Lia had always been there from the time they were both children, the first person he saw upon waking and the last before he closed his eyes. He didn't know life without her.

What are you doing right now? Are you all right? He stared at a small self-portrait she had painted years ago, willing her to hear his thoughts. *I miss you.*

A pounding on the door jarred him out of his

thoughts, and he fumbled for his crutches as a voice outside yodeled "Hello the house! Any lovely ladies in there?"

Geoff opened the door to find Keras leaning drunkenly against the jamb, and the sly trader gave a snaggle-toothed grin under yet another jaunty fedora. "Geoffroi! Lovely, yes, but not a lady… At least, I don't think so… Shall I check?" He made as if to reach out, and Geoff smacked his hand away, balancing on one crutch to do so.

"What do you want, Keras?"

The stench of alcohol and cheap perfume nearly made Geoff's eyes water. He leaned back out of reflex, and Keras seemed to take that as an invitation to enter, giving Geoff no choice but to take a few hopping steps back to avoid being spattered with the rain from the trader's tattered umbrella. Keras tossed it in the corner where it sat, steaming mournfully. "Well, that one's outlived its usefulness. Guess I'm here 'til the rain stops, then. Is there anything to drink?"

The thought of being trapped with Keras for the duration of the seemingly-endless downpour made Geoff faintly nauseous. "Again I ask, what do you want?"

As if Geoff hadn't spoken at all, Keras gazed around the shop with a hangdog expression. "No drink? Ah well, good that I've brought my own then." A flask appeared out of the flea-bitten fur coat and he downed a long swig, tipping the fedora back to do so. "You want a belt?"

"No. Thank you." Gritting his teeth, Geoff at least managed to be polite. Lia would have wanted that. No one was ever turned away from her home, if they needed shelter. "Did you need something, besides a place in out of the rain?"

Keras wandered past Geoff and into the depth of the shop, picking up Lia's paints and brushes, fingering them, then tossing them down negligently. "I saw the light on, thought I'd see if the lovely was home again." He cast a lecherous grin over his shoulder. "Didn't expect to find you here, Geoffroi. You keeping the home fires burning, are you? Lighting a candle so she can find her way back to your loving arms?"

"I'm just looking after things for her, until she gets back." He trailed along behind the unwelcome houseguest, putting Lia's things back in their proper places in the wake of Keras' passing.

While Geoff's motives in visiting Lia's home were mostly selfish and driven by longing for her presence, it also served the practical purpose of keeping squatters from claiming an abandoned dwelling. Which was, no doubt, what Keras had intended only to be thwarted by finding Geoff in residence.

"Downright noble of you, Geoffroi, fine and upstanding." His curiosity apparently satisfied, Keras sprawled into the chair Geoff normally favored, legs thrown over the arm, looking so much like a large wet hairball, topped with a dark purple fedora. "Always said you were a do-right kind of guy. Ask anybody."

In the distance, the clock on Olympus Tower tolled the hour, and overhead, the airships announced that curfew was in two hours. "If you want to catch a trolley back to the upper wards, you'll have to get going soon. They start cutting routes down here before Dark." Geoff had no idea where Keras actually lived. No one did, that he'd talked to. But Lost Lord of Tartarus, please let the annoying man leave. Geoff didn't dare leave him alone here in Lia's home. Spirits only knew what would turn up missing.

"Don't you worry about Keras, he always finds a nice warm bed to curl up in. Usually with a lovely or two." He winked. "You could come with, you know. I know several lovelies who would be more than happy to make you forget your troubles for a few hours."

Geoff felt his face grow warm, and Keras cackled. "No, thank you."

The older man shook his head, chuckling still. "Oh come now. You can't tell me that you've been dipping your brush in the pretty one's paint, can you? We all know you haven't."

The blush grew darker, but Geoff glared down at the scrubby little ratcatcher. "Whether we have, or have not, is no one's business but our own.

"Psh. What else do we have to do for entertainment but speculate?" Keras paused long enough to drink from his flask again, breathing a satisfied sigh. "There are quite a few service vouchers riding on the person who guesses when you'll cave. Because we all know it isn't her that's dragging her pretty little heels."

"This conversation is over." Geoff abandoned one crutch to hobble back to the door and snatch up Keras' traumatized umbrella. "Get out."

"Bah, Geoffroi! You're so high strung!" The shady trader flung his arms wide, sloshing liquor onto the floor, but making no move to rise from his seat. "You know what you need?"

"If you say a woman again, I'm going to beat you to death with my crutch."

That earned a laughing snort, and the shorter man finally pried himself up out of the chair. "Not just any woman. You need a certain type of woman." A thoughtful look crossed his ratty little face. "Matter of fact, c'mon. We're going out."

"I'm not going anywhere with you." He pointed to the door with the umbrella again, pretending that the cloth wasn't currently dripping off of the frame in melted puddles.

Keras grinned from under his battered fedora. "Tell you what. You come with me now, and I'll leave you alone for…at least a month. You don't come with me, and I'll just make camp here and talk to you all night."

Rolling his eyes at the ceiling, Geoff asked the dead gods for patience. "I take a trip with you, and you just…go away for a month?" Tempting. So very tempting.

"On my honor as a scoundrel."

"That doesn't…what does that even mean?"

Taking that for assent, the trader reclaimed his melted umbrella and steered Geoff toward the door by one elbow.

"But, it's raining!" No one in their right mind would brave the acid sludge that had been plaguing the city for a week straight.

"So? We'll take my car."

Somehow, Geoff found himself bundled up and herded out the door like a wayward herdbeast, unsure how he got where he was, or how to get back to where he'd been. And all he could really think was, *Keras has a car?*

A car it was indeed, and a fine one, parked only a few blocks from Lia's modest shop. How under the sunless sky no one had ever seen Keras driving it before was a mystery.

Tempered against the acid rain, the black paint

only had a few pit marks, and the rest easily reflected Geoff's bewildered face in the finish. Keras pushed his reluctant guest into the passenger seat, burnished leather squeaking with every movement.

"Mind those crutches, don't be snagging the upholstery," Keras admonished, and hit the starter with his thumb. With a few coughing chugs, the car rumbled to life, the whirring of the dynamos under the hood giving the entire vehicle a subtle vibration.

Geoff could only gape in amazement as Keras eased the throttle forward and the car rolled into action. As an afterthought, he folded up his greased canvas and laid it safely in the floor to keep any residual drips from marring the leather where he sat.

The wiry trader gave Geoff a sidelong grin. "You've never ridden in a car before, have you?"

"I've ridden on a trolley," Geoff answered absently, watching the street lights slip past faster than he could ever move under his own power. The rough cobblestones, such a bane to his wheeled chair, were barely noticeable as Keras' vehicle purred along.

"A trolley. Bah! That's like comparing a racing stallion to a plow mule." Keras tilted his head, scratching his fuzzy chin thoughtfully. "But then you won't know what those things are either, do you? Here, let's get us some music going, shall we?"

Keras fiddled with a few knobs on the dash, and a radio popped and sparked to life, the tinny music barely audible under the static. "Bah, no reception when it rains. Ah well, not like they're going to play anything new, right?" He cackled at his own joke, hands flying over levers and switches that Geoff couldn't possible fathom a use for.

The lights whooshed past faster, and the car

careened around a corner, pressing Geoff tightly against the door. He grabbed for a strap hanging above his head and held on for dear life. Keras laughed harder. "That's it, Geoffroi, hang on tight! No sense wasting time in the traveling, when the destination is so much more fun!"

Within blocks they'd left Deeptown far behind. In fact, they left behind all the districts Geoff knew, and the buildings they passed began to sag less, and were not so dependent on their neighbors to remain upright. They passed fewer glowing yellow gaslights, and more that put out the pure white light generated by electricity. The rain ran into gutters alongside the streets instead of swamping the roadways themselves, and twice Keras cut across the path of a trolley with only meters to spare, causing Geoff to cringe and brace for the crash that never came.

"Maybe we could slow down? Just a little?" As fascinating as the high-speed conveyance was, Geoff was more than a little queasy.

"Of course we will! Right here, in fact." Keras pushed a third lever, and the car's steel wheels screeched in protest. Geoff was forced to plant his hands against the dash to avoid meeting the windshield. "Everybody out, we're missing the party!"

As Geoff struggled out of the car in his tangle of crutches, he noticed that the rain had stopped. The scent of oil and acid still hung heavily in the air, but the toxic precipitation seemed to have ceased for the time being.

Keras noticed too, tipping his gaudy purple hat up to peruse the dark sky. "Hunh. Whaddya know. Things are looking up, Geoffroi me boy! Hey, that rhymes!" Delighted with his unintended poetry, the spry man linked his arm through Geoff's, heedless of the need for crutches, and practically dragged him down a short flight of stairs beside the street to a recessed door. He placed his finger to his lips, miming silence, and winked at Geoff as he rapped out some intricate pattern on the wooden portal.

A moment later, a panel slid open and a pair of bloodshot eyes darted back and forth between the two men. Identity presumably established, the panel slammed shut, and the door creaked open, letting out a thick cloud of clove smoke.

"Hello ladies, your darling has arrived!" Keras plunged into the smoke to a chorus of female voices calling greetings, and left Geoff to choke his way through the fog.

He heard the door slam shut behind him, the rattle and clank of gear locks falling into place seeming a bit final for his tastes. The heavy pall of smoke that hung about the room made his eyes water, and by the time he could get his vision cleared, Keras had installed himself at a large table across the room and was waving frantically for Geoff to join him. "Over here, Geoffroi me boy, best table in the house!"

Navigating the length of the room proved to be easier said than done.

The tables and low chairs made the cramped space even more so, and none of the patrons seemed inclined to make way for a man with crutches. After the fifth time he had to mumble apologies to someone he'd jostled, Geoff gave up. No one looked up at him anyway, hats down low down over their eyes or noses buried in glasses of gods knew what.

But the women, they noticed him. Hands appeared out of seemingly nowhere to touch his shoulder, his arm, to trail across his back or stroke a lock of his wavy hair. Painted lips curved in smiles that said much more than he could understand, and he nearly injured himself trying to find a safe place to rest his gaze. Everywhere he looked were corsets in satin and leather and heavy buckles, silken stockings that ended in tightly laced boots, and far more flesh than he was accustomed to seeing. It seemed they passed by him in a trill of laughter and a scattering of glitter, and the air nearly shimmered with the weight of their perfume.

He became aware that the low pounding he felt from the soles of his feet to the top of his head was in fact the deep base of some music, drowned to only impulse beneath the general tumult of the cramped lifeforms.

"Slide over girls, give my friend a seat!" Surely it was Keras' grip that pulled him off his crutches and into the plush booth, the deep crimson leather nearly swallowing him whole. "Lovelies, this is my dear friend Geoffroi, and we're going to give him a night to remember."

Darkest night, how many women were crammed in there with them already? Geoff quickly found himself pressed between two scantily clad, but very soft, forms, and did his best not to flinch when tendrils of curled hair tickled his ears and neck. *How under the black sky did I get here?* Better yet, where was here?

Keras caught him trying to get a better look at the room and laughed. "Let it go, Geoffroi. You only find this place if it wants to be found." That cryptic statement was followed by a cheer as a serving girl delivered a tray full of drinks to the table.

The redhead on Geoff's right leaned across him to grab a short glass full of clear liquid, then thought better of it and fetched two, setting one in front of

Geoff. When he looked up at her to murmur thanks, she slowly licked her first sip from her painted lips, and gave him a grin, reaching out to toy with a lock of his hair. "Go on, it's good."

Keras seconded the sentiment from somewhere within a sea of fiery embraces. "Drink! It's called the Waters of Lethe, and it'll help you forget all your worries, just for a little while. You have too much going on in that pretty head of yours."

"I don't want—"

"Drink!"

Reluctantly, Geoff picked up the glass and sniffed at the fumes rising from it. It made his eyes water, and he coughed. He gave Keras an uncertain look, but the trader just motioned him to drink with a cheerful grin.

At first gulp, Geoff was certain he was drinking heating fuel. Then the brew seared his taste buds and he could no longer taste anything at all. The liquid burned down his throat and settled in his stomach like a ball of flaming pitch. Reflexively, he gasped, and the inhaled fumes had him doubling over coughing until tears ran from his eyes. Dimly, he became aware that Keras was pounding on the table and cackling loudly.

"There we are! It'll put hair on your chest."

When Geoff could breathe again, he made it very clear that he did not want a hairy chest much to the amusement of all involved. The red-haired woman – and no one had hair that shade of crimson naturally, Geoff knew – cooed and nuzzled his neck, allowing him a glimpse of her very generous cleavage. The heavy buckles on her satin corset pressed into his arm, and where he might have objected to the discomfort a moment ago, he found now that he really didn't care so much.

She smelled of something spicy and thick, not like Lia's light floral fragrance. The strange woman's arms were plump, round, not slender and lithe like Lia's. Her voice, low and warm, like syrup… Not like…like…who? Though he tried to cling to it, the thought of Lia flitted away like the tendrils of smoke in the air.

Seeing his fascination with the clove fog hanging over the table, the sable woman on his left lit a clove and entertained him by blowing smoke rings that hovered and danced over the table at her whim. The women chuckled amongst themselves, and Geoff found himself chuckling right along with them, sipping from his glass every time one of them pressed it into his hands. Beneath the table, he felt slender fingers exploring the length of his thigh, and he dimly knew he should object, but couldn't for the life of him remember why. Even the ever-present pain in his knees was dulled, and he finally just dropped his head to the back of his seat, closing his eyes and savoring a few blessed moments of peace.

A pair of soft warm lips found his throat, and a flicker of a tongue tasted his pulse just below his jaw. He didn't care. It was warm here, and soft, and the alcohol nestled into a warm glowing orb in his stomach.

When they ran out of the potent alcohol, the waitress appeared as if by magic, bringing another tray full of small glasses. Geoff blinked blearily at the woman who seemed to sense his gaze. When she turned to look at him, he realized it was a man, not a woman, with features almost as delicate as his own. Another blink, another moment, and no, it was a woman again. Or was it? He watched him/her walk all the way across the room, and could never reach a positive conclusion.

Geoff eyed the glass in his hand warily.

Keras snickered, watching his confusion play across his face. "That's Andy. You don't really want to know."

"I don't?" He was answered with a laughing chorus of "no"s from the ladies surrounding them. "All right." It was easier to do what they said than to try and make his mind function past the Waters of Lethe.

"Here now, watch this, this is something special." He heard Keras' voice somewhere under the humming in his ears, and he obediently brought his eyes into focus, to watch in mild curiosity. "Thel doesn't sing for just anyone."

Across the room, another of the lovelies had ascended a table, and she stood there in a circle of light. Her hair, black as day and night both, had been pulled high, then heated into three fat curls that lay along her neck and over her pale shoulder into her cleavage. The black corset was adorned with buckles and stitching of gold, and her long skirt fell in many layers of ruffles to the table, affording no glimpse of her silk-clad legs, unlike most of the other women. Over it all, she wore an odd cloak of coal-black feathers. Without the Waters of Lethe, Geoff might have wondered where she obtained feathers in a world whose birds had been dead for millennia.

She stood there for long moments as if waiting for something, her hands clasped before her. When all eyes were upon her, the cue she had been waiting for, presumably, she drew a deep breath, her breasts straining the boundaries of her garment, and opened her mouth.

The voice that emerged was the most beautiful thing Geoff could ever remember hearing. High and pure like crystal even in the smoky air, it lifted every person present to another place. It didn't even matter what the words were, it was so pleasant to soar on the wings of her voice, flung high into the clouds and caught before plunging into the depths at the bottom. More than one person blinked back tears, stunned by the beauty and fearful that it would be over far too soon. Geoff felt his heart swell as if it might burst from his chest, and his world shrank to include only that pool of light and the singer within.

He was on his feet and couldn't remember how he'd gotten past his amorous companions. For once, his knees didn't hurt, and he hobbled his way to the singer's table without benefit of his crutches. There, he gazed up at her, rapt and enchanted (and more than a little woozy).

She smiled down at him, reaching a hand out and he took it in his. At that moment, he would have stayed at her side for the rest of time. As if she knew, her smile grew, and there was something dark and predatory behind the lovely voice. Geoff didn't care.

"Ah ah…none of that now." Keras retrieved him, extracting his hand from the siren's, and shook his finger at her, admonishing, "You know better, Thel."

Unabashed, she sang on.

Geoff allowed Keras to guide him back to his seat, and collapsed in the midst of the attentive ladies who purred and made over him. Thanks to the strong brew, he no longer possessed the capacity for embarrassment, and he took it all in stride, smiling through the fog of booze and smoke. There was very little his new friends did not attempt, and it never occurred to him to refuse.

There was no telling how long it went on. Surely the chimes on the tower had sounded, because patrons reluctantly began to depart, shadowy forms slinking back to their usual lives before Dark. Geoff fell asleep to a sweetly alluring song, cradled against someone's soft bosom, and only dimly remembered the ride home through the drying streets.

Later, he was certain he remembered Keras tucking him into his own bed, almost tenderly stroking his hair. "You sleep. It's well past Dark for all of us."

The strains of the raven-haired singer's lament echoed in his ears, carried on by the trader's multi-flute as the odd man sat in the chair in Geoff's outer room playing quietly for himself.

Geoff would wonder later at the odd things the alcohol made him see as he lay in his bed watching the world beyond his door swim in drunken circles. Things like prim little hooves poking out of Keras' pantlegs where feet should be, and the gleam of tiny horns in the trader's curly hair when he removed his ever-present fedora.

When he woke at First Light, Keras was gone.

When Artemis found him watching she and her maidens, she was so wroth, she transformed him into a deer, and set his own hounds up on him, tearing him to pieces.

~ancient Elysian myth

<u>CHAPTER 9</u>

Follow her. Watch her. Take the hounds. Of all the commands Artemis could have given him, that last disturbed Heracles the most.

The kennels were at once a place of solace, the smell of warm furry bodies and straw eliciting memories of days and hunting companions gone, and a place of unease as those in various stages of the transformation mingled unabashedly with their fully canine brethren.

Heracles walked the narrow aisles between the stalls, carefully keeping his eyes straight ahead and ignoring the muffled sounds of animalistic coupling from not entirely animal pairings. Several large flat heads poked out of the dens, nostrils flaring as they tested the scent of this visitor to their realm, their golden eyes following him down the walkway. From the farthest stall came meek whimpering, and the bitch kept a wary gaze on the demigod as he approached, hackles raised in warning if he got too close to her new litter. The female hound stood with her black-speckled head nearly at his waist, and he was not a small man. Her threat was valid.

At the end of the aisle, one of the huntsmen stood at attention and saluted his captain. Heracles felt obligated to speak. "All quiet?"

"Yes sir. The shift should be changing in about twenty minutes." The man's speech was only slightly slurred, the over-large canines in his mouth inhibiting some of the more sibilant sounds. His eyes had not taken on the golden quality of the hounds yet, and the black spots, while visible on the back of his hands, had not progressed to his face. This one was nearly human, still. Heracles didn't know his name. In a year or so, it wouldn't matter.

"Any of them needing exercise in particular?"

The huntsmen looked over the stalls thoughtfully, then nodded. "Number eight. He's been antsy for a few days, but he's almost too big for any of us to handle."

"Perfect."

Number eight was large as promised, even for one of Artemis' hounds. The massive male raised his head from his paws – the size of dinner plates – and watched Heracles with a golden gaze that, while not threatening, was most definitely not subservient. Instead of the usual speckled coat, this one was pure black, hints of blue hidden within the slick fur when the light caught just right. There was always one black hound in Artemis' kennel. Some preference of hers, he supposed.

Heracles rattled the chain lead once in command, but the dog took his own time standing and shaking the straw from his short fur. There was no mistaking that all proceedings would be on the hound's terms. The overly intelligent look in the golden eyes said as much.

In a way, it was nice to know that the transformation didn't break all of them. Just most of them.

Heracles clipped the heavy lead onto the chain collar, and brought the hound to heel. "Now I just need to get you a scent."

Heracles left the kennels behind him, a mixture of relief and revulsion making him desire a bath more than anything else. *Not a good way to feel about one's own troops.* They were his in name only, of course. It was Artemis who would always demand their devotion.

Despite his distaste at their creation, he was forced to admit that the Hunt was effective. Even those just beginning the change could outrun, out-jump, out-climb, and generally outperform any ordinary human, and once the massive hound form had taken hold, they were nearly unstoppable. The muscular animals could sprint for hours, and their jaws could crush steel pipes. Nothing escaped their keen sense of smell. They could track a scent across the length of the city, leading unerringly to their prey.

And to a creature, they were unfailingly, unswervingly loyal to their mistress. Even Heracles, their ostensible captain, did not warrant the rabid devotion Artemis commanded.

Though his dreams were only recently restored to him, Heracles had already had several nightmares about being chased down dark alleys by baying hounds, feeling those powerful jaws close on the back of his neck. He disliked turning his back even on the ones who still resembled the humans they'd been.

A glance downward showed the great hound looking up at him, as if the beast knew of his current keeper's disquiet. *I wonder if I knew you, before.* Best not to think on those things. The men these hounds once were had vanished at the whim of their goddess. Very little of the human sentience remained. Though this one, this black monster…he might be the exception.

It was easy enough to retrieve a bit of the young artist's clothing from the room where they'd kept her. Not two hours ago, Heracles himself had put her on a trolley bound for the lower wards, and depending on how well the transports were functioning this day, she should be nearing her home in another hour, just before Dark. He'd planned it that way, so she'd have to go to ground as soon as she left the trolley. That was how a hunter found a den. And surely, she would be living near her muse.

The ebon-furred male sniffed at the delicate slip of cloth Heracles held before his snout, ears perking with the first sign of interest. "Lead me to her."

The dog threw back his square head and bayed, the sound reverberating through the small room until Heracles' ears rang. From the far distant kennels, other voices answered, not all of them fully canine.

With a lurch that nearly jerked the large demigod off his feet, the hound was off, intent on one thing and one thing only. He would lead Heracles straight to the girl.

No one saw Heracles and his hound loping through the streets of Elysia. To be sure, there were people out, scurrying to finish the last of the day's tasks before Dark, but every eye was averted, every ear turned deaf. No one wanted to see the Hunt, no one wanted to watch one of their neighbors torn to shreds in those massive jaws.

It was just as well. If they'd truly paid attention, someone might have wondered just why Heracles himself was leading the Hunt with only a single hound at his call. Better that no one begin to ask questions or think of wild possibilities. That would lead to other things.

The girl's trail followed the trolley lines, as Heracles had known it would. He and the massive hound covered the distance at a ground-eating jog, the demigod being one of the few beings who could easily keep pace with Artemis' cunning hunters.

Several times they were joined in their hunt by a huntsman and hound pair, the loping canines exchanging some kind of silent communication before the patrol went its own way again. The huntsmen seldom glanced at their captain, already adopting the law that a direct stare was a challenge to authority. None of them would challenge Heracles. Yet. Perhaps someday, when Artemis had no further use for him.

The rain had stopped sometime in the last two days. As they made their way into the lower wards, the black silt left behind collected where gutters ought to be, clogging drainage lines and trolley tracks alike. They passed one car, stalled where it sat as the irate engineers squabbled over whose turn it was to clear the way. Upon seeing Heracles and the Lady's hound, the two men decided it was in their best interest to cooperate and hastily began the repairs.

Four times the girl changed cars. At first, Heracles thought she was trying to be cagey, but then he realized that wherever the young woman lived, the trolley service there was questionable at best. Her easiest route home happened to be the most circuitous, passing through more districts than Heracles could count. And the further out from the tower they went, the more deplorable the conditions where.

Nearest the tower, Elysia's heart, the homes were lighted with electric light, generated by the Factory's steam boilers. The buildings were sturdy, tempered and coated against the acid rain, and those passing in and out of them were dressed fashionably in their silks and satins and fine wools.

But the outer rings of the city, those beyond the tower's light... Here Heracles saw structures that were barely upright, and in some cases not even that. The cobblestoned streets had been scavenged for building materials, making them little more than mucky, gravelly trails. Twice, he was forced to skirt large sink holes, and in those neighborhoods the buildings were dark, no one daring to risk being the next to fall into the earth's gaping maw.

Here, eyes followed him from shadowy doorways and alleys. They were gaunt eyes, desperate eyes, wary eyes. The scent of rotten meat permeated the damp air, and hushed voices muttered at his passing. Lotus eaters, he knew, and made note of the location. The Hunt would have to come back in force and clear out this next before they swarmed.

None challenged him, though, scuttling back to the safety of the shadows as he and the black hound passed. Dark was coming, and no one wanted to be caught out with the Hunt running. Fear was an excellent teacher.

So intent was he on the area around him that he nearly ran over his quarry before he spotted her. The hound had led him away from the trolley tracks, indicating that the girl was at last on foot, and they rounded a corner only a few dozen meters behind her. With a hiss of breath, Heracles man-handled the hound back out of sight despite the dog's struggles. "Shhh...good boy, you found her... Good dog..." He kept a firm hand on the dog's collar and the animal quivered under his touch, anxious to lay claim to the prey he'd tracked across the length of the city.

The streets were nearly clear this close to Dark, and Heracles' own internal clock could feel the time winding down to first bell. A few voices called greetings to the sylph-thin artist as she darted across the street, but she did no more than wave. Her destination seemed to be a plain door set in the side of a building. It was an odd door, he realized, wider than one would expect, with the knob set overly low. The girl rapped her knuckles on it, hugging her tattered shawl around her shoulders as if it would ward off the impending darkness.

It was not her dwelling, he realized. One doesn't knock at one's own door.

The door opened inward, and for a few seconds, only the silhouette of a standing person was visible. The voice, though, it carried, breathless with disbelief. "Lia?!" A young man's voice, and as the girl threw her arms around the fellow's neck, he was pulled into the yellow gaslight. In fact, he nearly fell on his face, staggering with one hand clutching a rather crude crutch. The device seemed to be clamped around his forearm, and that was all that allowed him to keep hold.

His infirmity seemed confined to his legs. Heracles could see the outline of wiry muscles beneath his shirt, and his grip was steady on the crutch once he got his balance. The other arm pulled the girl close and he held her tightly. "Thank you, merciful Goddess." He turned his face up toward the black sky, tears trickling down his smooth cheeks, and Heracles' heart stopped.

It was Icarus. Or at least, the model for the painting still in Artemis' possession. Understandable that they had expected a woman - every muse Heracles had ever heard of had been a female – and who would have thought a man could be so beautiful? Even in the tainted sickly light, the soft waves of his chestnut hair gleamed with golden highlights, and his skin appeared flawless, perfect, as if it had never seen a razor in its life. There was a delicate cast to his features, without making him appear weak, and a grace inherent in his form despite whatever injury confined him to the crutch.

Where under blighted Olympus did you come from? And gods on high, there was no doubt in Heracles' mind that he had found the source of Lia's inspiration. Even at a distance, he could feel the tightness in his chest as if a steel band was wrapped around his heart. He was one of the few people left in the world who would recognize the sensation for what it was.

It was love, pure and simple. A great aching love emanating from the crippled man. It washed out from the muse in a wave, uncontrolled and unfettered, and no doubt everyone in the district would feel its effects. Flirtations would turn into passionate devotion, this night, total strangers would find soulmates in the eyes of those across a dingy table, and for those whose loves were long gone beyond reach, they might very well close their eyes and follow them across the River Styx before morning. So much raw power and not an ounce of control behind it.

Heracles leaned heavily against the wall next to him, trying to ground himself in the present moment. *Megara…I would follow you gladly…* She was so near, he could smell her perfume and the sea air near their modest hut. Tears stung his eyes and in thoughtlessness, he almost released the hound to wipe his face.

The beast lunged against his lead, sensing freedom close, and Heracles yanked the thing to heel, eliciting a pained yelp.

In the doorway across the street, both young

people looked up, startled, and glanced warily around. For one moment, it seemed the man, the muse, looked directly into the alley that hid Heracles, but a moment later he had drawn the girl inside and closed the door.

"Ha! Nearly got you that time!"

Heracles whirled at the sound of a voice behind him, and found a rather odd looking character lounging against the alley wall. The man might have been short and spry under the moth-eaten fur coat, but it was hard to tell. His face was mostly hidden by the wide brim of a garish fedora, but his snaggled teeth gleamed white as he grinned at the demigod.

Heracles frowned. "Who goes?"

"Who goes? Well, nearly everyone goes, sooner or later. Nearly, of course, not all, because there are always exceptions to prove any rule, wouldn't you say?"

The hound growled softly, a barely audible rumble, and Heracles tightened his grip on the collar. Distantly, on Olympus Tower, the clock chimed first bell. "Curfew comes, you should be off toward home, citizen."

The jaunty little fellow sauntered toward Heracles, twirling a thin cane in one hand, tapping out a subtle rhythm. "Home is where you lay your head, I say. That way, you're never far from it." Something about the tilt of his head, the pattern of his speech seemed familiar, but try as he might, Heracles could not place it. "Except you of course. You're far from home and hearth, and into strange territory here."

"All the city is my territory, at the Lady's behest." Still, the little man advanced on him, and he had to marvel at the nerve. Very few humans would face down one of the Lady's hounds, let alone her demigod bodyguard.

"And of course, when the Lady snaps, we all jump to, sharp as nails. Keeper of the world pillar, long may she reign and whatnot." The strange man stopped within arm's reach, and fished inside his mangy coat, finally emerging with a beaten grimy flask. "Have a belt?"

"No, thank you." Heracles tried to keep the incredulity out of his voice. It had been a long time since anyone spoke to him thusly. Hells, it had been a long time since anyone outside the tower had spoken to him at all.

"Suit yourself." He helped himself to a swig of whatever was in the flask, and the aroma of alcohol filled the alley. Up close, the scruffy man had a scruffy goatee to go with his scruffy coat. They were the same color too, apparently some shade of dun brown, though Heracles could see darker curls beneath the gaudy hat. "Never did appreciate the simpler pleasures in life."

The world seemed slightly out of joint, Heracles realized, as if a lens had fallen a hairsbreadth askew. Perhaps it was simply the reverberations of the muse's high emotional state, but the demigod felt a haze around his thoughts. They skittered out of reach like water beetles on a pond. "Do we know each other, sir?"

"Oh, I don't think we do." Again, the odd fellow flashed the toothy grin that at once seemed jovial, lecherous, and snide. "Sure you won't have a belt, before you go?" He offered the flask again.

"Who says I'm leaving?"

With a weary sigh, the scruffy man shook his head. "Perhaps I'm not making this plain. Shall I use smaller words?" He tipped the brim of his hat up, and while his voice remained as jocular as ever, there was something sharp and hard behind his watery eyes. "You are not welcome here." He pocketed his flask and sauntered out of the alley, turning to look back once as he stood in the street. "This place….it's for people who can appreciate it. Not for old soldiers who sold out their own kind."

Perhaps he flinched, the stranger's words echoing thoughts he had never voiced about himself. Perhaps there was a ratcatcher nearby that wanted chasing. Perhaps the hound just sensed his distraction. Either way, the great beast gave a lunge at his lead again, and it took a good while to get the dog under control again. The ebon hound growled, the muted sound promising to become a roar if he was truly provoked, but he finally yielded to the demigod's superior strength.

When Heracles looked up, the strange man was gone.

He looked up and down the alley, even daring to poke his head out and peruse the street. The second warning bell rang out, the airships overhead intoning their doleful message of pleasant sleep and the Lady's goodwill. Nothing stirred.

Forcing the stubborn hound to turn about they way they'd come, he began the long walk back to the tower. The last sign he had passed had said "Deeptown." He would remember that, and he would return.

CHAPTER 10

She knew the moment he returned to the tower. It was like a rubber band snapping back into place after being stretched thin. Such was her connection with the hounds of her Hunt.

Her coat was midnight blue this night – though midnight and high noon alike had been nothing more than pitch black for centuries – and it suited her mood as she stalked her way down to the kennels. She felt as turbulent as the roiling smoggy sky above, anxious to know if the hunt had been fruitful. She didn't know if she was more afraid it had succeeded, or hadn't.

Heracles was just manhandling one of the bigger hounds back into his stall when she arrived.

"Well?"

He straightened, wiping his hands on his trousers before he answered her. "Well what?"

"Well did you *find* her?" Something about his demeanor pricked her ire. He was obviously set to be obstinate again.

"The girl? Of course I did. Your hounds have never failed." The chain lead rattled as he hung it on the hook by the door.

"Not the girl, idiot!" The sound of her palm meeting his face echoed down the long walkway, and flat speckled heads poked out of stalls to watch the commotion. In contrast, the semi-human guard near the door averted his eyes discreetly. "The muse! Did you find her?"

Heracles rubbed his jaw for a moment, and she could see the rebellion glimmering in his dark eyes. It was answer enough. "You did, and she's put thoughts into your head hasn't she?" With a sneer, Artemis traced the darkening bruise on his cheek. "Would you like to strike me back? Reach out to snap my neck with one strong hand? I can see it in your eyes. You are thinking thoughts you have not contemplated in centuries, and it's because you were near her."

She drew back her hand to strike him again and he caught her wrist, his massive hand dwarfing even her muscled arm. "Perhaps it's simply because, like any hound, if you strike me enough I will eventually bite back."

The ebon-furred male growled a soft warning, echoed up and down the long aisle by the rest of the pack. The sound made Artemis smile and filled her with an almost giddy assurance that she was in the right.

"Perhaps you simply need a reminder of who I am and why you serve me, my ardent warrior." Her gaze found the guard at the door, his still-human eyes turned away from the brewing conflict. "Perhaps you need to recall just what I am capable of."

It was a simple power, possessed by many of her kin and used to greater effect by some than others. The power to transform those around her into the shape of her whim could be extremely useful. It could also be terrifying.

The guard, already a hound in the making, jerked stiffly to his feet, eyes going wide in horror as he felt what was happening. His mouth opened to scream, but the changes being wrought in his throat eliminated any human voice. Instead, a strangled bleat emerged, the man choking and gagging on his own tongue now grown too large for his mouth.

He hit the ground on all fours, seizing as the muscles crawled and knotted beneath his skin. The sounds of bone cracking were loud against the bare ceiling, and every hound in the place had emerged from its den to watch the spectacle.

Heracles made the mistake of trying to look away, and Artemis grabbed his chin, forcing it forward. "You will watch, my warrior. And you will remember." She could feel his jaw clench at her touch. She sank her fingernails in for good measure.

Fine brown hair had emerged over the tortured man's body, his clothing fallen away or absorbed somehow during the transformation. He shrieked as his pelvis fractured with a gunshot report, reforming itself, and his knees folded backwards to create the hocks of some four-legged creature. His ears lengthened, his skull flattened on the top even as his cheekbones and jaw crackled in their transformations, creating a muzzle with a broad flat nose. His eyes, pleading mutely with the goddess who commanded him, became large and round, deep brown pools of agony.

You do this at my will. You have given yourself to me and you are mine to do with as I see fit. Artemis smiled gently at those begging eyes. There was no greater act of love than giving himself to his goddess' purpose.

His fingers, braced on the floor, fused into two thick toes, the skin blackening and melting together as it shrank into a tiny hoof. The coat of fine hair now covered his entire body, down to the tip of the thin tail that had sprung from the base of his spine.

In a matter of excruciatingly painful moments, a tottering newborn calf stood where a man had once been. The pitiful creature shuddered, trying to find a balance on its new and unfamiliar hooves, knobby knees trembling with the effort of supporting its own weight.

The enormous hound in the kennel next to her butted her hand insistently, golden eyes turned up in entreaty. She caressed the black-furred head, and nodded with a smile. "Have your way, my hunt."

"No!" Heracles' protest was lost in the baying of the hounds as the animals descended on their one-time keeper.

The calf managed one terrified bleat before it was buried under the mass of muscular bodies, and soon the only sound was the cracking of bone and snarls as the hounds squabbled over choice tidbits amongst themselves.

Satisfied, Artemis turned to look at her bodyguard. "You are immortal. Can you imagine being torn apart like that every morning of your life, only to heal anew by Darkfall and face the same fate for eternity?"

He swallowed hard, no doubt trying to contain his gorge. He'd never had the stomach for the truly necessary things, in her experience. "Would it be so different from my life now, my lady?"

Ah, so we play the martyr now, my turncoat? "Perhaps not for you, no. But Persephone?" She shook her head. "It would be a pity for her to suffer for your obstinance."

"Leave her out of this."

"Of course I will. Of course." She patted his arm, the muscles in it corded with his clenched fists. "But fetch me that muse. Before she has a chance to contaminate anyone else with impure thoughts."

He was defeated, and she knew it. She could

sense it deep within her hunter's soul. Heracles turned
to go, and Artemis happily watched her hounds feast.
Piles of steaming offal disappeared down the lean
throats, and the irritated snarls had dissolved into growls
of contentment. One of the males mounted a female
there amid the carnage, the beasts coupling with no
thought at all to the humans they'd once been. For the
first time in days, the voices in her head were silent.

"Heracles?" She heard his boots stop. "Come to
my bed tonight." He didn't answer, but she knew he
would obey.

~*!*~

Geoff watched worriedly as Jon pronounced his
diagnosis. "Honestly, it's a miracle it hasn't snapped off
and dumped you in the street, Geoff."

The crippled man slumped against his crutches.
"So you can't fix it?"

Jon stood, wiping his hands on the rag he always
kept in his back pocket. "The axle is nearly rusted
through, and the wheels aren't even round anymore
they've been so eaten away. Look." A piece of rusted
wheel snapped off and crumbled between his fingers.
He ran a hand over his short hair, pursing his lips in
thought. "If I can get some metal, I can probably work a
whole new apparatus under it, but…there's no repairing
what we've got here. There's nothing left to repair."

Geoff's heart sank. Sure, he could get around on
his crutches, but on the days his legs were paining him
the worst, he'd be nearly bedridden without his wheeled
chair. "Well, thanks for looking at it. I'll figure
something out, I guess."

Jon gave him a small grin and punched him

lightly in the shoulder. "Hey, don't make with the long face. Have a bit of faith in me, all right? I'll magic something up."

Geoff managed a small smile, and when Lia passed within his line of sight, it became larger. Yes, a broken chair was a small inconvenience. Now that Lia had returned, so many other things seemed trivial and unimportant. "Whenever you have time. I don't want to be a bother."

"You're not a bother, Geoff. Deeptown wouldn't be home without you." Jon followed his gaze to Lia, who was helping Ambert recoat his awning against the acidic rain. Luckily, the precipitation seemed to have ceased in the last few days and the people of the lower wards were slowly making repairs.

Lia, dressed in a pair of borrowed trousers and a rough work shirt, clambered nimbly over the awning, even her slight weight making it sway dangerously. If she felt unsafe, it didn't show as she flicked spatters of the waxy fluid down at Rik who had smarted off at her.

Jon glanced away from his twin and back to Geoff. "It's good that she's back. It's not Deeptown without her, either."

Geoff could only nod, words catching in his throat again as he thought of a life without her, a life with Lia gone.

The night before, she had slept curled up in his bed, his arms around her where he could feel every breath, hear every heartbeat. She had come home frightened, angry, but unharmed. She was safe. He lay awake the entire night, repeating that to himself, his face buried in her mane of flaxen hair.

During those long, dark hours, he'd come to a few decisions. He would ask her to marry him, just as soon as he could find a ring suitable. Whatever his reasons for waiting before, they were inconsequential now. His Lia had been returned to him, and he couldn't risk losing her again.

The low hum of a dirigible passed overhead, and most who were working outside paused to look up. The airships typically didn't sweep the lower wards until closer to Dark, at least not on non-worship days. A spotlight split the smog and did a slow serpentine dance over the rough street.

"They're looking for someone," Jon frowned at the unseen airship. "I heard the Hunt was in the district last night. Old Wiles said he saw the biggest hound he'd ever seen, pitch black and breathing fire, with the biggest huntsman."

"Old Wiles would say he saw the Lady herself dancing naked atop the Wall, with what he's usually drinking," Rik interjected as he joined his brother. "But I passed Raffa this morning, and she was upset, even for her, and babbling about hounds and hinds, or some such."

"Probably some convict escaped from the Factory is all." Geoff couldn't take his eyes off the light, now moved on to the next block. A chill ran over his arms. How strange that something as simple as a circle of light could feel so ominous.

"Well more power to the poor bastard, whoever he is." Jon seconded Rik's sentiment, the twins nodding in unison. "Nasty way to go if the Hunt catches him."

"When the Hunt catches him." There was no if. The Hunt never failed, and there was nowhere to run. There was only the Wall, trapping them all within its protective and condemning embrace.

Life went on in Deeptown. Lia finished her

acrobatics atop Ambert's awning, and climbed down to help one of the new families patch up a leaking window. Geoff ended up managing the counter at Ambert's shop, as people seeking repair work began straggling in, sometimes with their marred possessions in carts behind them, sometimes with a plea for the carpenter to follow them back to their homes. The twins, having a day off from the Factory, were drafted into lifting a large staircase into place where it had collapsed.

Deeptown was bustling, which would explain why no one heard the airship return until the spotlight speared through the darkness above and fixed on Ambert's shop. When the light did not immediately sweep on, those in the street began concerned murmurs, and Geoff left the small stool he occupied to investigate.

All faces were turned upward, searching the smog for the ship, when something thumped down at the east end of the block. Geoff blinked at what appeared to be merely a wad of cloth, until he noticed the tendril rising from it into the clouds. Three more bundles of rope spiraled down out of the sky to land on the cobblestones with soft noises, and a moment later men began descending the lines.

They were dressed as the Hunt, in trim dark uniforms, goggles protecting their eyes from the contaminants in the air above. Alike enough to be indistinguishable, the four carried pistols on one hip, but no other visible weaponry. Each man paused as his boots touched the ground, and in unison their heads swiveled toward the beacon light, focused now on Geoff who stood in Ambert's doorway.

Geoff was struck by the odd thought that he was now prey. *Why…?* He didn't even have time to complete the thought.

From the west end of the block, the baying of hounds broke out, haunting voices from many throats. The people of Deeptown scattered with terrified screams, parents frantically rushing to get their children inside, nearly knocking their neighbors down in the scramble.

The Hunt appeared between the buildings, huntsmen and hounds alike, the large canines straining at their leads as they gave full voice to their efforts. The four men from the airship merely stood in the street, gazes fixed on Geoff, and the frightened residents rushed past them without notice.

They're coming for me. He knew that with certainty. For no reason he could fathom, the Hunt had come for him, in force.

The others knew it too, those who had loved and nurture him all his life.

"Geoff!" Lia screamed, somewhere in the throng that was pressing her away, and he caught a glimpse of Ambert's massive arms holding the girl back as she tried to reach him.

He lost sight of her as one of the huntsmen broke ranks, striding ahead of his fellows. No, it wasn't a huntsman after all, but Heracles himself, the colossal man scarcely pausing to avoid the fleeing crowd. His massive shoulders parted the tide of people like water, his inexorable steps carrying him straight to the man in the spotlight.

Geoff's mind was suddenly blank, flailing for some guidance that refused to materialize. His chest hurt. It was the only thing that anchored him to reality, and his thoughts coalesced into a babble of *someone help me!*

"Geoff! Run!" Jon's voice over the din, and

Geoff heard a hound give a yelp of pain. Heracles stopped in his advance to look behind him.

The twins had ambushed the Hunt from the rear, Jon's enormous wrench cracking the skull of a hound before the beast could even turn on him. Rik held his ground beside his brother, clubbing the dog's handler to the ground and snatching the pistol from the downed man's belt.

Run? How? Where? He stood frozen, watching the scene play out even as Heracles dismissed the interruption and returned his attention to Geoff.

The demigod filled his field of view, looming over him. For the briefest moment, Geoff entertained the notion of striking out with his crutch, fleeing into the alleys. The blond giant raised one brow, as if he could sense his quarry's thoughts. "I have no intention of harming you. Come now."

A pistol cracked, and Geoff stared in horror as he saw Rik's limp form disappear under the seething mass of hounds and huntsmen. Somewhere in there, Jon was forced to his knees, arms twisted behind his back as he tried to reach his brother. Geoff could still hear Lia screaming his name.

"This is not necessary. Please, come."

Perhaps it was the please. Perhaps it was the genuine pleading in Heracles' voice. Geoff nodded, stepping forward on his crutches. Immediately, four huntsmen surrounded him, matching their steps to his awkward gait.

They led him west, past Jon as they clapped chains on his ankles, past the steaming pile of what used to be Rik. The hounds were eating well, it seemed. Even the bodies of their slain brethren were disappearing down the spotted throats. Geoff swallowed hard, tasting the bitter vomit at the back of his throat but refusing to be sick. *I'm sorry. I don't know why this is happening, and I am so sorry...*

Something scuffled in the alley, and the four guards snapped their heads that way in perfect unison. But it was only Raffa, staring in horror as they escorted Geoff away. His last sight of her was the strange woman biting so hard on her own fist that she drew blood.

CHAPTER 11

"Simply amazing." Artemis prowled around the chair, touching the young man's silky hair, his face, whatever caught her eye at the moment. It never occurred to her to wonder if he objected. "I mean, just look at him, Heracles!" Her bodyguard had no response, merely standing at the door with his hands clasped before him as she examined the prisoner.

He was not what she'd expected at all. The very fact of his maleness, for one thing, was highly unusual. In all her admittedly fragile memories, she could not recall a male muse. They were water nymphs, and therefore female. She could not even recall a word for a male nymph. Had there ever been one?

And what a male. He was absolutely, stunningly beautiful, almost ethereal with his large eyes and delicate features. And yet, flawed as well. She kicked one of the offending appendages out of her way as she passed, and he winced, gripping his deformed knee.

"Perfect in every way, save the legs. I wonder

how that came to be." The young man's jaw clenched, but if he had something to say to her, it did not escape. Fear did that. Made him easy to control. Beneath the fear, she could feel the rage radiating off of him. It tingled across her skin. Pure, unadulterated hate. "You. Your name."

He glared at her from under his chestnut bangs for a moment before gritting out "Geoffroi."

"Geoffroi." She purred the name, sweeping her long gown aside as she crouched down to look into his face. "How did you come to be, Geoffroi? What tiny crack of Tartarus did you creep out of?"

"I don't understand your question. I was born in Deeptown." Confusion warred with anger in his eyes, adding a bitter tang to the sensations she felt seeping from his very skin.

They will come from the deep… No, that was not how the prophecy went. Was it? Coincidence, surely. "To what mother?"

"I…I don't know. I was found abandoned in the snow. Raised by others."

Artemis pursed her lips and stood. "Either he lies, or he believes his lies so much as to make them truth."

"I'm not lying." When she reached out to pet his hair again, he jerked his head out of reach. "Why did you bring me here? I've done nothing wrong!"

She snatched a handful of his hair and yanked, simply to prove to him that she could. "I brought you here because it was my will that you come. Do you need another reason?"

It took him too long to answer, and she wrenched his head again. He winced. "No, my lady. Long may you reign."

"You're how old, in your twenties? How under the dark sky did you manage to evade me for so long?" He didn't answer. She didn't really expect him to. *Who else did you miss in your genocide, sister dear?* Apollo's phantom voice taunted her gleefully. He was obviously amused by her incompetence. *Shut up.*

"Why have you not healed yourself?" She kicked his leg again, and his face went white but he made no sound. Stronger than he looked, then. And sturdy, despite his infirmity.

"I don't understand your question." He corrected himself a heartbeat later when she made to kick him again. "I don't understand, my lady. My legs have always been like this. From birth."

"You have control of water, yes? Water is the body's binding force, therefore you should have been able to correct the imperfection." From the look on his face, it was clear that he thought her barking mad. *Is it possible that he truly does not understand his own nature?* She turned to find Heracles still watching silently. "What did you observe in the people who have been exposed to him?"

"You met the girl. An artist of no small ability. He also dwelled in close proximity to a woodworker of some renown. Other than that, I saw no evidence of any particular influence. It would seem his effect has been largely passive, these twenty-some-odd years."

"Save on you, my warrior, no?" She smirked as Heracles refused to respond to that. He was going to require some reeducation, once she removed the muse from play. If he *was* a muse. She was still not convinced. *He is. You know he is. Can you eliminate everyone he ever touched? Everyone he ever influenced? The seeds may already be planted, dear sister.*

With a scowl at the incessant mockery in her head, she kicked the crippled man's leg again. This time, he bit back a yelp. "Get him up, bring him to the Greenery. There is pure water there, we'll see what effect that has."

~*!*~

He had entered a den of lunatics, he was certain of it. And chief amongst them was the goddess herself, long may she reign.

Geoff kept his mouth shut when they confiscated his crutches and plopped him into a wheeled chair – a much nicer vehicle than any he had ever owned to be sure, with a plush upholstered seat and padded armrests – and ushered him into the lift. It was already clear that drawing Artemis' attention to himself was counterproductive. He'd seen her go from sweet and almost purring to violent and raging in the space of two breaths. His own legs ached from the constant torment she seemed to be taking a perverse pleasure in.

And the poor servant girl she'd beaten, simply for coming too near Geoff in the expansive hallway. The girl had looked barely conscious when the vengeful goddess was finished. Geoff hoped she was all right.

Perhaps if he could get Heracles alone, he could plead a case for his own release, but… Once the stoic warrior had gotten Geoff into his car, he hadn't said another word, and he didn't seem inclined to offer any more conversation now, either. He merely marched along behind, pushing the chair as Artemis kept pace beside.

They were bound for the Greenery, apparently, a place Geoff had only glimpsed on worship days.

Something to do with the pure water there? Truly, Artemis' comments had made little sense to him. *Control of water?* If he had control of water, he'd have done away with the acid rain years ago. *Just what under the black sky does she think I am?*

The lift rattled and clanked to the lowest level, and Heracles wheeled Geoff into the hallway. The wave of humidity was like a slap in the face, and the thick smell of something living was nearly overwhelming. It was almost too heavy to breathe, and yet he could almost feel his skin soaking up the moisture as if he had been parched for years. The air tasted sweet when he opened his mouth to gasp. The sticky taste was faintly unpleasant, like the aroma given off by some great rotting corpse.

Artemis noticed his reaction as he struggled to make sense of the unfamiliar smells. "The air is kept moist here, because it is conducive to accelerated plant growth. The downside is that the water tends to degrade anything that remains inside for very long. Including the workers." Her gaze went to Heracles, behind Geoff. "Bring him inside."

The glass door was clouded with mist, the condensation dripping from the jamb as Heracles opened it. As soon as they entered, Geoff felt the wetness settle onto his skin, his hair, like a thin veil. *Like rain that doesn't burn...*

That in and of itself would have made the place a wonder, even without the strangeness spreading out before his eyes. As far as he could see, row after row of low metal tables lined a narrow walkway, and overhead sprawled an impossible tangle of copper pipes and glass bulbs, the white light throwing rainbows through the constant mist. *Rainbows....* He knew at once that was the word, though he'd only read of them. Nothing like the tainted riot of colors in a wet oil slick, no matter what anyone else said, and he'd be sure to tell them that when he saw them again. If he saw them again.

Past the pipes, the glass ceiling of the Greenery reflected the darkness, the lights of a trundling airship the only relief against the black smog.

Beneath the tinny rattling of the pipes overhead, a shuffling sound to his right drew his attention. Geoff caught just a flicker of something darting between the tables as he turned his head. Were there living things in here besides the plants? He peered that way, but Heracles pushed the chair on, and whatever it was did not reappear.

"What do you think?" He looked up to find Artemis looking expectantly at him, and his heart sank when he realized he had no idea what answer she might be looking for.

"It's…interesting. What do they grow here?" Asking questions of his own seemed a safe route to take.

"Whatever is needed." She gestured at the low tables, most of which were covered in a layer of black dirt, the first springs of green shoots poking up through the soil. "Every bit of food you have ever eaten in your life has come from this Greenery."

Except Raffa's rats, he thought, and he fought the urge to smile fondly. No doubt, the erratic goddess would misinterpret the expression.

Something scuttled behind one of the tables as they passed, and Geoff got no more than a glimpse of what appeared to be two very large black eyes staring at him before they were gone. *What the…?* That had been no ratcatcher.

Artemis noticed it too, if her frown was any

indication. "Make certain they stay back." At first Geoff was confused, then he realized she was speaking to Heracles.

"It doesn't look like it's going to be a problem. I've never seen them this skittish before." Heracles' voice was deep and a bit gravelly around the edges, but he didn't sound concerned by the unseen watchers. If anything, he sounded more curious.

They meandered through the tables until the condensation was fairly dripping from Geoff's hair. He tucked the wet locks behind his ears, very aware that Artemis was watching his every move. Whatever amazing feat he was supposed to be performing, she obviously wasn't seeing it and her frown grew darker the deeper they ventured into the Greenery.

They passed through several doors, and the scuttling noises grew louder, as if their interested watchers were multiplying in numbers. Geoff thought he could hear voices on occasion, but it was merely muttering at the edge of his senses and he could make out no words.

The doors seemed to separate sections in different stages of growth. The plants were taller in each one, straining toward the white lights above. Some of them even sported tiny buds, promising fruits or other delicacies later in their life cycle. The words for things he'd never seen sprang easily to mind, and he blessed Raffa for the steady stream of books she had supplied him over the years.

"Oh what under the dark sky is this?" Heracles puzzled question brought Geoff's gaze forward, and his eyes went wide. Apparently, the watchers had gathered enough courage to show themselves.

They were short, barely standing taller than Geoff

in his chair. It made sense now, the height of the growing tables. To a one, they seemed to be dressed in long coats that might have been white in earlier days, but were now streaked with soil and stained with unknown substances. Thick, dark goggles reflected the lights and made them appear blind. *The eyes I saw.* Most had stringy hair plastered to their scalps by the constant moisture and what appeared to be strands of green growth in the tresses. Their skin, too, seemed tinted by deep green and blue fungus until it was impossible to discern gender, and a faint scent of mold and mildew hung around them like a shroud.

Geoff tried to count them, and quickly gave up. There were too many, and they looked too much alike for him to keep his place. Some of them murmured softly amongst themselves, shuffling their feet, but otherwise they did no more than block the path.

"You will be gone!" Artemis' voice sent nervous chitters through the peculiar little drones, but not one of them moved to get out of the way. "Do you not hear me?"

One of the goggled creatures edged forward, and offered a broad smile, not to the goddess, but to her bodyguard. His – it was possibly male – teeth were yellowed and rotten, and the flesh of his pasty face seemed to have grown around the cumbersome goggles, but his smile was merry. "Return you! Happy she!"

Towering over Geoff, Heracles nodded his head to the little drone. "Send my greetings to the Lady Demeter, if you would."

The little man did a cheerful caper, and pleased murmurs sprang up amongst the odd throng. "Happy she! Happy we!" echoed from many throats.

"I ordered you to clear this path!" At the

goddess' barked order, the happy voices turned into frightened chittering, but they held their places.

The seeming leader shook his greenish finger at the goddess admonishingly. "Say she, stay. Stay we."

"You DARE?!"

Geoff could almost feel the waves of rage flowing from Artemis, and thunder cracked far overhead. The arc of the lightning through the smog clouds dimmed even the Greenery lights, and Geoff's chest ached as though a great hand had snatched him up to squeeze the very breath from his ribs. He gripped the arms of his chair, certain he was about to see the odd little fellow incinerated. *Please don't hurt him, please don't hurt him, please don't…* Suddenly, the pain in his chest vanished, and he drew a ragged breath.

The wheeled chair creaked, and Geoff realized Heracles had gripped the handles hard, the metal denting under his powerful hands and as one, the drones snapped their heads to look at Geoff with their hidden eyes, eerily silent now. Not one of them so much as breathed, as far as he could tell.

Artemis went suddenly pale and might have slumped to the floor if Heracles had not moved to catch her as her knees buckled. She clung to the large man, staring at Geoff in a strange mix of exultation and horror. "You…you dare try to use your power on me…?"

Whatever answer he might have given her – and he had no idea what that was going to be – was lost in the sudden excited babble from the swarm of drones. Their leader approached to tug at Geoff's hand, nearly pulling him out of the wheeled chair.

"Say she, come! Excited she! Excited we!"

They surrounded him, a myriad of moldy hands

touching and patting, words lost in a cacophony of voices. Geoff found himself and his chair carried away on the mildewed tide, leaving Artemis and Heracles to follow along behind.

They passed through several sections of the Greenery, the crowd of white-coated drones constantly moving and shifting around Geoff and his chair. He could not have even said which of them was pushing him at any given time. The bold one, the leader, kept pace at Geoff's left elbow, constantly patting and stroking Geoff's hand with his own doughy mitts. Geoff was hard pressed not to jerk away, especially after a large beetle, carapace an iridescent black, scampered out of the drone's sleeve, across Geoff's fingers, and away.

The plants in this section towered over Geoff and his strange entourage. *Corn*, his mind told him, though the stately stalks and heavy hanging ears were hard to reconcile with the colorless corn gruel he had eaten all his life.

"This is almost finished, right? Ready to be…" He had to search his mind for the word. "Harvested?"

The drone nodded happily, dislodging a few more beetles from his stringy hair. "Yes yes! Harvest soon, replant. Cycle on!" He seemed to take a great deal of delight in Geoff's simple question.

"Where are we going?" That question got him only an excited stream of babble from the horde, many hushed whispers of "Say she, come!"

"They're taking you to the Lady Demeter, if I had to guess." Heracles' voice was closer than he'd thought, and when he craned his head, he could see the demigod and his goddess still marching along on the outskirts of the drone throng.

Artemis had lost her fury sometime in the walk,

and now seemed to be coldly calculating something. The expression was more frightening than her rage had been before.

Heracles, marching stiffly at her side, looked strangely emotionless, as if afraid to react one way or another. But he allowed his gaze to drift to the chair-bound man for a moment. "Be respectful to her. She sees more than you might think."

The drone nodded cheerful agreement. "See we, see she!"

Only upon seeing the goddess did Geoff truly begin to understand the strange comments.

At first, he thought they had discovered a statue, carved of green-veined marble and lost amidst the mosses and molds of the Greenery. But the drones swarmed around it, caressing and petting it much the same way they had Geoff, and he understood that this was their goddess, their Demeter.

Deep purple vines twined through her raven hair, the tresses falling straight past her shoulders, nearly to her waist. Her gown was most likely velvet, but it was nearly impossible to tell beneath the layer of soft moss growing on the cloth. Her hands, white on the dark arms of her chair, were tinged a soft aqua blue, the same color Geoff realized as the mold on the drones' faces.

As they wheeled Geoff closer, she never moved, never acknowledged that she was aware of their presence at all. Her milky white eyes stayed fixed on some point far away.

Heracles nudged him from behind. "Greet her."

After a moment of confusion, Geoff managed to bow from the waist. "Lady Demeter. My name is Geoffroi."

The drones broke into happy chatter, their leader

nodding until Geoff thought the goggles would detach themselves from his face. "Happy she to meet the Geoffroi."

The sentiment was echoed around the room from many throats. "She…speaks through you. Through all of you." They shared one mind, he realized, one consciousness split into many bodies.

The drone grinned, exposing rotted teeth. "Say she, say we."

"What happened to her? Why can't she speak for herself?"

Artemis snorted. "She's done this to herself. Nobly sacrificed herself for the sake of the humans who no longer remember her name." Her scorn was evident, fairly dripping from her lips.

"Without the Lady Demeter's efforts, humanity would have starved to death in those first dark months after the war." Heracles' voice was low, respecting the serenity of the Greenery that their visit had disrupted. "She gives much of herself to maintain the cycle of life within these glass walls."

There was a sadness about her, Geoff decided. It was nothing he could put his figure on. Her face appeared as serene and tranquil as stone, but somehow, he could sense a pervasive sorrow that overshadowed this place and those within it despite the abundance of life that surrounded them. She was a prisoner. A willing prisoner, to be sure, but a prisoner nonetheless.

"They do remember your name, my lady. I myself have read stories to people, tales I found in old books. They do remember." It was all he could think to say, to alleviate the gloom that surrounded the still figure.

The lead drone smiled softly and patted Geoff's

hand. "Happy she."

"Why did she… Why did you bring me here?" It was hard to speak to her, rather than the drones, but he knew somehow that he should.

"Say she two things." The pasty creature grew solemn, his voice dropping to a whisper. "First say she, hope. Must hope, always. Life begets hope begets life, say she." He waited until Geoff nodded understanding – though what he truly understood was open for debate – before he went on. "Second say she, flee. The Geoffroi must flee. Now."

"Flee!"

"Flee!"

The cry was taken up by the drones surrounding the goddess Demeter, echoed throughout the room, and beyond. How many drones where there throughout the Greenery? All of them, urging him to flee, and in Geoff's mind, he heard Jon's voice. *"Geoff! Run!"*

"ENOUGH!" Lightning arced through the black clouds above, splitting the darkness in two as it struck a nearby rooftop in a shower of sparks. Before Geoff could blink, Artemis had snatched up the brave little drone and sent him spinning through the air, crashing into the tables and piping like a limp doll. The creature hung there, his coat tangled in the wiring, his head lolling at an impossible angle.

The throng fell into eerie silence, and Geoff felt a chill creep down his spine. For a long, breathless moment, he was certain he would be witness to a battle between the two goddesses.

When the spots began to dance at the edges of his vision, he remembered to breathe, and the tension broke. Artemis whirled on her heel, stalking past them toward the door. "Bring him."

As Heracles wheeled him away, Geoff looked back to see the countless pairs of goggles watching him like the faceted eyes of one great insect. And seated above them all, the Lady Demeter had turned her head, blind eyes watching him go.

Flee.

Chapter 12

For one heartbeat, Heracles had nearly jumped in front of the odd little drone, nearly taken Artemis' blow in his stead. His hands had crushed the handles of the wheeled chair as he resisted the muse's influence, the muscles in his legs and back quivering at the conflicting commands his body sent, and even then it had been a near thing.

Untrained, uncontrolled, the young man's power was unfathomable. It was ruled by his emotions, obviously, and made all the stronger for it. If he ever learned to consciously exert his influence, who could imagine what change could be wrought in the world?

Artemis could, obviously. What might be the world's salvation was her worst nightmare become flesh. *"Take him, kill him. Burn the body in the furnace. Send him back to Tartarus where he came from."*

The man, barely more than a boy, sat quietly beside him in the car, watching the darkened streets slip by outside the window. He knew, of course. Artemis was not one for subtlety, and a blind and deaf man would have known the sentence once she pronounced it. He seemed strangely calm, considering.

"You've not said a word since we left the tower." The young muse flinched when Heracles broke the silence.

"What is there to say? I'm condemned for… I don't even know why I'm condemned." He bowed his head, the chestnut locks falling down to hide his face. "You've never told me what I've done."

Heracles flexed his hand on the gear lever. "Your only crime is existing. A thing that can hardly be laid at your own feet, but there it is."

The muse – *His name is Geoff.* – turned to face him, the leather seat creaking at the movement. "Whatever it is she thinks I am, she's wrong. I'm just a man, trying to make a life for myself."

Heracles shook his head, keeping his eyes focused on the headlamps before the car as they split the blackness. "Artemis is many things, but in this, she is not wrong. I can tell you that with absolute certainty."

"Then I swear I am not trying to harm her. I'll swear anything she likes if she'll just let me go home."

"No!" Even to his own ears his voice was loud, and he grimaced. "No. Swear no oath. It's not worth it."

"I don't understand. What is it about me that she fears so? I'm nothing. I'm only human, my knees are busted up, what threat can I possibly pose?"

With a sigh, Heracles brought the car to a purring halt, idling quietly in the middle of the street. It was after Dark. They would be in no one's way. "Your threat lies in mere possibility." Looking at the muse, finally, he could see the confusion in the young man's eyes. "Have you never looked around yourself, and wondered why you were so blessed? I've seen the squalor that exists in the lower wards, and yet the people who have loved and cared for you seem to have escaped that bleakness. Do you understand why?"

He shook his head. "Ambert's good at what he does. So is Lia. If they earn a little more money because of it, it makes life a little easier."

"But *why* are they good at what they do? Why does no one else create the paintings your Lia does? Nothing new, nothing fresh, has come into this world since the war, because the powers of creation and inspiration were destroyed. Until now. Until you."

"But I didn't *do* anything!"

"Apparently, you don't have to. What other reason would there be to pluck a deformed infant out of the snow? How many people took a hand in raising you to adulthood? Fed you, clothed you, sheltered you? And all because, on some level, your mere presence made them think of *possibility*." How could the man be so blind to all that he could represent to the world? "Now imagine what you could do, if you could use your power with a purpose."

The young man shook his head and looked out the window. "I don't want to have any power. I just want to go home."

"Unfortunately, that is beyond my ability at this time." Heracles slid the car into gear again, and the dynamos whirred softly, propelling them forward. "She has ordered your execution."

They rode in silence for long moments before the muse thought of something else to ask. "So where are you taking me?"

"The Factory." The auto slid smoothly around the corner, and the structure in question loomed into view.

The Factory, the source of all of Elysia's power, took up almost an entire quarter of the circular city. It was nearly a city unto itself, divided into many structures that included a refinery, a manufacturing plant, and the huge boilers that churned constantly to keep the city warm and lighted. The resulting black smog belched continually from the imposing stacks, blanketing the city and turning what little rain they received into toxic acid.

Most tasks were taken up by citizens, anxious to earn a wage however they could and fortunate enough to return home at the end of each long shift. But the dangerous jobs went to the convicts, those who never saw the outside world again. They were the deep miners, the explorers of underground shafts, the handlers of explosives. Life expectancy amongst them was three years, if they were truly lucky.

Heracles received a scant nod at the gate as he drove the car through. The huntsmen had either been told he was coming, or simply were not surprised to see their captain there after Dark. It was not uncommon for the Hunt to deliver surviving prisoners to the Factory at all hours.

The demigod steered around to the eastern side of the compound, finding one small door set in the corrugated metal wall. He turned the car off, and faced his passenger.

"Listen very carefully to me for the next few moments, for I must say this quickly." He could tell the young man was paying attention, though he kept his eyes downturned. "The Lady Artemis has ordered your death. Because I have sworn to serve her, I cannot disobey her. But she never said *when*." The muse's gaze darted upward, brown eyes wide as he realized his death was not looming imminent. "I leave you here as a convict. You will serve in the pits, the foundry, wherever they can find a use for you. It is cruel, punishing work. It breaks a man. Most likely, it is a death sentence, and so I can honestly tell her that I carried out her wishes. If you have any chance at all…you will find it here."

"Do…should I tell you thank you?"

Heracles shook his head. "No. I do you no service here, and you will most likely grow to hate me more than you already do." With that he exited the car, and waited for the muse to struggle forth on his crutches. Those brown eyes, deep and fathomless, found him across the top of the vehicle.

"I don't hate you. We all do what we must to survive."

"If you are smart, you will." He took a firm grip on the young man's elbow, and led him toward the door.

~*!*~

"What in the name of Hades' black balls am I supposed to do with *that*?" Geoff winced at the foreman's blasphemy, but it seemed he was beyond anyone's notice. He had been reduced to a *that*, not even worth a name.

The stocky foreman, face flushed red with heat and ire, gestured wildly around the room as he expounded his opinion at length to Heracles. "You drag me out of bed for *this*? Woulda been kinder to leave it to the hounds! What the dank pits of Tartarus am I going to do with it?"

"You'll find something. I don't think you truly wish to go to the Lord Hephaestus and tell him you have no use for a crippled man." At Heracles' quiet words, the foreman blanched, going oddly pale under his ruddy skin.

"Well…mebbe I can find something. What's it here for? Is it dangerous? I got problems placing the dangerous ones, you know."

Heracles looked at Geoff across the small room

for a long moment before shaking his head. "No. He's not dangerous. Put him in with the general population."

I think the Lady Artemis would disagree with you there. Lost spirits watch over him, but how in the world had he gotten here?

Eventually, Geoff was left alone with the foreman who barely growled a command to follow as he left the small receiving room. Follow he did, attempting to draw as little attention to his crutches as possible. *Yes, because you can just hide them in your pocket.*

The heat from the Factory proper was almost enough to knock him down. It washed over him the moment the foreman opened the door, and by the time they had made their way across a small open to yet another unadorned door, Geoff was dripping with sweat. The air itself made his lungs burn and he could swear his lips instantly split from thirst. Distantly, he could hear the roar of the forge, the hiss of the steam. If it was that loud at a distance, he could imagine going deaf within a few weeks of working directly under them.

The foreman snorted, seeing him waver on his feet. "First time you pass out, the boys'll have your boots off you, and we don't supply no new clothes 'til you been here a year."

That was a comforting thought.

The foreman's office held no more than a rumpled cot, a few crates used as all-purpose furniture, and what looked to have been a desk in some previous life. The stocky man dragged a crate over for himself, making thoughtful noises as he rifled through the papers on his desk, but he never once asked Geoff to sit.

"Kinder with the hounds, but no, I have to put it somewhere…hmm… Who's got an empty space..?" The red-faced man produced a thin metal toothpick from somewhere and rolled it between his teeth as he worked, making a soft clicking sound.

The pervasive ache in his knees had progressed into a dull scream, and Geoff wanted nothing more than to get off his feet, even for a moment. *Just put me somewhere, already. They can have my damn boots.*

"Ha! I got it. Just put that new mech in with third shift, so they can't complain none if I saddle them with you, too." Satisfied, he scrawled something down in the ledger – a number, Geoff noted, but never a name – and slammed the book shut.

"Move it. They should just be coming off shift, so you can bunk down and start fresh in the morning." This thought seemed to amuse him, and he chortled to himself all the way to the barracks, frequently murmuring, "Start fresh!" which would set him off again.

The barracks themselves were scarcely more than four walls and a roof made of corrugated metal, buildings within the building. There were four, presumably one for each shift of convicts who worked throughout the Factory, and the foreman led him to the third one, a rusty number 3 marked on the door with rivets. Geoff could feel the heat radiating off the structure before he reached it, and he knew that sleeping inside would be like taking a nap in Kedrick's oven.

"In you go. Beds along the walls, showers in the back, just follow the crowd come meal time."

The beds – cots, really – were lined up along the outer walls with scarce room to walk between them. No doubt, at least fifty men lived in this barrack. Each cot seemed to have a crude metal box at the foot, probably holding the possessions of its resident. There didn't seem to be an empty one.

Head swimming with the confusion of the past

day, and legs nearly quivering with exhaustion, he sank down onto the foot of the nearest cot. *What now, Geoffroi? Your gears are seized up tight this time for sure.* The mocking internal voice sounded a bit like Keras. Merciful spirits, he even missed that annoyance already.

The door banged open, letting in a gust of heated air and the missing residents of Barrack 3. Geoff struggled to his feet, certain that no one would like finding him seated on their bed.

A chorus of catcalls greeted him, and he was thankful for the heat that made him flush, hiding his blushing.

"Look here, boys! Fresh meat!"

"Hells, that's a woman, look at those pretty eyes!"

"Nah, he's a stilt walker, he's entertainment. Walk on those stilts there, boy!"

It was hard to tell they were men, beneath the coating of black grime. Only their eyes stared out at him, bright against the soot and coal dust. They all possessed the corded muscle of hard labor, the uniform sleeveless shirts leaving massive biceps and shoulders bare. Some were short, some were tall, some stooped with age, or weariness, others still straight and proud. Not one of them wanted another person in their midst, someone else to compete with. That much was plain, even to Geoff.

Most of them moved past him without incident, though the owner of the bed did give him a glare, growling, "This one's taken."

"Are any of them not taken?" Lost Lord of Tartarus, just let him get off his feet.

His only reply was a grunt and a slight nod toward the back of the barracks. Resigned, Geoff began to hobble his way back, careful not to invade the personal space of his new bunkmates.

There did seem to be one unclaimed cot nearest the showers. Geoff sighed as he realized that it also caught a good deal of spray from the open stalls and that was probably why it was empty in the first place. *A few weeks of that and I'll look like one of the Greenery drones.*

Before he could even sit, a booted foot planted itself in the middle of the spare mattress. "This one's taken."

Geoff looked up to find a toothless man sneering at him, flanked by two more who were as big as Ambert in his prime. The few bristles of hair he had seemed to be sticking straight out of his ears, and his nose had been pulped so often as to be a shapeless mass in the middle of his face. "You're jesting, right?"

Toothless cackled. "'Jestin', he says. Boy this ain' no place for jestin'." He took his foot off the cot and made a show of straightening the ropes he used for suspenders. "Now, old Stan here, I'm a reasonable fellow. I'm willing to rent you this cot for…those boots you got there."

"I need my boots to work." Geoff knew he was only delaying the inevitable. He'd either sleep the night with no boots, or not sleep at all lest someone snatch them.

Old Stan sniggered again, and his cronies joined in on cue. "Work he says. Like a crip is gonna be working at all. You'll have a tragic accident soon enough, tumble into some deep mine shaft no doubt. Shame really. You was a hard workin' lad, despite your infirmity."

The two lackeys made mournful faces and shook their heads in mock grief. "Was taken too young, he was."

"So…I can have them boots now…or later." Stan grinned, the stench of rotten teeth proving that he hadn't lost all of them yet.

"Or I can crack your skull and pitch you into the slag pit." The voice growled from behind the bullies, and a hand grabbed old Stan by the collar. Before his minions could react he was sprawled on the floor, a heavy booted foot propped across his throat.

The cronies seemed to be at a loss for what to do without orders from Old Stan. And really, Old Stan wasn't going to do much more than gurgle with someone's weight pressing down on his windpipe.

"Thanks, I—" Geoff looked up at his unexpected savior and froze.

Jon gave him a half-hearted grin. "Hey there, Geoff." Stan twitched and Jon leaned harder. "Now you boys run off and play. The foreman isn't gonna like finding out you made me hurt my hands." He released Stan, watching to be sure the two brawny ones picked him up and retreated, then turned to Geoff again. "I'm a trained mechanic, and it's rare on the convict lines. Foreman will crack skulls if they make it so I can't work."

"I…don't understand. How…?" In his surprise, Geoff even forgot that he needed to sit until Jon gently pushed him down onto the cot.

"They dumped me here yesterday. Figure I'm lucky they didn't just feed me to the hounds, after…" He grimaced, swallowing hard.

Geoff's heart sank into his stomach. He'd forgotten. "Jon, I'm so sorry about Rik. It was all my fault."

It took Jon a moment to answer, and when he did, his voice was thick. "Nonsense. Rik was a grown man, same as me. We made our choice." He patted Geoff's shoulder. "I'll swap cots with one of the others, so I can stay close. Stan's been here a long time. He won't challenge the foremen by hassling me."

"You talk like you've been here years yourself."

Jon chuckled. "Rather feels like it. But no, I used to come down here and do repair work when they didn't have a mech of their own. I know some of the long-timers, most of the foremen. I'll look out for you, Geoff." He looked Geoff up and down with a critical eye. "You've been on your feet too much these past few days. I can tell. Hells, you've got blood seeping through your pants."

Geoff brushed at the dark stain on the knee of his trousers. "Must have just started."

"Lay down, rest. We've got a few hours before meal." Jon turned to go, then paused. "The hardest thing to get used to here isn't the heat. It's the light. It's never dark here, Geoff. Makes it a bit hard to sleep in the beginning."

Geoff nodded and reclined on the damp mattress, trying to block out the squabbles and scuffles of life in the barracks. *If Artemis and Heracles are right, Rik's death was my fault, Jon. And neither you nor he had a choice, not with me around.*

The Titan Atlas knew his time was near, so he bade the Lady Artemis to construct a column to hold the world in place upon his demise. And with the aid of the Lord Hephaestus, the pillar was forged of the purest metal, and Atlas could at last lay down his burden and rest.

~Emris Virit, Scholar, Second Olympic Dynasty

CHAPTER 13

The worst thing about waking was never knowing whether it was day or night. Artemis would always lie abed until the clock overhead chimed the hour, and even then it was anyone's guess if it was Dark or day. The windows surrounding her bedchamber were black, regardless, and the light in her room was ever burning. Never again would she sleep in darkness, lest it grab hold and not let go.

Her bed was empty this waking, and she frowned as she rose. She did not remember giving Heracles permission to leave. Upon further reflection, she couldn't even remember if he'd come to her at all this night.

Which night…? Nude, she padded to the windows, gazing out over Elysia. The clock atop the tower tolled the hour even as she watched the gaslights spring to life across the city. *Ah. Morning.*

She'd slept the night through, then. Peacefully, without reliving any of her usual memories. It was nice to be at peace.

Hear that? At peace. All is well, you taunting fiend. There was no response from any of the voices in her head, and her reflection in the window wore a satisfied smile.

Her bedchamber door swung open without notice, and Persephone invited herself in. The goddess' usual cool aura was prickly with agitation, and her anger showed on her smooth face.

In the tranquil mood she was in, Artemis found it within herself to smile graciously. "Persephone, good morning." She retrieved her silken robe from the foot of the bed and swung it about her shoulders. "Shall I have breakfast sent up?"

"What have you done to Mother?" she demanded without preamble.

"Done? I've done nothing to the Lady Demeter. Why would you ask such a thing? I care for your mother deeply, of course." Something niggled at the back of her mind, but she shoved it aside. She didn't like to think of Demeter and her eerie little cadre of drones if she could help it.

"Three crops have failed in the last two days. Failed! Destroyed beyond salvation. And all she'll say is that she mourns. What is she mourning for, then? What have you done?" Persephone grabbed Artemis by the arm and shook her once, displaying surprising strength. Artemis just stared at her in disbelief.

"You will remove your hand from me, Persephone, and remember your place." Artemis could feel her peace leaking away moment by moment. "I have been nowhere near your mother in…" *Days? Weeks? No, that's not right…* She did see Demeter…when was that? Why in the world would she have been in the Greenery at all?

Yes, sister, why go poking in that steaming wet hole? What might we have been doing there, hmm? Apollo sneered in her head, and she grimaced. "I last saw Demeter…"

"You last saw her three days ago, and she's been distraught ever since."

Artemis frowned as she tried to clear the fog in her head. She remembered being damp and hot, a constant state in the Greenery. She remembered one of the vile little drones, twitching in its death throes as it dangling from the piping overhead.

The boy, in a wheeled chair… *Tsk tsk, sister, an important thing to forget… But you do tend to block out the unpleasantries of life.* "Shut UP!" She only realized she'd spoken aloud when Persephone raised a surprised brow. There was contempt behind those beautifully serene eyes, the knowledge that she, Artemis, was inherently flawed.

With a snarl, Artemis lashed out and her fingernails scored bleeding marks across Persephone's pale cheek. "You keep to your place and don't ask questions you do not need answers to."

The other goddess pressed a hand to the bleeding marks, eyes flashing furiously for a moment. There was a breath, a heartbeat, where Artemis was certain Persephone was about to spring upon her. Then the blond woman nodded her head stiffly. "As you will. I will see if I can calm Mother." She turned and marched out of the room, head held high.

She believes you are not worth striking at, sister. You've done so much, accomplished so much, and she still believes she is above you. Apollo's voice was soothing, almost purring. *You are still my sister, I still defend you above all others. Is that not what siblings are for?*

"I am the queen of Olympus. I guard the pillar

that holds the world," she whispered, as much to quiet her ghostly brother as to remind herself. *Of course you are. None could stand before your might. None were capable of doing what needed to be done, in the end.*

Still, the feeling of peace had quite vanished, and the unease seemed to press in on her from all sides. *The muse is dead and the secret died with him. The pillar that holds the world is steady, and your darkest secret is safe with me.* Artemis hugged her arms around her, pulling the robe tight to ward off the sudden chill. *Go. Go see it if you must. Remember that it is solid and safe. The pillar holds the world, and Artemis guards the pillar.*

~*!*~

The pillar's blue metal gleamed somehow even in the darkened and cavernous room that housed it. Artemis watched her own shadowy reflection as she approached, the curve of the metal column distorting it into something ghostly and strange.

Alone in the circular room, the goddess rested her forehead against the cool pillar and spread her arms to try and wrap around it. It was impossible, of course. The circumference was easily three times her own span. But there was a comfort to it, a feeling of being something small in the presence of something great.

If she rested there long enough, she knew she would feel the smallest of vibrations, the minute changes in position as the world spun slowly on the great metal axis. It was those changes, those rotations that drove the great clock overhead. Even now, the great dial illuminated the chamber, each man-sized number shadowed across the walls in reverse. Around the outer wall, a staircase spiraled upward, and Artemis took it, holding her long skirt in one hand.

The top of the pillar was flat, but the edges were notched to accommodate the many gears that ran the great clock. The immense toothed discs seemed to hover in the air within arm's reach of the stairway, slowly ticking away their existence. And larger still was the enormous gong, mounted near the ceiling, and the great mallet that would strike it at the appointed hours. Either one of them would be capable of crushing a person if it fell, not to mention causing extensive structural damage to the tower itself. But the craftsmen had done their jobs well, and the clock had unerringly counted the passing moments of every dark day and night since the war.

The catwalks passing through the mechanisms were meticulously clean and carefully maintained, though no one was allowed beyond a certain point save the Lady herself. Even those denizens of the tower who were allowed in the clock chamber – her most trusted servants, if she had such – were not permitted to touch the pillar at the center or the workings of the great clock. That was Artemis' domain alone.

The walkway did not even sway beneath her feet, so securely was it anchored to the walls with rivets and welds. Her boots barely made a sound on the wooden platforms. It was a waste of a precious commodity, spending wood on mere flooring, but no one wanted to risk a metal spar snapping free and marring the pristine pillar. Who knew what would happen then? The only potential flaw in the column was the perfect hole, no bigger than her fist, directly in the center.

"But if you put a hole in the center, to the core, it will weaken the entire structure." Even in her head, Hephaestus' gravelly voice echoed around the clock tower.

"No no…it will simply allow for temperature fluctuations and such without putting undue stress on the metal." Artemis smiled as she murmured her explanation quietly, kneeling to run a hand across the smooth pillar's top. "I am not untrained in these things, Hephaestus. I do make my own arrowheads, after all." Even now centuries later, she could feel the lie to the words, but in her memory, she saw Hephaestus grudgingly nod his shaggy head and craft it just as she described.

Though she knew no one would follow her into the belfry, she glanced around to assure her solitude before directing her gaze upward. It was still there.

It might have been a simple piece of measuring string, left behind by some careless builder. It could have been anything, really, the delicate wooden shaft suspended from the apex of the ceiling. It was innocuous enough in the age of guns and machinery. Very few would understand what it was, even if it was explained to them. After all, the last bow had fallen to dust millennia ago. No one had ever seen such a weapon, let alone the ammunition for one. A single arrow, metal-tipped and lethal. The slate gray head blended with the shadows against the ceiling, barely visible.

She could feel its pull, even as it hung high out of her reach. *Adamantine.* The one metal capable of slaying a god. Toxic even in proximity, she had suffered illness herself for years after the war, after she used it to do what had to be done. And no one else could ever know how.

The last sample of the metal in Elysia dangled precariously over a hole drilled straight through the world's metal axis. At the bottom of that hole lay a disk of pure steel. And hidden behind a panel opposite the great clock face was the lever that would release the adamantine arrow to plummet into that smooth tunnel. The colossal spark it would create when it struck the steel would fracture the pillar, end the world.

That was not its original function, no. It had been meant for one heart, one man. Escaped and gone away, these long dark years, but the arrow waited for its chosen victim, like the rest of its spent brethren. There had been one for each of them, all those who had sided against her. Each arrow had found a home deep in a godly breast. All save this one lonely projectile, dangling above the ever-turning pillar.

Artemis caught herself giggling and bit her knuckles to stop. It was her secret. The fate of every living thing in the world rested in her hands. They lived at her whim alone. They would live her dreams, and no one else's.

No one else's? The mocking had returned to Apollo's voice, cruel and spiteful. *They dream new dreams, sister. He showed them the way.*

Artemis whimpered, drawing her knees up to her chest. "He is dead now. He can do no more harm."

But the seeds that were planted before? Your warrior, for one. Demeter. They have been contaminated. Every person who breathed his air, heard his voice, passed near his home. What dreams do they dream now?

He was right, she knew. Heracles was proof of that. The demigod was thinking thoughts he'd not had in centuries. He was forgetting his oath to her, and it was because he had been too near the muse. "He cannot be trusted any longer."

So few can be trusted. Who knows what dreams he touched, what sparks of rebellion he kindled?

"Only the ones he never touched… Demeter is lost, Heracles is lost. Persephone will side with her mother." Artemis bit her lip as she pondered her choices. "My hounds are loyal to my will, I have no worries there."

What of the smith? The crafter of these wonders you protect?

"Hephaestus…" Yes, she should check with the smith. He could not have been exposed to the muse, but if he had, she would know it by his eyes. "I will go to the Factory."

Heracles seemed to have disappeared, and Artemis thought briefly of sending a hound to track him, to watch his every move. But no, he would notice such surveillance, and the longer he believed himself safe, the less likely he was to move against her.

Instead, she summoned one of her huntsmen to drive the low black car and together they set out for the looming structure of the Factory. It was easier, she found, to watch the huntsman's hands on the levers, faint gray spots showing where the transformation was taking effect, his fingernails already blackened and sharp. This one would finish soon, and would earn the right to lope along at the side of another hopeful, doing Artemis' will.

She leaned her head against the back of the seat, soothed by the whirring of the dynamos that powered the vehicle. "You would do anything I asked, yes?"

The driver cast a surprised look at her in the mirror. "Of course, my lady."

"Without question or hesitation?"

"Yes, my lady."

"Even unto death?"

"Yes, my lady."

"You love me, don't you?"

"Of course, my lady."

She smiled to herself and remained silent for the rest of the trip. The Hunt was loyal, and they loved her. What more did she need?

While Artemis acknowledged the necessity of the Factory, it was truly her least favorite place in Elysia. It was too hot, too grimy, too full of stinking, sweating humans for her to enjoy visiting. And the master of the Factory, the smith-god Hephaestus, would be found in the very center of the tangle of machinery and scorching heat.

To no one's surprise, Artemis found him near the forge, bent over an anvil every bit as big as she herself. His human assistants scattered at her approach, but the god himself didn't bother to acknowledge her.

His auburn hair hung in sweaty tangles past his broad shoulders. The muscles rippled across his bare back, his shirt discarded who knew where, and his biceps bulged as big as her thigh with every stroke of the hammer. "You know, there are machines for that."

He didn't turn to face her, merely picking up his work with a pair of tongs and plunging it into a nearby vat, sending gouts of steam rolling toward the ceiling. "A machine can never duplicate what the eye can detect and hand can create." His voice, like boulders grinding together, carried over the usual mechanical din.

She stepped up onto the raised platform, careful not to get smut on her brocade coat. Already, she was too warm, the stifling heat of the nearby forge almost a palpable force. "What are you making?"

"Do you truly care?" He barely swiveled his eye in her direction, raising one brow. "What do you wish of me today, Lady Artemis?"

The goddess smiled warmly. "Is it so unusual for me to visit one of my kinsmen?"

"Yes." The word was punctuated with another jarring clang as the hammer met anvil. "I have work to do. What do you want?"

Gritting her teeth to ignore the grease and soot, Artemis found a place to lean one hip against a table. "Merely to see you. It's been some time since we've had a proper conversation."

"Our conversations have never gone well." With another clang, he laid the hammer aside and finally turned to face her.

Artemis kept the smile on her face, though her stomach rolled. "You're looking well."

The crippled god's left leg had never been sound, twisted at the knee until his foot nearly pointed backward. But that was the least of his deformities now. His left arm was blackened and shriveled, useless and bound tightly to his side. The left half of his face was similarly afflicted, the skin blighted, the bone structure fairly melted away. His eye, a diseased gray orb that neither saw nor moved, looked to spill out on his wasted cheek at any moment, and his mouth drooped on that side, displaying a glimpse of white teeth in blackened rotting gums.

Such was the price for the god who dared to forge adamantine.

"This pretty small talk, while appreciated, does not become you. Truly, speak what you want or leave me in peace."

Her smile faded into a frown. Why did everyone have to make things so unpleasant? "Has Heracles been here?"

The crippled giant shook his shaggy head. "No.

His visits are more infrequent than yours."

"Persephone?"

"She brought my evening meal, near a month ago. I've not seen her since, though she still owes me a game of stones if you could relay the message."

Long before she might have come in contact with the muse. The thought was so pleasant that she forgot to be annoyed at being given orders like a common messenger. "If they come here, you will tell me."

Hephaestus raised his one perfect brow. "My days of taking your orders are long since passed, Artemis. If you wish Heracles watched, set one of your hounds on him." He picked up his hammer, returning to whatever it was he was bludgeoning into shape. "I serve here of my own will, and for my own penance. But ask nothing else of me. I've nothing left to give you."

"Do you know what I could do to you for your impertinence?"

He chuckled softly, actually shaking his head as he laughed at her. "What could be worse than leaving me to die this slow death?" High on the tower, the clock chimed the hour. "Shift change soon. You'd best be off. I know how you hate to be caught in the crowd."

Had any other living creature been close enough to hear the Lady Artemis dismissed like an errant servant, they would have died on the spot. Instead, the ghostly voice in her head counseled her to patience. *He is no more intransigent than he ever was. He is uncorrupted. Turn your attention to the warrior.* And she would. Heracles was the one to watch.

Chapter 14

The convict work crews toiled daily within the depths of the earth. Using everything from pickaxes to great steam-driven borers, they continually carved new paths through the increasingly riddled bedrock, seeking out ores and minerals, gases and oils to power the city far above. And even in the deepest catacombs, with tons of rock above their heads, there was light. As they laid the parallel tracks for the steam carts to haul them to and from, they also laid lines and fixtures to carry the precious electric light into the dark tunnels. Never mind that one stray spark could ignite a gas pocket, or that one of the few oil lamps they burned could suffocate an entire crew in the airless caves. The tunnels must go on.

With every bit of required labor being so intensely physical, it seemed the only task they were willing to trust Geoff with was wheeling around the large drum of water, ladling out crucial hydration to the other convicts as they worked. In truth, it seemed to work well, as he could lean on the cart itself in place of his crutches, but being on his feet constantly was wreaking havoc with his knees. Luckily, even Old Stan and his crew would rather have the water than risk going without if they tormented him, so he was largely left to his own devices.

The wheels of the water cart creaked not unlike the wheels of his old chair, and the sound made Geoff homesick every time he heard it. Which was, admittedly, every single waking hour of his days.

He had no idea how long he had been there. Certainly, he could count the number of sleeping periods they'd been given, but without the regular rise and fall of Dark, counting the days seemed an exercise in futility. It wasn't like he was actually sleeping through the endless bright nights or the constant roar of the forge and furnace. It didn't seem to bother anyone else, though, and snores and mumbled dreams added another thread of sound to his already taxed senses.

As he lay on his cot, feeling the ever-present damp from the showers, a shadow drifted across his closed lids, and he heard Jon sit down on the cot next to him. "You need to sleep, Geoff."

"I am sleeping. See, my eyes are closed."

He heard Jon sigh as the bigger man stretched out on his own bed. "Seems like no one is sleeping tonight."

Geoff opened his eyes to look at his friend. "What happened?"

The mechanic shrugged. "Fons woke up crying again from that dream he's been having. Young Stan was going to thrash him one, but me and a couple others put a stop to it. Thought there was going to be a brawl for a moment, though."

Young Stan was one of Old Stan's two minions and had proven to have a quick temper only lightly leashed by the older man's will. But he was still smart enough to avoid taking on superior numbers. He was more of a catch-you-behind-the-dig kind of fellow.

"Everyone seems so riled up," Jon observed through a yawn. "Never seen it so tense down here before. When I worked down here with Rik, the convicts always seemed so cowed, so docile."

"Maybe they're just tired of being here." Lost spirits knew, Geoff was tired of it. Between the shower spray and the sweat, he was certain he'd never be dry again, and he could feel the throbbing in his knees up into his teeth and behind his eyes until he wanted to scream.

"Maybe. Get some sleep, Geoff. Morning comes damn early." A few moments later, Jon was softly snoring.

Geoff envied him. At this point, Geoff envied the beleaguered Fons. At least the man was dreaming, which meant he was sleeping. *I hope your dreams get sweeter and your sleep peaceful.* Someone ought to be peaceful, anyway, even in this horrible place.

His own sleep was usually chased away by the pain in his knees and an almost as painful longing for home. More importantly, he longed for the people he had come to call family. Was Ambert keeping up with the shop without him? Was Lia all right? The thought that Keras had possibly moved into his apartment in his absence made his stomach roll. The logical side of his mind knew that Ambert would never allow that, but the worry lingered. *I don't belong here.*

Far at the end of the narrow walkway, someone cried out in their sleep, earning a chorus of "Shaddup you!" and "Stifle, will ya?"

The distraught dreamer wailed "I don't belong here!" Whatever else might have been plaguing his dreams, it was lost in the snarls and grumbles of his fellow inmates.

The commotion died down without coming to blows, but after a few moments, Geoff sat up on his narrow cot. *None of us belong here.* He looked over the lines of sleeping convicts, trying to pick out whoever had called out. *Did he hear me?* Near the doorway, a restless form beneath a blanket stirred and whimpered in his sleep. Geoff focused his eyes on that shape. *Sleep easy. Dream of happy times. Dream of home.*

Almost instantly, the tossing and turning ceased and within moments silence reigned beneath the distant roar of the forge. Geoff watched for a few moments longer, then lay down himself.

It could be coincidence, of course. But the longer Geoff pondered the small event, the more he wondered if perhaps he was just what Artemis feared. *Tomorrow. I'll find out more tomorrow.*

As far as experiments went, the results were very hard to quantify. For two nights, Geoff spent his sleepless hours directing soothing thoughts toward the restless dreamers amongst the convicts. Sometimes they would quiet, sometimes they would not. It was impossible, of course, to know if his efforts were having any influence, or if it was simply the coincidence of cycling dreams.

He wanted badly to ask Fons what his dreams were about, the ones that woke the man screaming and weeping like a child. But such things were not discussed amongst the inmates, and a personal question like that would get him cuffed or worse, even with Jon's protection.

As he pushed the water cart amongst the men – the convicts were lounging against the heavy machinery on one of their brief breaks – he pondered how to get the piper alone and quiz him. It was that inattention that caused him to run over someone's foot with the rusty wheel.

"Hey! Watch it, gimp!" Young Stan, the seemingly injured party, lashed out with a heavy boot and caught Geoff just above the right knee, which gave out with an audible pop. Geoff hit the ground, his vision swimming and his stomach rolling from the pain.

"What'sa matter, Stan?" Geoff could hear others gathering around and wondered frantically where Jon was. Then he remembered. Jon had been called further down the shaft they were digging to investigate some problems with one of the steam drills. Jon wouldn't be coming to help this time.

"Gimp ran over my foot! On purpose!"

Through a haze of nausea and a humming in his ears, Geoff shook his head. "Didn't…"

"Shuddup, gimp." A boot landed somewhere in the vicinity of his rump, belonging to Old Stan, judging by the voice. "Toldja we were gonna have to school this one. Doesn't know his place."

The next kick hit his knee again, sending bolts of white light through his vision, and Geoff gritted his teeth not to spew his meager breakfast on their boots. He wouldn't give them the satisfaction.

"Hey, Stan, he's gonna pass out. Watch him!" A chorus of laughter greeted that prophecy, and then Geoff was doused with the very lukewarm water he was supposed to be dispensing. "C'mon, if you pass out it's no fun!"

The water trickled into his eyes, under the collar of his shirt, across his lips. He licked them and tasted the salt of his sweat. Dimly, he heard the men above him discussing his fate. "Strip 'im down, chuck him in the slag pit. Won't no one miss him."

"What about that mech? He's the foreman's pet at the moment."

Old Stan snorted. "What's he gonna do, bring the gimp back to life? Once it's done, it's done." There was a sound of a smack, someone's hand meeting the back of someone else's head. "You need me to take a piss for you too, since I'm doing all your thinkin' for you?"

From his vantage point, Geoff saw Young Stan's fist clench at his side. *You don't like that, do you? Always taking orders from him.*

"What's with you hitting me all the time, hunh?" Young Stan turned to look at Old Stan, forgetting all about Geoff. "Who died and made you lord and master?"

Water dripped from the downed man's hair, spattering on his hands where he lay braced against the stone floor. It made tiny rivers of mud in the dust. *The water…it's the water…* Geoff looked back to Young Stan, looming over the older convict, and focused his thoughts. *He's always acting so superior. Like you're nothing, lower than dirt. You don't have to take that.* Something in his chest clenched, a fist gripping his heart as he waited to see what happened.

"Watch yourself, boy, you aren't nearly as big as you think."

"You wanna know what I think?" Stan the Younger planted both hands against Stan the Older's chest and shoved hard. "I think I'm not going to take orders from you anymore, old man." They stepped behind the water cart, the drum blocking Geoff's view, but the sounds of a sudden scuffle were unmistakable. More voices shouted and there were running feet as the convicts came to watch the brawl.

Biting his lip to keep from making a sound, Geoff dragged himself away, finding shelter behind one of the large borers. He leaned his head against the machine, taking deep controlled breaths to think past the pain in his mangled knee. There was a splash of water as the brawl upended the water cart, and he felt a brief sense of near panic. If it was in fact the water that enabled his gift, his chance to do more had just drained into the dust and stone.

"Hey, what's going on there! Get back, you tunnel rats!" The sound of clubs on flesh joined the sounds of fighting, and the crowd scattered. The foreman had arrived, no doubt flanked by his own force of loyal convicts. They'd break up the fracas and crack a few skulls in the process.

The now-empty water drum clanged as someone threw it aside. "Where's Geoff? The water boy, where is he?" Jon's voice, tight with worry and anger. He'd come back with the foreman, then.

If you were a cripple, where would you hide, Jon? The thought made Geoff smile despite the pain in his leg, and the tightness in his chest faded away the moment Jon's head poked around the corner of the borer. "Knew you'd find me."

"The Lady's white tits, Geoff, what happened?"

"I'll explain later." Much later. When the rest of the barracks were asleep and couldn't hear the secrets he was about to impart. "My knee's busted good." The excruciating pain had faded into a low pervasive throb, but he knew the moment he moved, he was in for it.

"Gods, Geoff." Clumsily, Jon got Geoff to his feet, his shoulder under the smaller man's arm. "What in the name of lost spirits are we going to do with you now?"

The better question is, what am I going to do with you? The simple thought made him want to giggle and retch all at once.

His conversation with Jon had to wait until their

token medic had a look at his knee. Fons happened to be the one with the most medical expertise, and even he winced when he rolled Geoff's pant leg up to his thigh and looked at the purple, swollen joint. "Spirits, man, what did he do to you?"

"Look at the other one. They always look like that." In fact, the uninjured knee looked slightly better than usual. Certainly, it was still grotesquely shaped, and there were scabs where slivers of bone had worked their way out through his skin. It was hot to the touch indicating a constant infection, but the color was better, the deep bruising fading to yellow around the edges. *Maybe the constant dampness is helping me heal?*

Fons shook his shaved head. "How under the black sky do you even walk?" Geoff didn't have an answer for that, so he only sat and let the medic wind a tight bandage around his knee. "Honestly, there's not much I can do. I can't tell which is new damage and which is just…the way they are. Stay on the crutches, don't get kicked again." He departed with another shake of his head, leaving Geoff alone with Jon.

The big man took a seat on the edge of his cot and just watched him, waiting.

Geoff took a deep breath, wondering where to start. "I know why they took Lia from the market. And I know why they came back for me."

It took a long time to tell the story, unsure as he was still on some of the finer points. When he was done, he sat with his hands in his lap, waiting for something. Anything.

Jon looked at him for long silent moments until Geoff was afraid perhaps the mechanic hadn't heard him. Finally, the big man shook his head. "Gods, Geoff. I don't know who's crazier, you or her."

That, at least, was a response he'd expected. He wasn't too certain of the answer himself. "Questionable sanity notwithstanding, it worked. I turned the Stans against each other, but it only worked when I touched water." Geoff shrugged helplessly. "I don't know why, but the water was important."

"So you just told Young Stan to punch Old Stan's teeth through the back of his head, and he did?"

"No…not like that. I just…made him see how badly Old Stan was treating him. He chose his own course after that."

"A muse…" Jon shook his head again. "It's not possible. I mean, I watched you grow up. Don't think someone would have noticed before now?"

Two men shambled past, heading for the showers, and Geoff waited until their heads were under the stinging water before he went on. "Look at Ambert. Look at Lia. Their talents bloomed, because they were around me. Just from me being there. Imagine what I could do if I actually *tried*."

"That's what worries me." The mechanic frowned. "What gives you the right to control other people's minds?"

Geoff felt a sinking feeling of helplessness as he watched his friend get up to pace around his cot. *Please Jon, I need you. Trust me.* "That's just it, I can't. At least, I don't think I can. All I can do is…offer a nudge. An idea. They have to act on it however they see fit. In Stan's case, he punched Old Stan's nose cockeyed." He hoped he was relating things accurately. The last thing he needed was to be a liar on top of everything else. He raked a hand through his hair, the locks hanging limply around his face in the shower mist. "I'm guessing on most of this, Jon. But if I'm right, I think I can get us out of here."

"How is that, exactly?" Jon sat again, leaning his elbows on his knees, hands clasped. At least he was willing to listen.

"Well, I don't have a plan of my own." Jon raised a brow and Geoff hastened to explain. "But I don't have to. I just have to nudge some people, inspire them to come up with an escape."

"Do you realize how insane this sounds?" Jon lowered his voice. "Not to mention what would happen to you if anyone overheard you and reported you to the foreman? There are worse things than the work detail, Geoff. Much worse."

"Worse than being trapped here for the rest of our lives? I want to go *home*, Jon. I want to marry Lia, and work in Ambert's shop, and watch the Morrow children grow up, and…" He sighed, frustrated. The need to get out of the Factory was an almost palpable weight, sitting in the middle of his chest. He rubbed at the tight spot. "I don't want to be this thing Artemis fears, but if I am, I'm by the darkness going to use it to my advantage."

Jon took a deep breath and ran a hand over his close-cropped hair. "You're risking men's lives on a possibility, Geoff. I can't accept that. Sure, probably two-thirds of the men in this barrack don't really belong here. But they're alive. You're asking them to jam their foot in the gears for what? The chance that you might be able to work some kind of miracle? And even if you get out, what's going to keep the Hunt from tracking you right to your front door? Again."

Geoff's heart sank lower with every word. If Jon of all people didn't believe in him, who was going to? "Jon, I can't stay here."

"Yes you can." Jon flopped onto his cot and laid his arm over his eyes. "Not another word on it, Geoff. Even talking about it is dangerous."

Geoff sat on the edge of his cot for a long while after that, watching the inmates bed down for their sleeping period. The gong of the tower clock was lost in the general machinery noise, and Geoff couldn't help but wonder how anyone could track the time in the endless hours of blazing light.

Down near the far end, Fons whimpered in his sleep, and Geoff sent him thoughts of soaring free in the blue sky like Lia's painting of Icarus. *You'll come with me, when the time comes. I won't leave you here.*

"Lay down, Geoff. Go to sleep." Jon's usual admonition held a formal distance this time, and Geoff felt more alone than ever.

CHAPTER 15

So began a very subtle sort of rebellion. Geoff rebelled against Jon, knowing he only had a small amount of time before he was killed. Whether it would be the men or the place was open for betting, but death was hovering over him, breathing down the back of his neck as surely as if he could see it. He couldn't stay, and he wasn't about to leave anyone else to die in that pit of torture if he could help it.

Doling out the day's water turned out to be advantageous in more ways than one. To begin with, it allowed him contact with every prisoner in the barrack, regardless of his standing amongst them. Every man there would take water from him, unwilling to go thirsty for the sake of a grudge.

Easy access to water allowed him plenty of opportunity to experiment with his questionable gift. The first tests determined that it must be pure water. His own sweat would not work, tainted by salt and soot. The oils that lubricated the gears in the giant borers would not work. Certainly there were other available…fluids that he could have tested, but those were less than palatable, so clean water it would be.

He gradually grew to recognize the difference

between thinking simple thoughts and exerting influence. It took the form of a small warm knot at the tip of his sternum, a tiny point of pressure that would release like an unclenched fist when he pushed in just the right way. Perhaps it was a muscle, growing stronger the more he used it, much like his legs were growing stronger on every hour-long trek into the deep catacombs.

With every cup he delivered, his fingertips would linger in the liquid for just a moment. A moment only, but it was enough. Along with the water, each man got a tiny nudge, the simple thought that things did not have to be as they were. And with every nudge, the unrest amongst the prisoners grew.

It wasn't anything overt, at first. The borers broke down a little more often, requiring costly delays in digging to repair. The foreman, formerly obeyed if not respected, began to receive surly glances and backtalk from the boldest inmates. Supplies began to get lost, everything from sulfur flares to pickaxes to the simple tin water cups that held their daily rations.

The prisoners paid dearly for the misplaced equipment. Their rations were cut at first, then their work hours extended to make up for lost time. They were denied peace during their sleeping periods, the foremen stalking up and down the barrack aisle with demands for information. Finally, when no one would inform on their fellows, they pulled a piper named Skif out of the ranks and produced a wicked looking whip of thin chain links.

All of the prisoners were turned out for the display, even those from other barracks. Skif was tied to a metal pole set in the floor and his shirt was ripped down the middle and discarded. With a sadistic grin, one of the foremen stepped up and laid into the bound piper.

Geoff had never seen a flogging before, and never hoped to again. Every time he attempted to look away, a foreman was there with a kick and a curse, forcing him to open his eyes again. Skif shrieked and writhed as every lash flayed his back open to the bone and blood splattered over the faces of those nearest. The man begged and pleaded and wept, but the foreman doled out all twenty of the prescribed lashes before they released him.

The knot was there in Geoff's chest. He could feel it throbbing, and he swallowed his gorge. He had done this. If not for the fledgling muse's insidious influence, Skif might not have hidden away that pry bar. He might have returned it when questioned. He might not be bleeding and screaming before Geoff's eyes.

That night, Skif raved loudly in delirium and pain, and silence only came when he died quietly sometime before morning.

Jon cast accusing glances at Geoff after that, but there was no way he could hate the muse as much as Geoff hated himself. Skif was but the first to die, Geoff knew, and he wondered if he had the stomach for any more. Jon's words kept coming back to him. *What gives you the right?*

What indeed?

And while Geoff pondered his own moral dilemma, the fledgling rebellion stagnated, lacking the last push they needed from their secret source of inspiration to make the jump from talk into action.

Things might have hovered there at that brink indefinitely, hampered by Geoff's own reluctance, had Keras not been arrested.

The inmates worked in eight-hour shifts, not counting the hour or more it took them to march to and from the current dig site. Each shift overlapped by two hours with the shifts both before and after it, and Geoff came to recognize the faces of the men from other barracks as he watched them shuffle past.

The lead foremen of shift four were a quartet of burly thugs, no doubt promoted from inmates themselves once upon a time. They were quick with a curse and a blow, and their prisoners never raised their eyes from their shoes, never made a sound unless directly spoken to.

Therefore, when the fourth shift arrived to take over duties at the dig, and the sound of off-key singing preceded them down the tunnels by a good ten minutes, all the men from Barrack 3 stopped to watch the arrival with keen interest.

Geoff, dutifully doling out water for the last break, missed the commotion until a familiar voice yelled "Geoffroi, me boy!"

The young man was nearly knocked off his feet by a huge hug from the fur-clad shyster. Geoff blinked in surprise, his vision filled only with the gaudy purple fedora. "Keras?"

"In the flesh! And several other coatings of questionable substances." The ratty conman grinned with his yellowed teeth, even as the foreman from shift four advanced on him menacingly.

"You there, get back over here!"

"Shush, I'll be just a moment!" Keras waved a hand at the foreman dismissively, and the man's mouth gaped in mute astonishment.

"How…?"

"How'd I get here? It's a tragic tale of misunderstanding, Geoffroi, just tragic." Keras shook his head mournfully. "I still maintain that the lady was hard of hearing and misunderstood when I told her that the potion was *not* guaranteed to revive her husband's…er…vigor." He shrugged under his filthy fur coat. "How was I going to know it would turn the affected member bright green? Never had a problem before, and that's the truth. Post-production contamination, obviously, or user error…"

The men of third shift were missing out on their water, but none of them seemed to notice as they watched the spectacle that was Keras. The ratty little man, true to form, basked in the attention.

"Are these your friends, Geoffroi? I've been telling pretty Lia that you'd be just fine and you were probably living the good life somewhere with puffy cushions and fizzy drinks." Keras glanced around the now-crowded tunnel. "Not quite what I had in mind, but I can put a good spin on it I'm sure."

A calloused hand grabbed Keras by the scruff of his shaggy coat and dragged the man away before he could chatter more. Still, he waved merrily, calling back, "I'll see you later, Geoffroi! We'll have supper!"

A smattering of laughter sprang up amongst the convicts, and more than a few echoed the "See you later, Geoffroi." To his surprise, Geoff found he'd lost the ability to blush, at least over that.

"Either I'm going mad, or I just heard Keras." Jon dropped his bag of tools on the floor with a clatter and helped himself to the barrel of water.

"No, that was Keras. He's on fourth shift."

The big mechanic grinned a bit, the first time he'd shared such an expression with Geoff in days. "Well, better them than us."

Shift change soon came to be the most entertaining time of the day. The men of Barrack 3 anticipated the antics of the ever-daffier Keras with relish, and the scrappy fellow was more than happy to oblige. And no matter how infuriated his foremen became, he never seemed to suffer any ill effects from their punishments.

The only casualty of the situation seemed to be the purple fedora, whose brim drooped lower and lower each day as the constant sweat and steam wreaked havoc on its form.

"How under the black sky he hasn't died of heat stroke in that rat-mangled coat, I will never know." Jon shook his head one day, watching as Keras was once again dragged back to his line to do whatever it was they thought him capable of mastering.

"It smells like he has," Geoff smirked faintly, but his thoughts were elsewhere. Time was slipping away, and yet the men only sat and grumbled. There were plots, to be sure, plans and schemes whispered in the quiet sleeping hours. But no one had made that decisive move, that ultimate decision to act. And it was Geoff's fault.

You're a coward, Geoffroi. He'd thought saying it, even to himself, might shame him into action, but it hadn't worked. He was forced to admit that he was right. The first stages had been easy, convenient to explain away as testing his newfound ability. But to take it that last step, where no doubt men would die and failure was almost certain… No, he was a coward, and even his longing for Lia could not bring him to push that last button, trip that last lever. She would be so disappointed in him.

He lost track of the days, or what passed for them, measuring them only by the droop of Keras' hat. On the day the saggy brim reached the little man's pointed nose, Keras arrived for the shift change and came straight for Geoff.

"I have reached a momentous decision, Geoffroi me boy, and I think you should be included in it."

Geoff never paused in dispensing his water, barely glancing at Keras. "Yes? What is it?"

"The novelty of this place has quite worn off, and I have decided it is time to go. If you'll excuse me." The men of third shift watched in slack-jawed amazement as Keras borrowed a sledge hammer from the nearest inmate and calmly walked up behind his own foreman. He took a few running steps to get momentum, almost doing a strange little dance, and bashed the man in the head with the hammer.

The foreman dropped like a stone, and for one heartbeat, there was absolute silence. Geoff stared in horror, watching blood and gray brain matter seep out of the crack in the foreman's skull as the man twitched in his throes. *But I didn't do anything….!* He could still feel the knot in the middle of his chest, clenched tight and awaiting his will. Keras' actions were none of Geoff's doing.

Belatedly, there was a yell from another foreman, and even that sounded hesitant as if he couldn't quite believe what he'd seen. "Hey…! You!"

But the prisoners had seen one of their captors taken down like so much slag, and even as the other foremen and their loyal inmates ran for Keras, the men of third shift scrambled to their feet, taking up whatever they could grab for weapons.

Young Stan, a steam hammer in one hand, swung at the nearest foreman, the bit punching through the man's chest with a sickening crack of breaking bone. The foreman fell with a choke, blood spurting from his mouth and the bright light of surprise dimming quickly from his eyes.

Now there was shouting from all sides as fourth shift was bullied into defending their tormentors. Geoff saw one of them reach for Fons, and the sometimes-medic swung a steel lunch pail at the man's head, the jarring clang echoing against the low tunnel ceiling. *Don't kill them! They don't know any better!* Here at last was a target for the pent up urge to meddle, and Geoff let the pressure in his chest go, spreading it far and wide. The inmates of fourth shift hadn't had the blessing (or curse) of his influence, and they couldn't be blamed for their actions.

Responsible or not, it didn't stop the two groups of inmates from clashing in the cramped tunnel, pinned between rock walls and heavy mining equipment. Years of restrained anger and frustration came pouring out, tumbling into the crowd in the form of heavy blows, devastating kicks, and pummeling with any item that wasn't bolted down.

Only when a large prisoner loomed over him did Geoff realize he had been merely standing there, gawking. The giant reached for him with hands knotty and twisted from years of work in the tunnels, and Geoff knew he could never get out of the way in time.

"No you don't!" A length of pipe swung from the edge of Geoff's vision, doubling the big man over with a whoosh of air forced from his lungs. The pipe came down again, cracking against the back of his head, and he slowly pitched forward onto his face. Jon grabbed Geoff by the shoulder and shook him. "Geoff! Come on, we have to move! Two of the foremen got back down the tunnel; we're going to have the whole Factory crawling up our tailpipes in short order."

He was right. Somewhere, Geoff knew he was right. Unhampered by equipment and machinery, the trek back to the Factory proper wasn't that far at all. And the escaped foremen would bring back help.

With Jon at his side, gathering more convicts as they moved, Geoff followed the sound of Keras' mad cackling in the opposite direction, further into the caverns they'd dug with their own sweat and blood. He stumbled over bodies in the way, and didn't have time to see if they were still breathing or not. Jon was shouting, rallying the inmates that remained when in their bloodlust they might have pursued the rest back toward the Factory.

"Into the catacombs! No one knows these tunnels better than us!" Someone tossed a canvas bag around Geoff's neck, staggering him with the weight. He didn't know what was in it, and there was no chance to examine the contents to decide if it was necessary. He simply kept crutching along with the growing tide of men, men who just hours before would have been as happy to shove him onto the borer tracks as help him escape their mutual prison.

Either the men from fourth shift had been beaten into submission, or they'd fled in the face of third shift's almost single-minded desire to bludgeon anything in their path. Either way, nothing followed them down the tunnel. They even felt safe enough to stop and tip the last borer over on Jon's instructions, using pipes to lever it off its rails and creating another obstacle to pursuit.

They used the moment for a brief respite, catching their breaths and bandaging what wounds they could. Geoff found Jon by his side once more, the large mechanic's face grim. "They'll send the Hunt. We'll never outrun them in these close quarters, even knowing the territory. Some of the men are hurt and bleeding. The hounds will track us before we've even had time to think of a plan."

"So what do we do?" The bag hanging around his neck hampered his own attempts to sit, and he lurched against the wall with a curse. Jon caught him by one arm and relieved him of the heavy sack in one motion.

"I know what we do!" From somewhere in the crowd, Keras bounded through, grinning like a lunatic and mumbling flippant apologies to anyone he tripped over. His grin faltered as he looked at Geoff, though. "You didn't drop my bag, did you?"

"No, Jon has it."

The smile came back to Keras' face, and he gleefully rubbed his hands, reaching for it eagerly. "The answer to all your prayers is in that bag, JonJon. I took it upon myself to relieve the poor foreman of it, it looked so heavy."

Jon stepped back just out of the smaller man's reach, and gave him a wary look as he pawed through the bag himself. "Darkest night, Keras…I don't know if I should kiss you or be very afraid of you."

The men around them craned their necks then murmured as Jon drew out a handful of blasting fuses and a couple bricks of the doughy explosive they used on particularly tough sections of tunnel. The prisoners were never allowed to transport the stuff. That responsibility fell to the foremen. But when it came time to lay the charges, it was the convicts who often took the risk.

Geoff blanched, realizing that the explosives had been banging around his knees during the long run down the tunnels. "Lost Lord of Tartarus…"

Jon was quickly drawn into a fevered discussion amongst several of the inmates with explosives experience, and it was decided that they would press on until they found a place where they could safely bring the ceiling down.

The ragged troupe got underway again, following the rail tracks until they ran out where the digging had stopped. Two access tunnels branched off to either side, tiny one-man channels leading to previous shafts.

Jon eyed the low-hanging rock thoughtfully. "The surrounding walls are stable enough. If we bring the tunnel down here, they'll have to search both parallel shafts starting at the Factory, and that will give us some time to get ahead of them."

The arrangements were made quickly, and the men made their way single-file though the access shaft. Geoff's elbows scraped against both walls as he crutched his way through, and he tried to ignore the heaviness in his chest, feeling like the whole of Elysia was about to collapse down on his head.

They found shelter around a turn in the parallel tunnel, one that had been mined out years before, and hunkered down to wait. The lines of electric lights had long since been removed from the abandoned shaft, and the prisoners passed sulfur flares amongst themselves, preparing for the moment that the light from the other tunnel would be cut off.

Jon stayed behind with one of the blasters to set off the charges, unwilling to let any man take the risk alone, and Geoff watched his friend disappear back down the narrow tunnel. Something furry brushed his arm, and he looked to find Keras at his side. The scrawny man offered him some meat jerky, and he shook his head. "How do they know it won't bring down this tunnel too?"

Keras shrugged, chewing thoughtfully. "Oh, it probably will." Geoff blinked, and Keras gave him a grin, dried strands of meat stuck in his teeth. "Better to die free than live caged, Geoffroi. You remember that."

"Hsst!" They fell silent at the warning from one of the other men. They took up positions, arms folded over their heads to offer what little protection they could, huddled against the sides of the tunnel. Every man there held his breath, waiting for the blast.

Folded into a painful little ball, Geoff counted his heartbeats. He reached fifty-seven and was wondering if something had gone wrong with the blasting charges when the rock around them gave a small shudder, followed by an explosion of sound and dust that drowned out all existence.

For a brief moment, he was certain the rock ceiling had caved in on them. He felt the great pressure against his body, an inexorable force larger than any person could possibly stand, then it passed outward and beyond, leaving him mostly unharmed.

The first sound he could hear was a groan next to him and coughing. Geoff sucked in air, taking in lungfuls of dust instead, and coughed until he almost retched. In the absolute blackness, he could hear others doing the same. But the bodies on either side of him were moving, and slowly, people began to call out names, seeing who was conscious.

"Stan."

"Fons."

"Mikel."

"Keras!"

The voices were distant, tinny, and nearly lost in the ringing left in his ears. Geoff spat a mouthful of grit, croaking out "Geoff." Others answered around them, recovering, feeling their way to silent companions in the blackness.

Then, the name he wasn't sure he'd hear at all. "Jon. Bent's with me, but he's hurt."

"Get those flares lit, come on…Everyone up who can." There was scuffling as those who could stand found their feet. Geoff's reaching hands found his crutches, and he struggled upright. His flare was in his pocket, and he fumbled to find it.

There was a snap and hiss to his left, and a green glow swelled to fill the dark tunnel. All heads turned toward the flare and the face illuminated there.

Raffa, tangled mess of hair hanging around her sooty face, frowned at the group of bedraggled men. "Well it's about bloody time! Do you know how long I've been waiting here?"

CHAPTER 16

"Who the Hells are you?" Young Stan spoke first. He'd come from the middle wards, and unlike the lower warders, had never encountered Raffa and her carts of semi-edible rats.

Of course, Geoff quickly started to think that none of them had ever encountered Raffa. At least, not like this.

When Raffa didn't answer him, Stan reached to snatch the burning flare out of the woman's hand. Geoff couldn't see just what went wrong, it happened so fast, but in a blur of motion, Stan was on the ground, groaning and holding his arm with his wrist bent at an unnatural angle.

"Anyone else?" Raffa's slight frame, still covered in tattered rags, suddenly seemed to fill the entire tunnel. She was balanced on the balls of her feet, knees flexed, hands folded into loose fists, and Geoff got the feeling she could have leapt in any direction with no hint whatsoever. The usual fog was gone from her eyes, and she fixed every one of them with a challenging stare. For the first time in his memory, Geoff was afraid of her.

When no one answered, she seemed to relax. Her hands dropped casually to her sides, and her gaze swept over the crowd until she found Geoff. "You still have your crutches, bitty birdy?" The old endearment sounded different. Her whole voice sounded different.

Who was this woman?

Reluctantly, aware that all the men were looking at him now, Geoff nodded.

"Good." Raffa craned her neck to see over the group and raised her voice. "Goat-boy! You back there?"

It was Keras who answered. "Yessum!"

"Get them moving then, we're a few levels too high for safety."

It seemed the majority of the men were too dazed to question the orders, but Jon pushed his way to the fore. "Just where in the Hells do you think you're taking us, Raffa?"

The filthy woman grinned, teeth bright and white in her darkened skin, where before they'd been jagged and rotten. "Exactly.

It was a long march lit only by the green glow of sulfur flares, though Geoff had lost all ability to judge the passage of time. It seemed they walked for hours, then days, then weeks. The usual ache in his knees grew into a screaming agony, lasting until his mind simply turned off his ability to feel anything, and he kept hobbling along with the rest. If Raffa noticed his difficulty, she never slowed the pace, disappearing ahead of them for lengths of time as if to scout the way and returning to grumble at their lack of progress.

The men themselves didn't seem to care where they were being taken, so long as the Factory was far behind them. Jon and a few others who were not injured would backtrack along the path they'd taken from time to time, listening to see if they could hear any kind of pursuit. Each time, they returned with nothing to report. If the Hunt was on the move, they were coming silently. No one said it aloud of course, but every man there felt prickles at the back of their neck, certain they were about to feel the hot breath of a hound as it sprang.

Subtly, the tunnel floors were sloping downward. Adjusting his balance on his crutches to account for the decline, Geoff suspected he was the only one to notice.

At first, the walls curved like every other mining shaft, scored with ridges from the massive borers. He wondered if the men he walked with had carved their path years ago, or if it had been the work of some long-dead convict. *Lost spirits bless him wherever he is.*

Then, then walls changed, as well. The ceiling grew higher, the floor smoother. Where the light would reach, Geoff could see that the walls met at right angles, nice sharp corners. No borer had carved these paths. They still marched downward, but the baking heat of the Factory had long faded behind them, leaving in its wake something that spoke of cool damp spaces, open and inviting.

That promise was fulfilled when they came out of the tunnels into an immense cavern, split in two by a river running silently through the darkness. It was there they decided to make camp. Or rather, it was where Raffa ordered them to stop. No one argued. The water seemed to be blocking their path in all directions, and even those men who were not injured were growing weary.

"Here, set up a perimeter and post look outs back up that tunnel. If they follow us down, we don't want to be caught unawares." Jon directed part of the men to organize supplies, and the rest sank down with weary sighs to treat their own wounds.

Raffa snorted at their efforts, but remained at the edge of the black water, gazing off toward the opposite bank. Even in the flares' green glow, Geoff could not see the far shore, and he wondered what it was that captivated her so.

The strange woman seemed like someone else entirely, and Geoff watched her prowl the riverbank like the large cats of his childhood storybooks. Gone was the daffy scrounger and purveyor of dubious edibles. Who was this woman in Raffa's place? She moved like a warrior. Like Artemis moved, he realized. She no longer hunched in her scuttling pose, and the dazed look in her eyes had been replaced by something keen and calculating. The filthy rags, once worn to hide her form Geoff realized, couldn't conceal the strength in her legs, the defined muscles in her arms.

Perhaps she felt his gaze on her, and she turned to look at him as he huddled next to the tiny oil fire they'd kindled. She seemed to be thinking of something, and pursed her lips as though about to speak, then changed her mind. Her pacing resumed, sharp eyes watching the darkness ahead of them.

"Here." Jon crouched beside Geoff and offered a hunk of hard bread. "It's not much, but it'll tide us over until we can see just what we have to work with." A gash above his right eye had crusted over with dried blood, but other than that, he seemed uninjured. His gaze followed Raffa's pacing, as Geoff's had. "Who is she, Geoff? What is she?"

Geoff could only shake his head and choke down the dry bread. He had no answers, and more questions than he knew what to do with.

A splash from the river drew every eye, and Geoff turned to see Raffa stalking away from the edge, growling to herself. "Thrice cursed… he was supposed to *be* here." Her furious glare fixed on Keras, who had been doing his level best to keep toward the edge of the crowd. "You there! Goat-boy! Get over here."

Every movement screaming reluctance, Keras got to his feet and approached the strange woman, looking like he might bolt back the way they'd come at any moment. He kept his eyes on the stony floor, the fedora pulled low over his eyes. "You know, that's not very nice. I don't call you names."

"Because I'd twist your scrawny head off. You have your pipes?"

It was obviously not the question Keras had been expecting, and he raised his head, blinking in surprise. "Yes?"

Raffa nodded. "Pipe up a tune. He'll hear that, if nothing else. And take off that hideous hat. I've always hated that thing." She snatched the purple fedora from his head before he could protest and tossed it into the fire. There it smoldered with a foul-smelling smoke, but no one noticed.

They were too busy looking at the two perfect little horns nestled in Keras' dark curly hair. They resembled aged ivory in color, nothing more than two little cones curved slightly back. The trader ran a self-conscious hand through his curls, feeling the knobs, and shrugged a bit. "Surprise."

"Pan." Geoff didn't realize he'd spoken aloud until the men around him began to echo the name in whispers. All this time, a god had been amongst them. "You knew. You knew what I was."

Keras-Pan shuffled his feet sheepishly, but before he could answer, Raffa gave him a rough shove toward the water. "Play, Goat-boy. We'll work on introductions later."

Meekly, the unmasked god pulled out his multi-flute and began to play, something low and mournful. The sound seemed to echo and rebound from the unseen cavern ceiling, creating an entire horde of pipers calling out their lament over the still waters.

The men tried to turn their attention to making camp and doling out what food they had hoarded between them, but most of them noticed when Keras shed his heavy coat, revealing the nub of a furry tail sticking out of the back of his trousers. Without the concealing fur, the odd shape of his legs was plain within his pantlegs.

As his steps turned into a small caper, at odds with his mournful song, Geoff knew he could hear the click of tiny hooves on stone. *I've seen you before, like this. You played me to sleep that night, but I remember.* Pan had always been with him, near him. Using him.

A foot nudged his thigh and he looked up to find Raffa dropping into a crouch next to him. "I need to talk to you."

The glimpse of bare thigh peeking through her tattered rags was dirty, yes, but young and muscled. How could they have ever thought her elderly? "I don't know that I should talk to you, when I don't even know who you are." There was no mistaking the glimmer of pain that flashed through her eyes when he said it, and he immediately felt guilty. This was Raffa, of course. Perhaps a different Raffa than he'd ever known, but still the strange woman who had shown him nothing but kindness his entire life.

"I suppose I deserve that. You'll be angrier with me long before this is done, so I may as well get used to it now." She picked up the remains of his bread, nibbling as she talked. "Once Goat-boy over there pipes us up a ride, I need you to come with me. Across the river."

At the corner of his vision, Geoff saw Jon shake his head subtly. He agreed. He didn't want to be alone with this strange woman. "I don't want to go anywhere but up and out."

Raffa snorted. "What, you think I'm going to eat you?"

"No." He looked up finally, meeting her eyes. "I think you'd take me, and leave them here to rot. It's me you want, right? You sent Keras to yank me out of there."

She nodded thoughtfully. "I did, it's true. Craven little thing that he is, he'll still follow orders. So how do you propose to solve this impasse?"

"We all cross the river, or I don't go at all."

Whatever Geoff expected, it wasn't for her to throw her head back and cackle. "Oh bitty birdy… They cross that river, it's a one-way trip for them. You, I can bring back."

"Why?"

She chuckled. "You'll see. In the meantime, I will promise to return you to this very spot, and escort you and your hardy band of noble warriors to the surface as soon as you've seen what you need to see. Fair?"

He looked to Jon, who wasn't even pretending not to listen. Jon nodded. Geoff looked back to Raffa. "Swear it. Swear it by something that matters to you."

She frowned, thinking, then settled on, "I swear it in the name of the Lost Lord of Tartarus, who has never been quite so lost as some might have hoped. Will that do?"

"I suppose it has to."

"Um…hrm…hello? He's um…he's here." Keras appeared at Raffa's shoulder, glancing back toward the black river with a small shudder. All eyes turned to look.

The boat had approached silently, without even the slightest splash of water. It was a shallow craft, riding low on the water with stem and stern rising into the snarling heads of fanciful creatures. A tall figure stood at the prow, draped in black, shrouded hands holding the long pole that had propelled the boat up on to the rocky beach. It stood still, unmoved by the slight rocking of the small craft it piloted.

"Ah, there we are. Your ride awaits, bitty birdy." Raffa hopped to her feet and looked at Geoff expectantly.

It was a struggle just to stand. His knees had stiffened as he sat, and the muted ache had renewed itself into screaming pain. No one offered him a hand up, however, and he wouldn't have taken it if they had. He got his crutches seated on his arms, and looked to Jon.

"Give her a day. If I'm not back, try to get them out anyway."

The mechanic nodded. "Be careful."

"What about me?" Keras fingered his multi-flute nervously, weight shifting from foot to foot. *Hoof to hoof,* Geoff thought.

"You stay here, Goat-boy." Raffa smirked. "Wouldn't want you falling in and wetting those pretty curls, now would we?"

The scrawny man's relief was palpable, and Geoff had to wonder what was on the other side of that wide river that could frighten a god. He eyed the black water, and a chill prickled the skin on his arms. "Don't let them drink the water, Jon. Only what you brought, understand?" He couldn't have said where the warning came from, but he felt the truth of it deep in the knot his stomach had become.

"As you say. Don't leave us here in the dark, Geoff." Jon gripped his shoulder once tightly, then let go.

Raffa snorted and stalked down to the water's edge, tapping her foot as she waited for Geoff to hobble the same distance.

The cloaked figure did not seem to acknowledge Raffa at all, but when Geoff neared, it turned its hooded head slowly. The shadows within the hood were impenetrable, at least by the rapidly fading light of the sulfur flares. Was there a person in there?

He got his answer as the thing stretched out one hand and the black robe fell away. Skeletal fingers reached for him, the bones gleaming and metallic. Silver and gold shown against joints of tarnished iron, and a few remnants of white bone stood out in the mechanical construction. The golden gears in the wrist clicked softly as it beckoned imperiously, demanding...something.

Geoff looked to Raffa, confused.

"Coin, dolt. Silver for the ferryman. Didn't you *read* anything I brought you?" Without waiting for his answer, she fished inside her own clothing and retrieved a handful of copper and bronze coins. "Here, it'll have to do. Beggars can't be choosers, after all." She thrust the money into Geoff's hands, then gestured for him to hand it over.

Hesitantly, Geoff deposited the coins into the upturned hand, fully expecting them to fall through the bones and clatter into the bottom of the boat. The coins tinkled musically against the metal fingers.

A disapproving noise rose from inside the cloak, a mechanical whirr that clearly expressed its displeasure. It leaned forward to peer at Geoff closely, and the young man caught a glimpse of two glowing red orbs deep within the hood, unblinking eyes set in a skull of steel. He swallowed hard and stepped back.

Raffa growled and the sound sent ice lancing through Geoff's veins. "You take what you're given, and bill the Lord for the rest. You're lucky you're getting paid at all, you wind-up charlatan."

The hooded head swiveled to look at Raffa for a long moment, unseen gears humming and buzzing as the thing debated its options. Finally, the bony hand withdrew into the folds of cloth, and it moved back to allow Geoff and Raffa to board. Geoff took the seat furthest to the rear, putting as much space as he could between himself and the strange pilot. *The ferryman…Charon. And this is the River Styx. She's taking me into Tartarus.*

As if she could read his thoughts, Raffa nodded. "You see now why I couldn't take your men. You'll need them later, and they're no good to you, trapped with the dead."

"But I won't be trapped?"

She settled into the shallow hull of the boat, propping her feet up one seat and pillowing her head on another. "Oh no, bitty birdy. You're as free to fly as the rest of us. Get some rest while you can. This will be a long voyage."

The long pole pushed the boat off the beach with a grating of gravel against the hull, and the light from the convicts' fire dimmed immediately, the green glow of the sulfur flares dying away as across a great distance. The mechanical ferryman poled them into the darkness, the gears beneath the cloak marking each stroke with a soft click-whirr-click.

Despite his fear of the coming unknown and the.

pain in his knees, the repetitive sound and rocking of the boat grew into a soothing rhythm, and Geoff finally dozed. Somewhere between Elysia and Tartarus, he dreamed of Lia dancing through a meadow of flowers in the sunlight.

CHAPTER 17

"I swear to you, I will let no one harm you again. My oath on my blood."

How often would those words come back to haunt him? They were words spoken with the best of intentions, out of the noblest of urges. And the world had paid a terrible price for his misguided honor.

Dimly, he could still hear her shrieking, her spittle peppering his face in her wrath, but the words were lost hours ago. The occasional shriek would penetrate the ringing in his ears, or the sharp crack when her fist met his face. But other than that, he was largely insensible. It did not seem to matter to her. He was on his knees already and still she beat him, drawing blood with the ornate rings on her knuckles.

"Thirty-two men! Thirty-two prisoners escaped! You did this! You let this happen!" Every word was punctuated with a blow until he could barely feel each new pain.

He made no move to defend himself. The punishment was just, after all. What else did he think would happen when his deception was discovered?

The sharp tip of an elegantly laced boot caught him in the ribs, and the air left his lungs in a whoosh. He doubled over, coughing as he tried to regain his breath. Blood dribbled from his cut lip, splattering his knuckles as he braced himself against the marble floor. Easy enough to wrap those hands around her throat, simple enough to snap her neck like a twig. He did not.

"Stop it! You have no right!" Persephone's voice, screaming her futile defense of him. He appreciated it, and he would tell her later, but he wished she wouldn't. Best not to draw Artemis' attention to anyone but him. Keep her ire focused, spare the others. And Artemis had every right. He had earned this, well and true.

If Artemis heard the other woman, she didn't show it. "You swore an oath to me! You traitorous halfbreed! Filthy base-born trash! Child-killer!" She kicked him in the head once, and blessedly her screams faded from his consciousness.

The man, the half god who was once Heracles, escaped into soothing darkness and the past.

She held the tattered edges of a robe around herself, her shaking visible even across the room. He lit a twig in the lamp flame to kindle his pipe, and she flinched at even that slight noise. What had happened to make the great huntress so skittish?

"Tea?" He wasn't certain he even had any tea. He usually kept to stronger drink. But it seemed the thing to offer her, in her current state.

Mutely, she shook her head. He sighed softly, inhaling the sweet tobacco as he watched and waited for her to find her voice. Women were so unpredictable, and goddesses more so. It was anyone's guess what had brought Artemis to his doorstep this day.

His patience was getting shorter as the silence wore on, and he nearly snapped at her until he heard her stifle a sob.

"Artemis?" Never in his life had he seen the huntress weep.

"Forgive me…I should not have come here." She made to flee out the door, and nearly made it when his hands touched her shoulders. Her startled gaze was wide and shimmering, tears hovering on her lower lashes like drops of dew.

"What has happened to upset you so?" He had never been particularly close to her, this god-kin of his, but she had come to him for a reason. He could not ignore that.

For one heartbeat, he thought he had erred grievously. There was a flicker in her eyes, something that bespoke a predator about to lunge, and then she dissolved into tears, burying her face against his throat. "He…he violated me…"

Heracles tightened his arms around her, a cold rage settling over him. No one would harm a woman, goddess or mortal, in that way if he could help it. "Who?"

"Ares…"

"And where is he now?"

Something cold trickled down his cheek and into his ear, leading him to believe that he was lying on his back. He raised a hand to brush the discomfort away, and someone pressed it back down.

"Don't, you're still healing. She gave you a bad turn this time." Persephone. Her cool hands removed the damp cloth from his eyes, but no light returned. They were swollen shut, then. At least for now. He heard her wringing the cloth out, water dripping into a bowl, and then it was replaced.

"How…how long?"

She snorted softly. "You've been unconscious for three hours. If your skull wasn't so damn thick, it would be longer." Her disgust was evident, and familiar. "I don't know if I should be glad you woke, or sorry that she didn't finally kill you and end it all."

Ah, that was a pretty thought. "Hoped she'd kill

me."

"I'm well aware of what you hoped." His bed jostled as she rose, and her voice placed her across the room. "Though you'll never get what you want. If she killed you, she couldn't make you suffer anymore."

"Truth." Forming the word cracked his split lip, and he tasted blood. "Hurt you?"

She snorted. "Of course not. My welfare is her only bargaining chip if her worst fear is about to come true. There isn't a mark on me."

There was a soft snap, and he felt the bone in his forearm reseat itself, knitting together even as he focused his attention there. He was healing. Bless his father's blood then, even as he cursed it.

"Is it about to come true?" He dragged the cloth off his eyes and managed to blink them into usable slits. His world was limited to the scope of his damaged vision, a slit of light and redness where the blood still stained his eyes. "Are they still free?"

Persephone came to sit beside him again, dabbing at his bleeding lip with a clean cloth. "Last I heard, yes. But she's left orders that we're not to be informed of any news, so rumors are slow filtering up the tower." Her hands dropped to her lap, her eyes clouding with anger. "She's sent the Hunt into the catacombs."

Heracles attempted to sit up, and was pleased to find out he could with a minimum of pain. "Knew she would. That's what they're for, after all."

"It doesn't bother you at all that those men will be slaughtered?"

"Maybe they won't be." Even with the half-sight his swollen lids allowed him, he saw her incredulous look.

"The hounds cannot be tricked, or avoided, and

they can barely be killed. How under the dark sky can you see this ending well for those poor men?"

He had no answer for that. It was an irrational supposition. No one had ever escaped the Lady's Hunt. And yet…he dared to hope. Another legacy of his brief contact with the muse.

"Did she go with them?"

Persephone shook her head again. "No. She's up in the clock room, still venting her wrath on anything that can't get out of the way." To confirm her story, lightning arced past the window to strike a luckless building to the east. The thunder cracked a moment later, rattling even Olympus Tower.

Heracles glanced upward, as if he could see through the layers of steel and concrete to find the goddess many floors above. "Best hope the Hunt does catch them, then. If this goes on too long, she'll lose what little grasp on sanity she has left."

"I think you overestimate her current state." The blond woman tucked a lock of hair behind her ear with a jerky motion. "Why did you do it? You had to know this was going to happen, why didn't you just do what she asked and execute that man?"

Heracles swung his legs off the bed, forcing her to stand. He braced his arms on his knees until the pain in his broken ribs subsided. "So killing one man is preferable to the deaths of thirty-two?"

"It won't be just the escaped prisoners and you know it. She's decided the whole of the Factory is contaminated, and it's only a matter of time before she decides to have it razed. Every person in there will die, and without the power and warmth, the Greenery will fail, and then all of this is over." She gestured out the dark windows to Elysia, sleeping beyond the glass.

He pushed himself to his feet, grimacing when he felt two ribs pop back into their allotted places. "Think on one thing, my lady. You said yourself that your noble husband was still in hiding somewhere, waiting for inspiration. Consider that I have delivered just that. If the Lord Hades is going to move, he'd better do it damn quick."

~*!*~

The shade of her long-dead brother paced the suspended walkways on the other side of the pillar, always just out of her direct line of sight. But she could hear him quite clearly.

Who can you trust, dear sister? Even the one sworn to defend you at all costs has betrayed you. Perhaps he already knows the secret. Perhaps he will come to your chamber in the darkness, and he will end your suffering with a quick stroke of metal.

Artemis moaned and hid her face in her skirt, hugging her knees tightly to her chest. How long had she huddled here once her rage was spent? Hours perhaps had gone by, counted out in perpetuity by the great clock. Her skirt was soiled and torn, and bore spatters of something thicker than gear oil. "They are all against me. *He* turned them all against me. I am alone in the dark." The gears overhead shifted positions, the metal vibrating as each tooth slid into its mate.

I am with you, dear sister. Always with you. I am your light in the darkness.

It was true. As much as she hated his constant taunting and incessant mockery, she still loved him as well. He was her brother, her twin. She needed him.

"What do I do? The contagion has spread."

She could swear she felt the platform creak with

extra weight, feel the soft thump of footsteps not her own. He was behind her now, circling the outer wall of the tower. *You do what must be done. First, you must find those you know are tainted, and cleanse them before they can infect anyone else.*

"Yes…yes, the Hunt will find them and destroy them. And if *he* is still with them, he will die as well." Bolstered, she got to her feet, hands gripping the thin railing before her. "And then…?"

And then, you will punish those responsible. The warrior, of course, but who helped him? Do you believe the smith was blind to it? Demeter and her get? They have conspired against you. They want the secret for themselves.

"They have always wanted it. They would tear me down as I did my father before me."

Ghostly hands caressed her shoulders, and she felt her hair stir as though something breathed lightly on her neck. *What need have you for other gods? Are you not the most powerful, the inheritor of Zeus' might? They not only threaten you, they distract the humans from their rightful worship of you.*

The clock's innermost workings trembled again, gears turning at their appointed times. Artemis stared at the great pillar, trying to discern its movement, no matter how slight. "There is so little metal left. Only the arrow. It would take planning, lest one warn the others."

You will not kill the warrior. He who has betrayed you and forsworn himself.

"Yes. He must suffer. No peaceful release is to be allowed." How alike they still were, she and her twin. So often, it seemed they shared one heart, one mind.

But the others…are expendable.

"Yes." A thought occurred to her, and she turned, puzzled when she did not find him standing just behind her. "But what of Hades?"

What of him?

"Any harm to Persephone will no doubt bring terrible retribution." Her answer was a low disapproving hiss.

You are the Queen of Olympus, the keeper of the world pillar! Who is our uncle to presume to threaten you? You hold all of our father's power. You will make Hades kneel.

A series of staccato sounds marked the winding of the spring that would power the massive hammer above. Artemis looked up to watch it coil back, poised to leap forward and bludgeon the gong. "If he dares to even show his face."

Exactly. Only a fool would emerge from hiding to challenge you now. Just be who you are, sister, and all will be well.

Again, she felt the whisper of a touch across her back, though it was pressed tightly against the railing. No one could be standing behind her, and yet she knew he was. Phantom lips traced the column of her throat. "I am sorry, brother. You do know that, yes?"

Of course I know. Are we not two halves of the same whole?

"It had to be done, to protect the secret. It was not done out of any malice."

I know. I hold no grudge.

"I loved you."

Hush now. You have plans to make.

"I do? What plans?"

You must be prepared, sister. To do what must be done in the end.

Her gaze traveled up to the adamantine-tipped arrow, suspended over the world's pillar. "Yes. What must be done."

CHAPTER 18

Geoff woke in time to see the far shore of the river approaching, and had no idea how long he had slept. Jon and the other convicts were long out of sight, the lights from their flares and fire extinguished like they had never been. It was an even greater blackness than Dark, where they at least had the constant glow of Olympus Tower to orient themselves.

And yet, somehow, he could see. The black waters rippled as the boat split them. The carved prow of the small boat gleamed in some mysterious light source. Threads in the ferryman's cloak twinkled as he poled them along. The faint whirr-click-whirr of Charon's gears was softened by the cheerful chatter of the disrupted river.

Raffa was awake before him and crouched near the stern, just behind the mechanical ferryman. Without looking, she tossed him a hunk of bread. "Eat this now. You shouldn't eat or drink anything once we get out of the boat."

He choked down what he could without water and watched flickering lights appear on the opposite shore. "Are we almost there?"

"Soon." The strange woman's shoulders were tense, and her hands opened and closed at her sides, searching for a weapon perhaps, or maybe just something stable to cling to. The fact that Raffa seemed nervous worried Geoff more than any other part of this madness he'd tumbled into.

Fine gravel grated against the hull of the narrow boat, but Charon poled it up onto the sand with little effort. The hooded gaze swung toward his passengers, watching silently as Raffa helped Geoff clamber out.

"You will remain here until we need to return, understand?" There was no response from the cloaked automaton, but Raffa seemed to take it for assent. "Are you ready, bitty birdy?"

Geoff eyed the line of torches – real torches, with real flame, not yellow gaslights – that lined the path from the beach, and wondered, *Ready for what?*

Without waiting for his answer, Raffa struck out across the gray sands, leaving him to struggle along as best he could. His crutches sank into the soft soil, and it slipped out from under his feet in the most irritating fashion. *It doesn't want me here.*

The path itself was little more than large pebbles strewn in a semi-orderly fashion, but it was at least easier to navigate than the sand. With a little effort, Geoff managed to catch up to Raffa. "Where are we going?"

"You'll see." She looked neither right nor left, her strides eating up distance without even winding her.

"This is Tartarus, isn't it? You took me across the River Styx, and we're in the underworld now."

"You're a shiny cog, bitty birdy. You always have been. Such a smart boy."

He sighed, realizing he wasn't going to get much else out of her. "Why do you call me that?"

He caught the hint of a smile that twisted her lips in the moment before it vanished. "Because when you were an infant, you would open your mouth so wide when you were hungry, just like a baby bird begging. It just...stuck."

"Raffa." He caught her elbow, and she stopped in her tracks, surprise showing on her face. "Who are you?"

For a moment, he thought she might actually answer him. It was there in her eyes, in the way she reached one hand up to touch his cheek, to tuck a lock of hair behind his ear. Then it was gone. She dropped her hand and turned away. "You'll learn soon enough. Come on, he's waiting."

The path soon widened out into what Geoff could only call a road, curving gently for no other reason than it wanted to. The torches burned brightly, but put off no smoke that he could see, nor did they ever seem to burn low.

A glow appeared ahead, the same red-orange as the torchlight, and he was not surprised when a massive stone archway came into view, flanked on either side by two roaring braziers. These guttered smoke, and almost obscured another doorway – smaller yes, in the way that Jon was smaller than Heracles – in front of which lay a heap of gleaming metal bars.

Only when the bars moved did he realize that they were not bars, but in fact massive links of chain, each curved piece as big as his own torso. It clanked loudly as something within the second doorway stirred.

"Ah wait, he gets so few opportunities to do his job these days." Raffa stopped them on the path and whistled sharply.

Out of the darkened doorway came a distinct growl, and then three pairs of glowing golden eyes appeared.

Geoff had seen Artemis' hounds, and even they could not prepare him for this sight as the creature emerged. All black fur and jaws big enough to bite him in half, the three canine heads took turns sniffing the air. The chain rattled as it stepped out of its shelter, revealing one massive body to support the thick necks. How its shoulders fit inside, Geoff couldn't figure out.

It apparently liked what it smelled, three sets of ears perking up, and the left-most head swung toward Raffa with a curious whine.

"There's a good boy. I'm home now." To Geoff's very real amazement, she walked up to the gargantuan hound and scratched its jowls with both hands. The thing made a rumbling sound of contentment, all six eyes closing in pleasure. Raffa grinned at Geoff. "Come on, let him get your scent. He's really quite gentle."

"This is…Cerberus?" Geoff approached slowly, quite aware that if the thing took exception to his presence, he had no chance to outrun it.

"A descendent of the original, but yes. I think he calls this one Panos." The three-headed dog nudged Raffa as she grew distracted from her ministrations, and she chuckled despite nearly being knocked over. "He's a lover more than a warrior, but he'll hold this gate as long as he must."

"And what happens if he doesn't like me?"

Raffa smirked. "Then each head will grab a body part and pull in opposite directions."

"That's a pleasant thought." Swallowing the churning dynamos in his stomach, Geoff reached out one hand to let the great mastiff sniff it. The right-most head did so, the other two more interested in Raffa. Moist breath bathed Geoff's face, and he did his best not to grimace at the smell. The wet nose pressed into his palm, snuffling for a few moments before finding the young man to his satisfaction and the head withdrew.

"See, he likes you. Come on." Giving the dog one last pat, Raffa headed off through the stone archway.

Geoff watched the black, three-headed hound as long as he could, certain it would change its mind and spring at him, but he made it through the gate without incident. *And now I am truly in Tartarus. Lost spirits, watch over me.*

And watch him they did. He felt the eyes on him the moment he passed through the archway, but he didn't associate the sensation with the blue wisps of mist flowing across the road until Raffa spoke.

"They can't harm you. Pay them no mind and keep walking."

"They?"

She nodded toward the vapors, eddying around their very feet. "The dead. This far from the center, they can barely hold form at all. They don't usually come out this far." She cast him an amused look. "They're curious about you."

The dead? Geoff watched the swirling mist with new wariness. He couldn't take a step without a tendril beneath his foot, and he had to wonder if it hurt when he stepped on them. He squelched the urge to apologize to the wispy phantoms, certain that Raffa would laugh at him.

True to her word, the farther they walked, the more solid the ghosts became. Geoff explained away the first few faces in the mist as fanciful constructions of his already taxed mind, but they began to appear with more regularity. Once, he was almost certain someone walked at his side for almost ten minutes, an intangible arm around his waist as if to support him. When he attempted to look directly at it, it wisped away into nothing. The road was lost now in a layer of blue fog that seemed to ebb and surge with odd sentience.

Before long, he began to hear the voices, whispers at first, but soon rising into something pitched just at the edge of his hearing. The keening, barely heard, made his heart clench in his chest. "Such sorrow."

Ahead of him, Raffa nodded without looking back. "They've much to be sorrowful for. The scars from the war linger even here."

The landscape began to take shape, distant hills and swells visible in the flickering torchlight. There might have been trees or clusters of small dwellings, but every time Geoff tried to focus on it, it would shimmer like forge-heated air and fade away.

"You'll give yourself a headache. Once we get closer, things will settle."

Closer to what? And how much farther did they have to go? Between his flight from the Factory, Raffa's long march into the deepest catacombs, and now this seemingly endless trek through Tartarus itself, Geoff had been on his feet longer than he could ever remember. "Can we rest a moment? Please?"

She cast a scathing glance over her shoulder, flipping her matted hair aside to make certain he saw it. "You know, distance here is only a figment of your mind. If you weren't so damn reluctant to get where you're going, we'd be there by now."

Geoff felt the nettle of being called a coward, and bridled at it. "You haven't even told me where we're going. A little information might be helpful."

Raffa sighed. "It isn't my information to give." She stopped, though, and let him rest on a boulder that seemed to materialize out of nowhere. "I only ask that you trust me, bitty birdy, as you've always done."

There were many retorts he could have made to that, but he did not. Certainly, she had lied to him all his life, and it was possible that even now she was leading him into the depths of Tartarus with no intention of returning him to the surface again. But she had also been kind to him, bringing a small injured boy countless books, pretty baubles from times gone by, and the occasional tidbit of food when times were lean. *I will trust, until you give me a reason not to.*

The knot was still sitting nestled in the curve of his sternum. He could feel it there, tight with anticipation. He had not used it to influence anything since the escape from the Factory, nor had he pushed any of the men to wait for him on that dark riverbank. It ached to be released, to be used. If Raffa proved herself to be an enemy, she would make a convenient a target as any. *I don't yet know what I will do, but I will not make it easy on you.*

As if she heard him, Raffa smiled and urged him to his feet again.

They lined the road, face upon face upon face, all staring in mute silence. They had been tall in life, and short, and skinny, and round, and all manner of races and creeds. They wore everything from archaic armor to the latest in Elysian fashion. It reminded Geoff of the most macabre Liberation Day parade he'd ever seen.

Raffa nodded her head in approval. "Good, you're getting us there faster. Shouldn't be very far now."

From time to time, Geoff thought he caught a glimpse of a face he knew. The old man who had frozen to death in Deeptown last winter. The little boy who had taken sick in the spring and died of wetlung. Twice, he was certain he saw convicts from the Factory, men he had seen alive just the previous day. *Charon has been busy today, and it was my doing.* He couldn't decide if there truly was accusation in their ghostly stares, or if it was his own guilt speaking to him.

"There's so many."

"Mm-hmm. They've nowhere to go but here, with the wall up."

Geoff frowned. How often had he offered a prayer to the "lost spirits" to aid him, without truly thinking about what it meant? "The wall around the Elysian Fields. The wall Artemis built."

"Yes. No one goes in, no one comes out. So they linger here, just waiting."

The phantom escort closed in behind the pair, leaving only the path before them open. Raffa seemed unconcerned, but Geoff had to wonder how certain she was that the dead could not harm them. They looked solid enough to him.

"Ah, here we are."

Wrenching his gaze away from the ghosts at Raffa's words, he looked ahead and blinked to find them standing before a large house. There was no way such a large dwelling could sneak up on them, and yet he hadn't seen it coming. *Strange are the ways of Tartarus.*

Three stories above their heads, it was constructed of the same dingy gray brick as most of the nicer row-houses in Elysia. Shutters graced the windows, the white paint standing out in stark contrast to the dark building, and the black shingles above seemed neat and orderly. The windows revealed no light to betray whether someone might be in residence.

Geoff blinked, and the structure wavered. For a moment, he saw tall columns of white marble, like the floors in Olympus Tower, and a wide open courtyard with fountains in the shape of fantastic creatures. The smell of fresh water wafted across his face, and he heard the musical tinkle as it trickled through the sculptures. Lamps hung on lines strung between the columns, little flames guttering cheerfully as they gave off light. Another blink, and it was simply a house again, dark and brooding. "What...?"

Raffa ignored his question, which seemed fair since he wasn't certain what he'd intended to ask anyway. Some things were just without explanation. She took his shoulders and turned him to face her square, looking him over. "Well, your clothes are ratty, and you smell like a week-old pig corpse, but...I suppose you'll do." She licked her fingers and attempted to smooth his hair until he batted her hand away.

He looked down at himself, noticing for the first time how tattered and frayed the cuffs of his pants had become. Amongst the other long-time residents of the Factory, his own clothing had been practically new by comparison. His shirt was stained with sweat and dirt, and there was nothing to be done for it. He made certain it was tucked in, then shrugged to Raffa. "This is as good it gets, unless you can find me a bath down here."

Her smile faded, and she quickly shook her head. "No, no baths. Too easy to get water in your mouth that way." She clutched his elbow tightly. "Drink and eat nothing, bitty birdy. I can't say that enough. No matter how small, let nothing pass your lips but air. Understand?"

Her grip started to hurt, and he grimaced. "I understand. I do, really."

She released him and stood there, biting her lip

hard.

That was disturbing. "What are you so afraid of? You brought me here, it has to be safe right?"

She shook her head, matted locks falling in front of her face. "Oh no, never think it's safe here. I brought you here because he told me to, but I don't have to like it."

"Who told you to?"

She smiled, and he thought he saw a trace of sadness there. "Go through the door. Find out."

Reluctantly, he began hobbling up the steps, stopping at the top when he realized she wasn't behind him. "You're not coming with me?"

She shook her head. "He didn't ask to see me. Just you. Go on." Her hands were clenching and unclenching at her sides, and he got the impression again that she was seeking a weapon she didn't have. "It's all right, bitty birdy."

Funny, he didn't feel like it was all right. Juggling his crutches a bit, he managed to turn the knob. The door swung inward into darkness, and Geoff could sense a great open space beyond, as if someone had created the façade of a house without truly knowing what lay within.

He glanced at Raffa once more, but she offered no more than an insistent gesture, urging him forward. Taking a deep breath, he stepped through the portal.

CHAPTER 19

The door swung shut behind him, and for a
moment, Geoff was encased in blackness. The windows
on the front of the house were apparently decorative
rather than functional.

"Oh, my apologies." The man's voice came from
the black, impossible to pinpoint a location, but it was
smooth and soothing. "It's been so long since I've had a
guest, I forgot to light the lamps."

Light bloomed all around, and Geoff shielded his
eyes on instinct. Still, they watered furiously as they tried
to adjust to the sudden brightness.

The room within looked nothing like the house
without. The light seemed to glow from no source in
particular, the lamps on a few scattered tables merely
there for authenticity. The walls themselves wavered in
his light-dazzled vision, at one moment the hewn stone
of the tunnels beyond, and at another, wood paneling
that gleamed in the lamplight. There were rugs upon the
floor, thick patterned fabric with heavy tassels, until he
blinked. Then there was rough stone…no, white
marble…no, the rugs again. And the ceiling was either

nonexistent, or like the cavernous roof of Tartarus itself, too far above to be fathomed. Already, Geoff could feel an ache beginning somewhere in the front of his head.

A heavy desk across the room seemed to trade places at will with a richly upholstered couch in red velvet, and the bookshelves against the ever-changing walls flickered in and out of existence with no logic whatsoever, the tomes on them rearranging themselves at their own whim it seemed. He closed his eyes as the swimming room stirred nausea, and he feared he'd lose the few bites of bread he'd managed earlier.

"Ah, apologies for that as well. It helps if you concentrate on one thing, picture it as you wish it to be. That much should at least be solid."

Grasping at that, Geoff pictured the red velvet couch, holding it firmly in his mind, and when he opened his eyes, it was there, very solid and real. He sank onto the cushions, feeling the bones in his knees grind with the sudden bending, and buried his face in his hands.

"Easy there. Give it a moment, it takes some getting used to." A warm hand came to rest on his shoulder, squeezing gently, and the couch shifted as someone took a seat beside him.

"I may be ill."

The man chuckled, the sound rolling and curling around the room until it came from all directions at once. "You wouldn't be the first."

After a few moments, Geoff dared to raise his head again. The floors still shifted beneath his feet, but if he didn't look directly at it, it wasn't so noticeable. Concentrating on the bookcases made them stop their odd dance as well, and that hid the indecisive walls. Satisfied that he was not going to vomit on the floor, he turned to look at his mysterious host.

He was a brunet man with the lines of a hard life etched on his face. His hair was close-cropped, and the small mustache and goatee were neatly trimmed. Before Geoff could open his mouth, the man was bronzed, with ash-blond coils of matted hair hanging past his shoulders, no older than Geoff himself. In a heartbeat, he was silver-haired and pale-skinned, a strange agelessness to his smooth cheeks. He wore white robes, then a nicely buttoned gray suit, then a pair of brown trousers and a stained linen shirt, open at the neck. Only his eyes, black and piercing, remained steady.

"That's rather unsettling, you know." What else could he say, given the ridiculousness of the situation?

The man smiled, his image settling into the older, dark-haired fellow. "So I've been told. I don't notice anymore."

Geoff frowned. "Who are you? Why am I here?"

The man chuckled again, proving that the lines on his face were as much from smiling as age. "The first question is easy. The second will require more time." He rose, walking to idly peruse the books on the now-stable shelves. "I am Hades, of course. Neither lost nor hiding, contrary to what you might have heard. Lord of….this. " He flipped a hand dismissively at the room, and presumably the world beyond. "As to why you are here… Sentient beings have been asking that question for millennia."

"I meant why am I—"

"No. You didn't." Hades turned to fix him with that sharp black gaze. "You know why you are here, in this physical location. You are here to speak to me. What you truly wish to know is why are you *here*? Why do you exist, and what purpose do you serve? And I can tell you that the answers to those questions were formed centuries before your birth. Fortunately for you, I was there, so I can relate the tale."

Something tight in Geoff's chest relaxed, and for a moment, he thought he'd inadvertently tried to use his influence on the Lord of Tartarus himself. But no, that knot of warmth still nestled in his sternum. It was relief, he realized. Pure and simple relief that perhaps now, he would find the answers he'd been seeking.

"Then tell me."

Hades smiled a bit, a hint of sadness flickering across his features. It was hard to tell if the expression was his, or belonged to one of the other appearances he'd worn. "We have to go back a long way. Centuries, millennia… Strange how one tiny event can create such catastrophic repercussions as the ripples spread outward. I expect you to despise me, by the way, before I am done with this telling. It is all right for you to do so."

How many more people were going to freely invite his hatred, he wondered? Everyone seemed to have a universally low opinion of him, if they expected him to assign hatred so freely.

The raven-haired man fell silent, long fingers running over the spines of various books. Books, Geoff realized, that looked very similar to those Raffa had brought to him his entire life. *Found in the catacombs, eh?*

"Your life, or rather, the path that would lead to your life, began with a wager."

The lights around the room snuffed out, leaving them in total darkness.

Out of the blackness, Hades' voice continued, coming from nowhere and everywhere at once. "What do you know of the great war, Geoffroi?"

Geoff could no longer feel the couch beneath him, nor the floor under his feet. His hands groped at where his legs should be, and not only did they touch nothing, he wasn't entirely certain they were still there to touch with. *Is this death?* "I…know that the gods warred on Olympus for thirty years. And that the Lady Artemis won."

"Ah, but do you know why?"

No, Geoff realized. The why of it was lost in the centuries after.

"It began with a virgin, and a scoundrel's wager."

Light blossomed, wavering like a warped mirror, and Geoff found himself facing a flat, faded image. It reminded him of the moving cinematics they showed at market some days, the fixed images in their rotating box stuttering along in a mockery of motion. In the odd moving picture, the colors bled out to shades of brown and red, a light-haired woman ran through stately trees. She wore a skirt that barely skimmed the top of her muscled thighs, and she gripped a slender length of wood in one hand.

A bow. It has to be a bow. "Artemis."

"Very good. As she was then, of course, not as she is now. The goddess of the hunt, the goddess of the moon, the virgin goddess, twin to the god Apollo."

The woman paused in her flight, holding up a hand to someone unseen, and raised her bow, fitting an arrow to the string. Even in the shaky image, Geoff could see the muscles in her arms bunch and flex, attesting to the power it took to draw the weapon.

"Sworn to forever preserve her innocence, she accepted neither suit, nor seduction." The arrow was loosed, streaking out of sight, and the image vanished, leaving only a warm glow of light. "But someone took that vow as a challenge."

The man that appeared had darker hair, though the color was impossible to tell in the sepia-toned cinematic. He stalked through the scene dressed in stiff clothing, adorned with metal studs. Armor, Geoff knew, of the ancient days. The set of his shoulders bespoke arrogance, and he moved like a fighter. "Ares. The god of war. And what is seduction but another type of battle?"

The image flickered, changed, and the next scene was hard to discern at first. Gradually, bare limbs and thrusting hips became clear, a couple joining vigorously on a blanket. Geoff tried to turn his eyes away, only to find that he could not. Even if he closed what he thought were his eyes, the scene played out before him regardless of his discomfort.

"It took centuries, but our huntress was a virgin no longer, believing herself to be conquered by love." The couple rolled apart, the woman's hand clinging to the darker man's arm as she looked up at him in adoration. "Her view of things was not shared by her lover. His conquest claimed, his wager won, Ares departed with little regard for what he left behind." Geoff could see the man throw back his head and laugh scornfully, could see the moment of shocked hurt on Artemis' face. "Nothing is so dangerous as a woman scorned. Remember that."

The light flickered, and a picture of an immense mountain bloomed. The peak was wreathed in clouds, flashes of sepia-toned lightning arcing through to spear the ground below. Indistinct shapes swarmed over the mountainside, armies clashing in silent fury. "The war began because Zeus would not accept Artemis' claim of rape and punish Ares. Sides were chosen, those who stood with the huntress, and those who stood with her father."

Hades, somewhere behind Geoff – or perhaps off to his left, it was hard to tell – chuckled. "I suppose it never occurred to them that a war between beings who cannot die was an exercise in futility.

"For two decades, Olympus was bathed in blood. The armies were mortal enough, of course. Humans and the old kinds alike died on that mountain. Entire races were slaughtered, made extinct. But still Artemis pressed on, her rage and humiliation blinding her to all else. I don't know, perhaps she actually believed by that time that Ares had taken her against her will."

The battle washed away leaving behind a sad-eyed man with light hair hanging in curls around his bared shoulders. "Apollo. He loved his sister beyond reason, and it was at his request that his muses gave over their gravest secret." A throng of slight females, every bit as slender as Lia, clustered around the huntress while Apollo looked on. One of them went on tiptoes to whisper into Artemis' ear.

The light extinguished in guttering fits, plunging Geoff back into darkness. "With the knowledge she gained, Artemis begged Hephaestus to fashion a weapon. She brought him the metal and bade him create arrows for her bow. I do not know if he understood then what she was asking. Perhaps someday, I'll be able to ask him."

The glow that came next was not in shades of warm browns, but was instead lifeless, cold and gray, the desolation almost palpable. An old man with white hair and a full beard lay dead, his sightless eyes staring upward at something unseen. An arrow sat in his bare chest, the flesh around it turning black and putrid even as Geoff watched. He swallowed hard, feeling the bile rise in his throat. Ravens flew down to pluck at the cloudy eyes, and almost immediately fell over dead, the feathers curling as if from immense heat.

"Even as she stepped over the dead and dying, Artemis knew that her victory was not secure. Not until she made certain no one else would ever learn how to kill a god." Corpses sprawled everywhere, the same lithe females that only moments before had cavorted so playfully across the scene. Their mouths were open in silent screams, throats torn out, limbs severed. They had not been merely killed, but butchered, cut down even as they tried to flee.

"I don't want to see anymore."

"You must. The story is only beginning."

Apollo turned to face Geoff, and for a moment the young man thought the god was actually looking at him. But the expression became a fond smile, and Artemis moved into view, her back to the watchers. They spoke for a few moments, their words undecipherable, then the goddess moved to embrace her brother. His fond smile suddenly became a look of shock, and when Artemis withdrew, he clutched at the arrow shaft protruding from his stomach. Blood poured from the wound, more than was warranted, and Apollo slumped to his sister's feet.

"Because the muses were his, she deemed him a danger to her, and so she killed him. But wait…it gets more interesting. Here is the part I play."

Apollo's body lay rotting, black corruption spreading from the wound to claim the flesh, and in the distance the sun was burning its way past the horizon for the last time. Artemis was gone, it seemed, but another shape moved into the picture. In the waning daylight, a raven-haired man crept up to the corpse, looking warily over his shoulder. He reached to close the dead god's eyes, head bowed, then drew a dagger from inside his cloak. His actions were hidden, but whatever it was happened quickly and he slipped away as the sunlight died.

Once again, the flickering picture vanished, leaving blessed darkness. Geoff's stomach churned, and he knew he'd never be able to erase those sights from his mind. His skin felt cold and clammy, which was an odd sensation when he had a hard time locating his body at all.

"And the god Hades crept from the underworld, and from Apollo's body he stole his seed, and Artemis mourned in the darkness for she had lost her brother twice. Isn't that how the tale goes?"

Slowly, the lamplight returned, and Geoff found the velvet seat cushion beneath him. He sank his fingers into it, holding on for dear life. The bookcases wavered only slightly, and the floor settled into the patterned rugs and changed no more.

Hades returned to the seat beside him, and shook his head sadly. "I am guilty, you know. The Lord of Tartarus is nothing more than a thief. I stole Apollo's seed, and then I fled into the depths of Tartarus where not even Artemis could find me."

Geoff cleared his throat, wishing for water to clear away the sour taste in his mouth. "Why?"

"Why?" He laughed, finding mirth where Geoff saw none. "Well first off, I didn't want to die. Artemis still has an arrow with my name on it, quite literally. And second, because I knew the people would need hope. What good is a world in darkness if there is no chance the sun will shine again?" He leaned forward, staring at

Geoff until the young man felt compelled to look away, the intensity of the god's gaze unnerving.

"While I was away from my throne, Artemis ventured into the underworld. Some human seer had spat up a prophecy, and Artemis was sure she could keep it from coming to pass if she could imprison all those she had killed in her madness. She erected a wall around the Elysian Fields, and since that day not one soul has passed in or out. All the dead you see out there are waiting for their due, waiting for passage into paradise, and Artemis has denied them that."

The thought of those ghostly, hollow faces brought a shudder, and Geoff couldn't help but look back toward the door, half expecting the dead to be pressing their spectral faces against the windows. "It's your realm. Why don't you just take the wall down?"

Hades nodded. "I could. I could, easily. But she has my wife, my Persephone. One chink in that wall, and I don't know what Artemis will do to her." Hades gripped Geoff's hand until it hurt. "And that is where you come in, Geoffroi."

Instinct prompted Geoff to lean back, putting space between him and the lord of the underworld. Hades nodded, smiling his acceptance of that subtle rejection.

"When I deemed it safe, I took Apollo's seed, combined it with the last traces of any muse I could find, and I tried to create life. You have to realize, this is not my strength. Never has the Lord of Tartarus been a life-bringer." He grimaced faintly. "The early efforts were…unsuccessful. Perhaps the seed was tainted before I could retrieve it. Most likely it was my own ineptitude. Regardless, for those same mysterious reasons, I just as suddenly succeeded."

He smiled, wrinkling the corners of his neatly groomed goatee. "You were flawed, to be certain. Male, though I hadn't intended that. Your legs were…not whole. But aside from that you were so strong, so determined to live." Hades stood to pace, and the walls seemed to recede to give him space. "It was rapidly apparent that, despite your origins, you would be mortal, and that this was no place for an infant. I summoned the one who would be your guardian, and I gave you over to her, and I sent you to the surface."

"Raffa." Always hovering at the edge of his vision, always turning up just when she was needed. The one to pluck him from the snow. *There was no snow, idiot. A false tale to explain away an unnatural child.*

"That is the name she took, yes. She had another name, once. She and her sisters. At their deaths, she took on all of their names and became the Erinyes alone. I suppose you should continue to call her what makes you comfortable."

Erinyes…the Furies. Purveyors of justice. Turned into a nursemaid for a crippled child. "Why? Why go to so much trouble?"

"Because the humans up there are so much cattle without you. They cannot think for themselves, without the influence of the muses. They don't dream of anything beyond those thrice-damned walls and the darkness and that lunatic bitch in the tower." He knelt, something feverish glimmering in his black eyes. "But with you there, perhaps someone will dream of a different way. They'll dream of change, and they'll act."

"You're speaking of rebellion. You want them to rise up against Artemis, don't you?" The scenes of battle recently seen played out again in Geoff's mind. How many more would die?

"Don't you? How many has she killed in her madness? Think of all those people, trapped within that wall with the very ground crumbling away beneath them. Has no one ever wondered what might be beyond? A better life? Freedom? Think of all these souls down here, unjustly kept from resting at peace."

"All for what? So you could rule in her place?"

"No. Never." Hades shook his head and resumed his pacing. "Everything has a life cycle, Geoffroi. Even immortal things. And we…we have long outstayed our purpose. No, I just want to rest, to leave things to the humans. It should be your world now."

The statement sounded hollow. To date, every deity he'd run across had used him in their own way, whether he'd known it or not. "Then what's in it for you?"

The god opened his mouth to answer, then hesitated for a few moments. "I suppose… After all this time, I just want to see my wife again. That is what I stand to gain from this. I think you of all people could appreciate that."

Lia's face came to him so strongly he could almost smell the oil paint and linseed oil. Geoff closed his eyes to hold the image as long as he could. "I could. Yes." The last time he'd heard her voice, she'd been frantically screaming his name. *If you spirits have any power at all, watch over her.*

"So will you do it?"

Geoff opened his eyes to find Hades watching him. Was that a glimmer of uncertainty in the god's dark eyes? A hint of pleading in his voice? "I'm still not exactly sure what you're asking me to do."

"It's very simple, really, once you get past the

logistics of it." The god stroked his neat beard with one hand and smiled jovially. "I want you to return to the surface and kill Artemis."

<u>CHAPTER 20</u>

The hounds were hunting. Man and beast and those caught somewhere in between, the Hunt ranged far and wide, searching for their elusive prey.

Artemis could feel each one like an extension of herself. She felt keenly the searing heat of the Factory through short speckled fur. Smooth rock alternated with rough cobblestones under calloused paw pads. Scents tantalized her quivering black nose, and floppy ears perked at distant hints of sound.

They were scattered throughout Elysia, pairs searching door to door in the lower wards. A woman screamed and cowered in a corner, clutching her child to her chest as the powerful hounds padded through their dwelling, showing not the slightest interest in her or her squalling offspring.

They were beneath the city, hunting parties plunging through the dark catacombs with only the light of sulfur flares. Rats and ratcatchers alike scampered out of the light, but the dogs never gave chase. This was not their quarry.

High and low, they prowled the blackness. Each huntsman carried a scrap of cloth with the desired scent on it. There was nowhere the escapees could hide from their preternatural pursuers.

As the goddess gazed out her window over the city, she could have pointed to any one of her creations at any point in time. They were hers, to the last thread of their being.

"Find them. Bring them to me," she murmured softly, and across the city, the Hunt leapt to obey.

Her back was to the door, her conscious mind absorbed in guiding her canine soldiers. She never heard the soft footfalls across the marble floor or the tiniest chime of a metal blade as it left the sheath. It was the breeze that snapped her out of her dangerous immersion. The slightest change in air pressure against the back of her neck brought her to full alert in the space between one heartbeat and the next.

The point of the blade glanced across the back of her neck, drawing a thin line of blood that healed almost as quickly as it appeared. The hand holding the knife slapped into the goddess' palm as she stood and whirled in one motion, a snarl on her face. "You dare?!"

Persephone faced her with ice in her eyes, her voice steady. "Obviously I do." She'd even dressed for her new role as assassin, wearing a coat of blue-black taffeta over trousers and boots of black.

Artemis twisted the other goddess' wrist until Persephone grimaced in pain and dropped the blade. "You can't kill me with that. You know that."

"I thought it worth the try." There was no quaver in her voice, nothing to show that she held the slightest bit of fear.

Artemis increased the pressure, forcing Persephone to her knees in a rustle of taffeta, and still the other goddess displayed no concern. "I should kill you now. Kill you and toss your body from the top of the tower as an example to all traitors."

"I am no traitor, Artemis. I am simply loyal to something other than yourself." Her blue eyes were hard as steel – *Hard as adamantine, dear sister.* – and she raised her chin proudly.

"There *is* nothing other than myself!" She sank her fingers into Persephone's carefully coifed hair and wrenched hard, eliciting another gasp of pain. "I am the Queen of Olympus! I am the keeper of the world pillar! All who exist do so at my whim!"

"All who exist are dying. You're killing them. Elysia itself is dying because of you and your madness. When all that worship you are dead, they are no longer yours, Artemis. You may rule Olympus, but the underworld is mine." Even on her knees, neck craned awkwardly, Persephone looked poised and calm. Oh, how Artemis hated her.

As she stood there, glaring down at her captive, that hate grew into a red, seething fog at the edges of her vision, humming in her ears like the high constant whine of a tiny dynamo. She bit the inside of her cheek hard enough to taste blood, and it only added to the scarlet haze surrounding her. With a wordless cry of rage, she backhanded the kneeling goddess hard enough to sprawl her across the floor, the sound echoing sharply against the high ceiling.

Persephone's hair came loose from its pins, tumbling around her face in tangles and disarray. Artemis eyed her smugly as the other woman pushed her mane out of her eyes and spat blood from a split lip. "Shall I send you to join your faithful throng, then?"

The captive goddess did not answer, and the new wariness in her eyes sent a surge of pleasure through Artemis' body. "No, that would be too easy, too final…I know a just punishment for a traitor."

She latched onto Persephone's hair again, setting out with a long stride that forced the goddess to scramble to her feet or be dragged. Through the halls they went, Artemis' grip on her captive's hair cruel and unbreakable. Only once did Persephone attempt to jerk free, at which point Artemis slapped her against the wall again and continued on, all the way to the clock room.

Up and up the stairs they climbed, spiraling around the inner wall until they reached the top of the scaffolding high above the pillar itself. Artemis gave Persephone a hard shove, sprawling her to the slatted walkway, and began pulling down lengths of the chains dangling from the brackets above.

"Promethean chains, dear Persephone. If they'll hold a Titan, they'll hold you." Artemis felt almost giddy as she clamped the manacles around the other goddess' wrists, feeling the god-forged metal shrink to hold her securely. Yes, seeing the queen of the underworld in chains was definitely the highlight of her day. "And from here, you will be able to watch the end of all things."

Artemis clamped the other end of the chains to the bracket in the wall, allowing enough play for Persephone to pace this single length of walkway. The blond woman yanked a few times, testing her bonds with a rattle of metal, then glared at Artemis in cold fury.

The Queen of Olympus smiled happily, reaching out to pet Persephone's hair though the other woman jerked away from her touch. "You watch that arrow, Persephone. Watch it closely." The weapon in question still hung above them, though a bit of clambering on the railings would enable a tall person to reach it. It dangled from its string in perfect stillness, poised over the core of the world pillar with silent menace. "That is for your husband, and I will end him one way or another."

Persephone's eyes followed the invisible line from arrow tip to pillar, a look of horrible recognition dawning on her perfect face. "What have you done, Artemis?"

She didn't bother to answer the question. "All the world exists at my whim. I am the Queen of Olympus, and the keeper of the world pillar. All will raise their eyes to me in adoration, or they will have no eyes to raise."

With an insulting pat to the cheek, she left Persephone there and began the long walk down the scaffolding. Halfway down, she heard the goddess call to her. "They will come from below, Artemis! Never forget that! And when all are beneath you, *everything* is below!"

As the huntress turned to retort, she felt massive hands close around her throat. Her eyes bulged and her voice came out as a mere gurgle, her chest heaving as she fought for the suddenly denied air. Raising her hands to claw away the inexorable grip, she found only her own skin beneath her nails.

She fell to her knees, the staircase shuddering faintly at the impact, gasping for breath even as she fought the taste of bile at the back of her throat. The grip loosened, then fell away, leaving her drenched in cold sweat. Gingerly, she felt at her neck, probing for the soreness of impending bruises and finding nothing. *It is not me.*

Someone was killing her hounds.

~*!*~

Heracles released his grip on the hound's throat, watching its black tongue loll out of the dead mouth in grotesque fashion. The creature had not even twitched in its death throes, facing its demise with an eerie acceptance in the golden eyes. Out of respect for the man the dog had once been, Heracles closed its eyes and laid it down gently.

Across the aisle, one of the bitches watched him, hackles raised but silent. Her speckled pups gamboled about her feet, oblivious to the drama playing out just beyond their small stall.

He held up one hand, palm out, careful to keep it out of snapping distance. "Easy. I am not a murderer of mothers and children." *Not anymore.*

If the she-hound understood him, she didn't believe him. Her hackles stayed up and her golden eyes followed him as he left the kennels. Impossible to tell if she was one of the hound-born or if she had at one time been human. Regardless, her litter was too young to survive without her, and they were as yet innocent. Never again would a goddess drive him to slaughter innocents.

The hounds, save the few elderly or whelping left in the kennels, had been scattered throughout Elysia. That much he knew. And the ones who weren't on the hunt for the escaped Factory inmates patrolled the hallways of the tower, four-footed wardens in a very pretty prison.

I have vowed that no one will hurt you, Artemis, and I shall hold to it. But these abominations must go, and disposing of them brings me no dishonor. The ones in the tower would be first, he'd decided, and then he would walk out the door to find the ones in the city. There would be no more hunting of the innocent.

He bore no weapon beyond his belt knife and he didn't expect to need one. The huntsmen rarely carried anything more than a pistol or crop. The whip wouldn't harm him in the least, and the pistol would only slow him down for a few moments at most. There was a small glimmer of unease at the thought of slaughtering men, but he quelled it by reminding himself that even the ones who appeared human were not. They were her creatures whether their transformation was complete or not.

He found the next of the beasts in a corridor leading to the Greenery. The hound approached warily, no doubt alerted somehow of its comrade's demise, but it clearly was not expecting the danger to come from a man whose scent was familiar and accepted.

Heracles was upon the dog before it truly understood what was happening, his massive arms wrapping it up in an inescapable vice. Grim, he squeezed the struggling body until it went limp, then snapped its neck for good measure. He placed the dog's corpse in a nearby alcove, wondering with macabre humor what the cleaning servants would think upon discovering it.

Footsteps sounded down an adjoining corridor, and he crouched where he was, waiting. The paces were not hurried, one pair of boots accompanied by the faint click of nails on the marble floor. One huntsman, one hound, patrolling at a sedate pace. Whatever warning may have passed amongst the Hunt, this pair at least was not worried for their own safety.

The man-shaped hound went down without a cry at one crushing blow to the back of his head. It helped to think of them thus, the human form merely a shell from whence a monster would emerge. Heracles knew how to deal with monsters.

Attacking the huntsman first left an opening for the hound to spring, and the powerful jaws closed on Heracles' forearm. Heedless of his own blood trickling out around the thing's slavering jowls, the demigod spun and bashed the dog against the wall. It dropped off his arm like a speckled leech, temporarily stunned. Heracles took that opportunity to fall upon it, squeezing the breath from its lungs as it lay pinned.

Once satisfied that the hound's life had been snuffed out, he examined the huntsman and broke his neck too. Upon examination, the punctures in his forearm were already closing, and he thought no more on the injury. *They have my blood now, smeared over their dead. They'll hunt me now.*

Oddly, that thought brought peace. Not murderer then, but survivor.

A low growl interrupted his thoughts, and he turned to find another hound haunting the end of the corridor. It was the ebon hound, the big intelligent brute, and its gaze flicked between him and its fallen packmates.

Heracles stood, hands loose at his sides, and waited. The big hound's ears were pressed tight against its skull, its hackles up, but it made no move to spring. For long moments, each gazed at the other, two prime specimens sizing up an opponent. Finally, the dog whuffed softly and backed a few paces into the adjoining hallway. It waited long enough to be certain Heracles grasped its intent, then bolted.

You want me to hunt you. The demigod broke into a run, not bothering to match the animal's sprint. He could keep his pace forever, and the faster hound would eventually tire and slow. *In hunting you, I lose precious time killing the others. You're protecting them.*

He couldn't have said how he knew that, save that it was what he would have done in the ebon hound's place. *Ah well, so be it.* It was only a matter of time before Artemis located him and struck him down anyway. Let him spend his last hours tracking a worthy opponent.

The chase – if it could be called such – led outward, the black hound spiraling into the outer hallways, and finally into the Greenery itself. It was never out of sight for more than the length of two strides, and would often look back to be certain its hunter was still following. But amid the cluttered tables and low-hanging pipes, pursuit became difficult.

You led me here on purpose. The first rule in battle was to choose your battleground to your advantage, and the ebon hound was doing just that, another display of its eerie intelligence. Heracles could do no more than follow, his admiration for the animal growing with every twist and turn. Where would the strange hound finally make his stand, he wondered. Would he lead Heracles into ambush with his packmates, or find a place where they could truly conduct this contest alone?

He was answered when the sounds of scrabbling feet ahead fell silent, and the demigod found himself in one of the empty sections of the Greenery. The metal tables had been scrubbed down recently judging by the antiseptic smell overlaying the mildew, and the pipes above were dry. It was an expectant room, waiting for the next round of whatever life would spring forth once planted. *No collateral damage. I see.*

The drones, usually skittering around at the edge of vision, were noticeably absent, and Heracles had to wonder if they had fled in fear, or if Demeter had consciously withdrawn them to preserve her neutrality.

A low growl rumbled through the room, bouncing off the metal tables and overhanging ductwork, impossible to locate. There were too many shadows cast by the ever-glowing lights, too many nooks Heracles would have to go on knees to examine, putting him in a vulnerable position. Which of those black shadows concealed the ebon hound?

Heracles walked the narrow aisle between tables, eyes searching for the tell-tale shadow that did not belong. The hound was stalling, giving its brethren time to rally or hide. "Enough of this. I thought better of you." In answer, the growl sounded again punctuated by the faint click of nails on the concrete floor.

Come on, make your move. When it came, it nearly caught the demigod by surprise.

The table to his left slammed hard into his thigh, pinning him against the one to his right, and the hound came over the top, clawed feet barely scratching the steel tabletop. Heracles missed his grab for the creature's throat, but managed to catch most of the momentum against his chest, the pair of them toppling back over the second table and sending the first spinning away into its fellows with a resounding clang.

Sharp teeth snapped a hairsbreadth from his face, and Heracles heaved the dog to the side. The creature twisted in the air to land on its feet and sprang at him again, saliva splattering over them both in its fervor. This was no mad dog frenzy, however, and each snap was calculated to herd the demigod where the hound wanted him.

Heracles, feeling the glass wall looming behind him, stepped into the next attack, deliberately stuffing his forearm into the thing's gaping maw. The massive jaws clamped down, fangs sinking all the way to the bone, and the hound shook its head violently as it would smaller prey. The demigod grabbed the thing's collar, lifting it clear of the floor.

As intelligent as the animal was, instinct still won out and it refused to relinquish its hold on his arm even to save its own life. With a tremendous heave, Heracles flung it away, into the dark glass wall. There was a yelp and a cacophony of shattering glass, and Heracles shielded his eyes from the flying fragments until silence resumed.

One glass panel was simply gone, reduced to so much glittering dust on the concrete and the cobblestones outside. It crunched beneath his boots as he stepped through the frame, approaching the still form on the stones outside. The hound was imprisoned in a tangle of piping and hoses, torn from the ceiling on its abrupt trip out the window. Jagged shards of glass seemed to sprout from the black pelt like the porcupines of old, each gleaming wetly with blood.

The streets, lit by the Greenery's constant glow, were empty save for the sound of Heracles' steps and his own breath in his ears. The houses that lined the square were dark, the inhabitants huddled fearfully inside, praying that their goddess' Hunt would pass them by on this night of nights. Even the trolleys, whose incessant trundling stopped for no man, had fallen silent, and Heracles could see one on a side street, sitting abandoned on its tracks.

The humans knew. They had no imagination to fathom what might be passing by outside their windows, but they knew enough to fear what it could mean. Their world was changing somehow, a thing that had not happened in living memory.

The massive hound's chest rose and fell once…twice…and was still. Kneeling, Heracles could see the fragment of the glass wall that had penetrated its jugular, spilling its lifeblood over the uneven cobblestones. Despite the gleam of sickly light from the Greenery, the blood was black.

He rested his hand on the still-warm body, patting it. He was a good hound, doing just what his goddess had asked of him. Heracles couldn't fault him for that. "Be at peace."

Standing, the one-time warrior wiped his hands on his trousers, indifferent to the bloodstains he left behind, and he surveyed his surroundings. It seemed that, since he was already outside, he should continue his extermination of the Hunt with those who were even now roaming the city on a hunt of their own.

Something tinkled behind him, the sound of glass falling lightly to the cobblestones. Heracles turned, frowning into the lighted square, trying to discern who or what had caused the slight disruption. It came again, nearly at his feet he realized, and he looked down in puzzlement.

A piece of glass embedded in the black hound's back fell from the corpse and broke in two on the stone pavement. As Heracles watched, three more pieces visibly moved, working their way out of closing wounds to shatter on the street. The dog's barrel chest shuddered once, then began to rise and fall in a regular – albeit slow – rhythm.

Heracles barely registered the pain in his knees as he dropped beside the hound, staring in sick fascination as the appalling gashes knit themselves together. He ran his hands over the black fur, coming away sticky with blood, but finding the cuts healing as soon as the glass dropped free.

Artemis' hounds did not heal like that. They were mortal, the same as the humans they'd been before. Only gods healed from otherwise fatal wounds.

The dog's golden eyes opened to slits, watching the big man warily.

"Darkest night," the warrior whispered. "Who *were* you?"

CHAPTER 21

Hades' voice plagued Geoff through the long
boat ride back across the River Styx. Not even the soft
splish of the pole in the water, or the quiet whir-click of
Charon's gears could drown out the constant replay of
his memories.

*"And just how do you expect me to accomplish this
thing?" Geoff congratulated himself on holding his voice steady in
the face of such an unfathomable request.*

*"Somewhere in that tower is the arrow she prepared for
me. I do not know how they work, only that they do. Find that
arrow, prick her with it. Even the smallest cut should prove
fatal."*

Because walking into Olympus Tower and asking
to search from top to bottom was such an easy task to
accomplish. No doubt, Artemis herself would give them
a guided tour.

*The length of wood the god handed to him stood taller than
he himself and was as thick as his own wrist. A heavy length of
cord spanned it, loops at each end loosely attaching it to the staff.
"If you get a chance, you can shoot the arrow with this. It was*

hers, once."

Geoff could see how the object could be bent into the weapon from the moving images, a bow, but for the life of him he could not see how to make it submit, despite the considerable strength in his own arms. "I can't even bend it."

"Find someone who can."

Oh of course. Giants walked the world all the time, what was he thinking? He toed the unstrung bow as it lay in the keel at his feet. Somehow, being given a weapon no one knew how to use did little for his confidence.

"Be aware of the hounds. She keeps tenuous contact with them, and once they start dying — you will have to kill them, you know — she'll be aware that someone is moving against her. It is possible to use wolfsbane to confuse their tracking abilities. Demeter may have some in that forsaken Greenery if you can get to it."

Instructions upon instructions upon directions upon warnings. Geoff's head ached with the holding of it all, and he dropped it into his hands with a groan.

"Are you well?"

He'd almost managed to forget Raffa's presence, so quiet had she been since he'd left his rather strange audience. "No." He raised his head to look at her.

While he'd been occupied with Hades, she had cleaned herself, washing away two decades of grime and soot. Her cords of matted hair were pulled back into a more manageable tail and her rags had been exchanged for an armored breastplate and guards on her calves. The metal was tarnished and dented, obviously having seen much use. A sword hilt peeked up over her right shoulder. What use was a sword, he wondered, against pistols?

"What am I going to tell them, Raffa?" He

looked ahead of the boat, but the far shore and the men waiting there were still out of sight. "Hello gents, would you mind coming along to Olympus Tower so we can find a lost weapon and kill a goddess? Why? Oh, because I'm some sort of constructed demigod and Hades asked us to." Geoff knew he sounded petulant, but he couldn't bring himself to care.

She smiled faintly in the odd dark-light. "If you like."

"I don't even know what to call myself," he muttered. "I don't know what to call you."

The warrior woman sat in silence for a few moments before answering. "Raffa has always been good enough until now."

"It's not your name." She was one of three sisters, the Erinyes. Which had she been, once upon a time?

"It's the name I claim, now. What came before…I am no longer that woman." She looked distinctly uncomfortable, shifting on the plank seat before speaking again. "For a very brief time…I had hoped that you would come to call me mother."

Her presence in his life at least made sense now, given what he'd learned. "You've been guarding me all this time. Grooming me. For this?"

"No." She shook her head quickly. "No, never for this. I didn't know…" A sigh escaped, and her shoulders slumped. "I didn't care. That's the truth of it. I didn't care what he planned after the first moment he put you in my arms.

"Even then, as an infant, you gave us hope. I didn't care overly much about anything after that. Just you, this tiny life entrusted to my care. You made me dream of things I never had before. Family beyond my sisters…children…"

"Then why give me to the people of Deeptown? Why the lies? A foundling in the snow?"

Raffa smirked, but there was sadness in her eyes. "Look at me. Do I look like someone capable of being a mother? I took a chance that your very nature would inspire them to keep you, care for you. You were better for it."

They fell into silence again as Geoff debated whether or not a life in the lower wards could be considered "better" than anything. The times with lean food, the bitter winters with none at all. Predation by lotus eaters and the Hunt. Sickness, back-breaking toil, fighting tooth and nail for every single moment of happiness… *If I'd have known, what would I have done differently?*

Not Lia, certainly. He couldn't imagine his life without her, regardless of his origins. Ambert, the Morrows, Jon… All people without whom his existence would have been very bleak indeed. Instead, he had grown up warm, loved, valued. They gave him those treasures. *Please be safe. Please be happy.*

At first, the distant glimmer of light seemed to be a trick of the eyes, gone when Geoff tried to look directly at it. But as Charon poled them ever onward, it resolved itself into a flicker of yellow flame, surrounded by the dying green glow of sulfur flares. Dark silhouettes huddled around the light, eventually resolving themselves into the forms of his fellow escapees. Most appeared to be sleeping, but several heads raised as the boat ground ashore.

Geoff struggled out of the boat with the cumbersome bow, thoroughly soaking the cuffs of his pants in the dead river but managing to keep the bowstring dry, and looked to Raffa when she failed to follow him. Instead, she stood just behind the clockwork ferryman, biting her lip.

"Aren't you coming?"

Sadly, she shook her head. "No. I've been ordered to let you go on alone." Her hands clenched at her sides. It was obviously not an order well-received.

"Why?"

"He feels this has to be done by humans alone. Otherwise, it's just a new battle in an old war, and nothing will truly be decided." Her legs gave out suddenly, and she collapsed to the plank seat, face a study in agony. "Oh bitty birdy...I don't want you to do this. I want you to go on and life a safe and happy life in Deeptown or wherever you find a home. But I think Hades is right. None of you will live a truly free life unless she is destroyed. I just...I wish I could help you."

Driven by sudden emotion he truly didn't understand, Geoff stepped back into the river to reach for her hand, which she gave over quickly. He squeezed the calloused fingers gently. "Will I see you again?"

She shrugged, her armor clanking faintly. "Who's to say? Everyone has to pass through Tartarus eventually, bitty birdy. Nothing is going to change that." She released his hand and gave him a nod toward shore. "Go on. Do what needs to be done. Send the goat-boy back this way, it'll keep him out of trouble."

Geoff was halfway up the beach when another thought occurred to him and he looked back. "Raffa? How do we find our way back to the surface?"

"Just put one foot in front of the other, bitty birdy. Trust me."

Oddly, he did, and he tried to cling to that confidence as he rejoined his comrades.

~*!*~

"He's out of his gear-stripped mind!" It was one of the nicer things that had been said thus far, Geoff thought.

He'd tried to explain things as honestly as possible, beginning with his own dubious heritage, up to and including the charge he'd been given by the Lord of Tartarus. Reactions ranged from disbelief to outright hostility, which was no more than he'd expected, really. They were hungry, they were injured, and they, like Geoff, only wanted to go home. None of them had signed on for a suicidal assassination attempt.

The ex-prisoners grumbled and snarled amongst themselves in the dying light, and the young man despaired of reaching any decision before they were left in the darkness.

Only Jon had remained silent, watching from the edge of the lighted circle with a thoughtful frown. When he finally stepped forward, most stopped to watch out of sheer curiosity. The big mechanic picked up the stout length of wood Geoff had carried with him, turning it this way and that, examining the grain and cord, the worn leather wrappings where presumably a hand would hold it. Unstrung, the bow was nearly as tall as the man himself.

After a moment's thought, he braced one end of the long bow against his boot, and slowly bent the upper end down until he could secure the loop of cord around the notch at the top. The taut weapon hummed softly.

"I can do it." The quiet proclamation seemed to echo against the cavernous roof above them. "If we can find the arrow, I can shoot it." To illustrate, he pulled back on the massive bow, holding it for long moments without a single muscle quivering.

"Why? Just because this gimp says we're supposed to?" Young Stan, broken wrist now neatly splinted and bandaged, gestured wildly with his uninjured arm, earning affirmative murmurs from the rest of the group.

"Why not?" Jon deftly unstrung the bow, laying it down again beside Geoff's seat. "What do we have to lose? We're dead men with the Hunt on us. We've already heard them in the tunnels above. It's only a matter of time before they find a path down here, or even just start digging through the ceiling at us."

Geoff looked upward in alarm. They hadn't told him that part.

Jon went on. "You there, Van. How many friends and family did you lose in the Serenity sinkhole last year?"

The man in question scrubbed a hand over his salt-and-pepper hair. "More'n I'd like to think about."

"And Elvin. Did you ever see your brother after he was hauled off to the tower? That was what, five years gone by now?"

"Something like, yeah. We never heard another word from him."

"And the rest of you. In all honesty, how many of you actually committed a crime to get condemned to the Factory?" Jon was one of three with raised hands, and if anyone was surprised by his confession, it didn't show. "This is no life for anyone. Year after year, crushed against the Wall? Nothing to look forward to but deep pits and hot forges."

"You're only talking like that 'cause he's here." One of the convicts jerked his chin sharply toward

Geoff, making all eyes turn his way. He did his best not to squirm.

To his surprise, Jon nodded. "You're probably right. But so what? It doesn't make it any less true. If Geoff being here means I can think like my own man, instead of being some wind-up drone for the Lady in the tower, I have no quarrel with that."

A thoughtful murmur sprang up amongst the men, and Jon barreled on. "What if there's life beyond the Wall? What if somewhere, the rain doesn't burn and the ground is solid under our feet? Wouldn't you rather leave that to your children than this?"

He was winning them over. Geoff could feel the mood of the group swaying with every word. And all the while, the warm knot of his power curled peacefully in his chest. Somehow, that made him breathe easier. If they marched on Olympus Tower, they'd do it on their own volition, not because he pushed them into an insane and futile battle.

"They got weapons!" Murmurs agreed with that word of caution.

"So do we." Jon pointed at the pile of picks and shovels and pry bars that had aided their escape. "If we can tear down solid rock with nothing but our sweat and muscle, what chance does a creature of flesh and bone stand? I killed a hound once already. They're not invulnerable, and their numbers are finite. If we can gather aid, we have them."

That earned more discussion, which trailed to a halt as yet another sulfur flare burned itself out in a sputter of sparks. Time was running out.

Geoff struggled to his feet, settling his crutches firmly on his forearms. "If we stay here, we're going to wind up in nothing more than a black tomb. I'm returning to the surface. What you all decide to do once we get there is your own concern."

Jon came to stand beside him, bow in hand, making clear where his allegiance lay.

The men glanced at each other for long moments, looking for the first one to speak. Finally, one of the old gnarled veterans shrugged. "If I'm going to die, I don't want it to be in a dark hole in the ground. And if I can take one or two of those furry bastards with me, so much the better."

"You know, if we can get to Rambling Ward, my brother might be willing to help us." The one named Van got to his feet.

"My cousin Karl would help to, if we could get to Shameless Row. He's got some big friends, too."

"Some of the men from Worryville might pitch in, if they're off shift at the Factory."

One by one, they rallied, gathering their meager supplies and haphazard weapons. Only when they all turned to look at Geoff did he realize that they were still relying on him to show the way out.

One foot in front of the other, bitty birdy. Trust me.

"See if we can save the light, only burn one at a time. I don't know how long this will take, or where it will bring us out." If they noticed his uncertainty, they didn't say.

"Let's move." Perhaps they weren't trained soldiers, marching back into the tunnels, but they did their best to move in step, leaving the River Styx behind them in the dark.

We're just getting out of the tunnels, Geoff insisted to himself. *I've committed no sin, started no war. We're just getting out, and then we'll see what comes after.* It was easier, that way, than thinking of himself as an assassin.

CHAPTER 22

The tunnel was suspiciously without branches as they made their way upward, and much shorter than their trip down. Perhaps in the almost total darkness, the men assumed that Geoff had followed a different path, but the young man knew that there were other influences at work. *Thank you, Raffa. I think.*

There was no change from square-cornered tunnels into the rounder steam-bored ones. They seemed to be traversing an entirely god-made channel. It was no surprise, at least to Geoff, when they reached heavy wooden doors bound in brass. Geoff held the bow while Jon and one of the other men put their shoulders to heaving the portal open.

They stepped cautiously from the tunnel to find themselves exiting a building in the lower wards. The rough cobblestones under their feet were welcome proof that they were indeed home and the fresh air made every man realize just how long they'd been underground.

It was obviously after Dark. The streetlights were black and not a soul stirred around them. After some discussion, it was decided they had surfaced in Vilemont, on the easternmost side of the lower wards.

"Watch your step along here boys, the ground's like paper."

Geoff found himself near Jon. "What now?"

The big mechanic frowned thoughtfully, visible in the faint glow from Olympus Tower. "Thirty men moving through the streets after Dark is noticeable. We need to split up, gather what reinforcements we can."

The men around them agreed quietly, and the group was soon split into six groups of five or more.

"Listen. The clock is just past eleven. We meet in Shameless Row at one with whoever you can muster. If you're not there, we'll assume the Hunt found you first."

"And if they *do* find us?"

Jon nodded. "Kill them. Quickly and quietly if you can, but messy will do just as well in the end. Once they're dead, move fast. The rest of the Hunt will be on you in a blink."

After a few more agreements on which group would go to which wards, the rag-tag band of rebels parted ways and Geoff found himself in the group with Jon.

"I'm going to slow you down. You should leave me somewhere. They're most likely after me anyway."

"We're not leaving anyone behind to get ripped apart by those things." Jon's face was grim, and Geoff knew he was thinking of Rik. "Keep up, Geoff. As best you can."

The first door they knocked on went unanswered, even when one of the men called to his cousin within. The second and third also yielded nothing.

Geoff frowned in consternation. "Where have they all gone?"

Jon shook his head. "They're home, Geoff. They're just too scared to open the door tonight."

Geoff looked back and saw the curtain twitch on the house they'd just left. He couldn't blame them, really. For too long, the Hunt had been the thing of nightmares and dire warnings to misbehaving children.

The fear was ingrained in their very marrow. But if everyone huddled behind their locked doors, nothing was going to unseat Artemis.

"I think… I think I should do something."

"Like what?" They took shelter in the space between two buildings. The upper floors of both structures leaned so drunkenly that they touched at the top and shared one roof.

"No one's going to help us. They're too scared. Maybe…they just need some inspiration." Ignoring the pain in his knees, he hobbled out of their hiding place and into the street.

"What are you doing?" Jon's voice hissed from the shadows.

"I'm not sure yet. But it's probably going to bring the Hunt, so be ready."

The street was empty and eerily silent. Had it always been this quiet after Dark? Not even the constant clatter and churn of the Factory reached them here. The air was heavy and expectant, a rain in their near future no doubt. No breeze stirred, and even the swaying, creaking tenements seemed to have settled, cowering as they waited for something dire.

Geoff leaned on one crutch and laid his other hand at the point of his sternum, just over the clenched knot of heat. This was going to be different, he realized, than nudging one person into action. His targets were not in front of him where he could see and touch them. He didn't even know them.

What do you want? He could almost feel them, clinging to each other behind the locked and barred doors. *What is important to you?*

He could only look at himself. What did *he* want? *I want to go home.* Deeptown was almost on the other side of the city, but he could have pointed to it unerringly. And there in Deeptown he'd find Lia, and Ambert, and everyone else that he had grown to care for in his two decades.

The only reason he wasn't already making slow awkward tracks in that direction was that he knew the Hunt would follow him there. So long as Artemis was looking for him, the people he loved would not be safe.

And that, he realized, was his answer. Despite the fact that the thought of killing another living creature, even a mad goddess, made his skin crawl, he was going to do it. Because his family was dependent upon him. And because deep down, he believed that it would make their lives better. He had hope.

He took that hope and he fed it to the flame in his chest. It grew. He took the fierce determination to protect his family, and fed it in too. The knot slowly began to unravel, uncoiling like a tightly wound spring.

All of you. Hope. Believe. With every deep breath, he could feel the power expanding in his chest until suddenly it eclipsed his own body. With his eyes tightly closed in concentration, he could still see with something beyond his sight.

The father in the building to his left, holding his wife as the woman held the small boy in her arms. A pair of squatters in the uppermost floor of the tenement to his right, each in his own corner and shaking in the darkness. One block over, a young woman had snatched up her only kitchen knife, dull as it was, and she hid beneath the table that also served as her bed.

He could see them all, no matter their hiding places. Block by block his awareness expanded, finding them in every crack and crevice. *Hope. Believe.* Further still, he found members of his own small rebellion, slipping like lost spirits through the black. He added their burgeoning hope to his own, finding strength in their faith.

He recognized Lia blockaded inside Ambert's shop, as he passed over Deeptown. *Hope. Believe.* Would she know his touch, if she felt it?

And out of alleys they came, black empty places in his mind. *The Hunt.* Drawn by the feeling of his power, they were coming. One, four, a dozen. They coursed through the night, fleet as thought. Geoff pulled his mind back from them. He only had moments, he could not afford to be afraid.

Hope. Believe. The words of the Lady Demeter came back to him, and he added those to his message. *Life begets hope begets life.* He whispered to all of them, every mind he could touch, every soul he could find. He felt them become aware of each other, in some abstract way. Neighbors thought to check on each other. Families wondered about distant relatives. *Yes. Hope. Believe. Together.*

The black shapes were drawing closer. Blocks away now, and coming on hard. He had only time for one last thought.

YOU ARE NOT ALONE!

Like a spring at maximum extension, Geoff suddenly snapped back inside himself. He staggered and only his crutches saved him from falling face first onto the cobblestones. His chest felt hollow, spent, and yet there was an odd sense of satiation about it too. His purpose had been served.

Strong hands grabbed his arms, lending him support. "Geoff?" Jon almost picked him bodily up off the ground in an effort to help him stand straight.

"They're coming. The Hunt is coming." Geoff

gasped the words out as soon as he could get air.

"You heard him boys, move!" Jon hefted his pick and pressed the bow into Geoff's hands and gave him a shove. He found himself in a stumbling run along with the rest if the men, not even realizing that he'd left one crutch behind until much later.

They didn't get far.

The first Hunt-pair materialized out of an alley, man and hound springing on the nearest escapee in utter silence. The prisoner went down with a gurgle, but it was enough to alert his companions.

With a roar, the men descended, Jon leading the pack. The huntsman froze in sheer astonishment as he was bowled over by four armed Factory escapees. Obviously, he had never imagined people fighting back. There were thuds of fists on flesh, grunts from all involved, and one sick crack as someone's shovel shattered the top of the huntsman's skull.

The hound left off worrying the miner's corpse and launched into the men with a snarl. Someone screamed as massive jaws closed around a forearm, snapping the bone. Jon dropped his pick and wrapped the beast up in his arms, the hound writhing and twisting to get its fangs into the big mechanic. The remaining men tried to get in for some crippling blows, but there was no way without hitting Jon too.

Geoff knew more of the Hunt was en route. This pair had simply been the closest. Jon could wear the hound down, he was certain, but they didn't have the time.

A voice shouted, "Drop him boy, I'll do for him!"

Jon heaved the struggling dog onto the cobblestones as hard as he could, and stepped back.

Almost immediately, a fireplace poker stabbed through the creature, skewering it to the street through its ribcage. The animal yelped and quivered a bit more, but a few solid blows from the rest of the men ended that soon enough.

Geoff blinked, finding himself looking at a stranger, an older man with white hair standing at frantic angles to his head. Once the dog quit twitching, he moved to retrieve his poker.

Jon nodded to the newcomer, chest pumping like a bellows as he tried to catch his breath. "My thanks, friend."

"My name is Colm. And you boys look like you could use some help." The elder fellow wiped his poker on the dead hound's fur with a matter-of-fact efficiency.

"We wouldn't turn it down, that's the truth."

Of the six prisoners, one lay dead in the street, mauled by the hound, and another was glass-eyed with pain and shock, cradling his broken arm to his chest. They could use all the help they could get.

"Then we best be getting where you're going, hmm?" Colm grinned, showing more teeth missing than present.

Jon pilfered the dead huntsman's pistol, tucking it into his belt. "Come on. Least we can do is make them chase us to Shameless Row."

As they ran down the street – hobbled really, between Geoff's own gait and the injured man's dazed shuffle – Geoff looked back to see faces poking out of doorways, watching them pass. Out of two of them, three men emerged with bats and pipes in their hands, following the group. They were now nine.

By the time they reached Shameless Row, they'd passed through four different districts, and gathered more followers on every block. Men and women, young and old, armed with everything from rolling pins to spikes torn from the trolley tracks. By the end, they were joining in groups of ten and twelve.

They'd also lost seven more to the Hunt, but by darkest night, the Hunt had paid the price dearly. Two more pairs were dead in the streets of the lower wards, the last taken from behind as they tried to flee toward Olympus Tower. The Lady was calling her soldiers back, it seemed.

Geoff himself could only follow along in a sort of daze. He had a hard time keeping his thoughts from straying into nonsensical tangents, and it didn't even occur to him to clean off the drying blood he'd been splattered with at various points in the night.

The clock was tolling the hour of one when they entered the square at Shameless Row and found it teeming with people. It was obvious that there had been more skirmishes with the Hunt in other parts of the city. The air smelled like old copper, the tang of blood heavy over the crowd, but the majority appeared to be standing and able.

"Darkness… There's gotta be five hundred people here."

Geoff seconded the amazement he heard in that voice. He felt like commenting on it, but a dim reflection in a nearby window caught his attention and he promptly forgot about it.

"Geoff."

"Geoffroi!" Jon's concerned face appeared in his vision. "Come, sit a moment. You're done in."

He felt done in, that was sure enough. He couldn't even feel anything below the hips and his tongue had long ago cleaved to the roof of his mouth in thirst. He allowed Jon to seat him on a nearby stoop while the rag-tag rebellion organized itself.

Artemis' bow lay across his tortured knees and he kept a death grip on it, knowing only that he couldn't lose it no matter what. Even when someone pressed a cup of water at him, he only took it in one hand, loathe to relinquish his grip on the solid wooden shaft.

The water, lukewarm and tasting of the pipes it had come from, seemed to clear his head a bit. He finally realized just how many people had come to their aid.

The square was packed full, and more were still trickling in from other districts. Someone had organized them into loose units, and Jon stood on a crate to be seen and heard.

"She knows we're coming, make no mistake about it. We've all seen the Hunt running with their tails between their legs. The Lady has pulled them back to the tower for defense." That was greeted with a chorus of catcalls and jeers, to which Jon held up a quieting hand. "I say this so you realize that we have a hard fight ahead of us. People are going to die. Anyone who wants to go home can do so, with no ill will held against them."

The crowd murmured amongst themselves, but Geoff didn't see a single person leave. One man near the back called out, "So what's the plan?"

Before anyone could answer, a shaft of light speared down from the sky into the midst of the milling throng. All faces turned upward, some shielding their eyes against the brightness, and as their voices died away, they could finally hear the low rumble of the airship above.

"Citizens. You are in violation of curfew

mandated by the Lady Artemis, long may she reign. Please disperse in a peaceful manner and return to your homes."

"Get bent!" The one taunt from the crowd spawned others, and Geoff found himself ducking for cover as several glass bottles were lobbed upward without a hope of reaching their target. They tumbled back to earth to shatter against the cobblestones, thankfully hurting no one.

The tinny voice from above sounded again. "If you do not return to your homes, you will be arrested and remanded to the custody of the Lady's Hunt."

That threat was greeted with more shouts, drowning out any further communication. Geoff was startled when Jon suddenly loomed at his side. "What are they thinking? They don't have the numbers to take on this crowd."

"Looks like they're set to try, though." The mechanic pressed his stolen pistol into Geoff's hand. "Take this. Things are about to get bad."

The angry crowd continued to shout and throw things at the hovering airship, the lights just barely visible along the bottom edge of the ever-present smog. The spotlight stayed fixed, illuminating the cramped square, and casting the outer edges in even greater shadow.

That was why no one saw the approaching swarm until it was too late.

They boiled from the side streets and alleys, tumbling out into the open area in a blind panic, driven on by the howls of the hounds on their bony heels. There were more than could be counted, made worse by the fact that they were tripping over each other in tangles of wasted, filthy limbs.

The lotus eaters might have gone plunging through the crowd, oblivious in their frenzy, if not for the scent of fresh blood that lingered over the would-be rebels. The leading edge of the swarm faltered for a heartbeat, one single moment, but it was enough. Geoff saw the moment that a balding head turned, sniffed the air, and then the creature sprang on the man nearest to it. The unfortunate victim went down with a scream that died in a gurgle of blood as his throat was ripped out by filed, pointed teeth.

That was all it took for the swarm to turn deadly, the cannibalistic need to eat flesh overriding the frantic flight from the pursuing hounds. Which, of course, had been the purpose all along. The emaciated creatures flung themselves upon anyone who could not get away fast enough, and the rest of the crowd turned to fight this new threat.

Right behind the lotus eater swarm, the hounds themselves piled into the crowd, coursing swift and silent now, threading their way around small pockets of combat in obvious search of one particular target. Their huntsmen dropped from the ships on long ropes, joining the fray, and gunshots cracked from the air above, those left on the airship picking out members of the rebellion from the seething mass of bodies on the ground.

"Anyone who can climb, get those gods-damned guns!" Jon towered above the men around him, taking out lotus eaters with wide swings of a pick he'd scavenged from somewhere, and he was the first to scale the swaying lines.

Men hit the dangling ropes, swarming up them with the strength of long work in the Factory. More than one was picked off from the first vessel, plummeting to the ground below, their bodies immediately lost under the claws and fangs of the lotus eaters. Still, Geoff could make out the murky silhouettes far above him as the first few reached the ship, clambering over the railing and out of sight.

Close, too close for comfort, Geoff heard one of the massive hounds let out a baying call. Whatever they were searching for, they'd found it. He caught a glimpse of the speckled head through the jostling crowd, saw as it swiveled to focus solely on him, and then the beast charged, bowling over all in its path. Fumbling his crutch and the bow into one hand, he took aim with the pistol Jon had forced on him.

The first clumsy shot went wide, barely grazing the dog's shoulder as the animal galloped across the blood-slicked cobblestones. The second hit it square in the chest, and the creature never broke stride. It was all Geoff could do to get the wood of the bow between the thing's teeth as it ploughed into him.

He saw bright lights streak his vision and realized belatedly that his head had cracked against the street. The hound snarled and slavered around the bow in its jaws, fetid breath bathing the downed man in the scent of rotten meat. Geoff gasped for air regardless, the beast's massive weight crushing his chest.

There was a sickening crack, and the hound abruptly collapsed atop its prey. For one heart-stopping moment, Geoff was certain he would remain pinned under the massive carcass until the lotus eaters noticed him, and then he would be ripped to shreds. Instead, blessed air flooded his lungs as someone heaved the hound's corpse off of him.

"No layin' down, gimp! We got work to do!" Young Stan gave him an unexpected grin as he retrieved his pick from the back of the dog's skull, then turned it on the lotus eater that had crept close enough to spring. The gaunt thing was smashed to the stones like it weighed less than paper, and didn't rise. With a triumphant yell, Young Stan vanished back into the melee.

There were more hounds in the throng. Geoff could hear their throaty voices above the rest of the cacophony. Though they would defend themselves if they had to, they were, to a one, fighting their way through the crowd toward him. The ground was no longer safe for him.

Before he could convince himself he'd lost his mind, he lashed Artemis' bow to his crutch with the bowstring and started a quick hobbling run for the nearest rope. Twice, he was nearly flattened by corpses falling from on high, but notably, both were huntsmen, and Geoff saw that both had been stripped of goggles and pistols before the bodies were buried under a swarm of lotus eaters. The battle above was going in the rebels' favor, at least.

With bow and crutch hooked around one shoulder, Geoff reached as high as he could and hauled himself off the cobblestones. The rope itself was rough, almost bristly, but his hands were calloused by long years on the metal wheels of his chair. His muscles, strengthened by those same actions, pulled him upward at a steady pace, and he allowed himself a smirk as the hounds below bayed out their frustration. He worked his way ever upward, out of reach of the four-footed predators, at least.

The hull of the airship had no doubt once been silver, shining proudly against the Elysian skyline. Now, the metal plates that protected the wooden keel were dark and pitted from a lifetime in the smog, and there was more than one hole where the hull had been eaten clean through. Those provided footholds as Geoff neared the top, forcing his legs to work for him whether they liked it or not.

Crawling over the railing, he dumped himself gladly onto the deck, only to find the barrel of a pistol pressed tight against his forehead.

"Don't shoot!" Jon's voice, and the pistol was batted away. "Lost Lord of Tartarus, Geoff! Are you mad?!"

Geoff just started laughing, conceding that yes, he may just be. "Hounds below. Wasn't safe." The bow was digging into his shoulder blade, and he squirmed to free it. "Only way to go was up."

"Not much safer up here. Keep your head down." Jon patted him on the shoulder. "We're going to go clear that second ship."

Geoff sat up warily, then immediately hit the deck again as someone swooped low over his head with a whoop. He watched in amazement as Fons swung out over the emptiness between ships, holding nothing more than a length of rope. The huntsmen on the other ship fired, bullets whining dangerously past Geoff's head, but they were unable to hit the moving target.

Fons hit the deck in a roll, tumbling into the shooters. Three more ropes went across the dead air, with men dangling over certain death if they fell. Even as they engaged the armed huntsman, more ropes were tossed across, and the airborne rebels boarded the other airship where the battle raged on.

Geoff crawled his way to the railing to watch with a strange mix of horror and exhilaration. Any one of those bullets could pierce the balloon above, any spark could ignite the gases within, creating a fireball that would no doubt decimate half the city.

One of the combatants was pitched overboard with a strangled yell, and in the darkness Geoff couldn't even tell if it was friend or foe. He leaned far over the railing, watching the body disappear into the mob far below. The spotlight was darting all about the scene below, the ship that held it shaking with the fighting on its deck. He could see only glimpses, frozen moments.

Someone who might have been Young Stan was taking a pick to yet another speckled hound. Two lotus eaters leapt in unison to drag down a woman, only to be buried beneath armed defenders in turn. In the flicker between strobes, at least three huntsmen retreated into the dark streets, fleeing toward the safety of Olympus Tower.

In hours or moments – Geoff was never certain which – it was over. The rebels had won.

They were not without casualties, of course. The bodies of the dead and dying littered the cobblestones below, rebel, Hunt, and lotus eater alike. The two airships drifted forlornly above, Geoff the only occupant for long moments as Jon and the others returned to the ground to make hurried plans.

The young man huddled gratefully against one of the long spars that supported the balloon above. He wasn't entirely certain he could have shimmied down the rope if his life depended on it. His arms and legs were shaking as the adrenaline faded, and if he dwelled too long on his frantic ascent, he got faintly nauseous.

The airship rocked in the gentlest of breezes, then shuddered as someone latched onto a rope below and began the long climb back up. Jon's head appeared over the railing first, followed by others. Geoff realized the small group was all that was left of the escapees from the

Factory.

"You ready, Geoff?"

Geoff struggled to his feet, leaning on the bow-crutch. "For what?"

Jon grinned, pulling a pair of goggles off his head to toss them at Geoff. "We're going flying."

CHAPTER 23

They swarmed up the steps like the ants of old, crashing against the line of huntsmen and hounds with a roar that Artemis could hear even from her suite above. And even more disconcerting was that the hard and fast line of her defenders seemed to be buckling.

"No…" There was a small gap in the line, on the north side of the dais where she normally led her worship services. A tiny flaw, no bigger than one man or one hound. But the invaders found it, picked at it, pried at it until they plunged through, the flood making the hole bigger. "No!"

The window before her cracked under the pounding of her bare fists. This was not supposed to be happening. *You knew this could happen, sister. You are prepared.* Apollo's voice forced her to take a few deep breaths. Yes, they had planned for this. Such heresy and insult would not be allowed to stand.

Artemis knew what she had to do.

The elevator ratcheted its way upward with protesting clanks, almost like the tower itself intended to thwart the goddess. At the top, she wrenched the accordion doors open, then bent them inward so they would not shut again. If the doors would not close, the elevator would not move. Climbing the endless stairs would slow down this invading army.

The clock tower was empty, the servants having fled no doubt to their traitorous kin on the lower levels. *For all the good it will do them.* There was a dark sort of satisfaction in that thought. They could revolt all they wanted, but *she* was still their goddess, and they were still hers to do with as she pleased.

"Artemis!"

The one-time huntress looked up, and smiled coldly. The clock tower was *not* empty after all. "I'd nearly forgotten you up there, Persephone."

The imprisoned goddess glared down from her catwalk cell. Her time near the toxic adamantine was showing. Her golden hair hung limply around her face which was drawn and pale, and her lips were cracked and bleeding. "What have you done? What is going on down there?"

Artemis gathered her skirt to climb the spiral stairs, one hand gliding elegantly along the railing. She was quite pleased with the tranquility she was projecting. And why would she not be calm? She ruled the world, she guarded the pillar. "Nothing that cannot be handled in but a moment. How are you? Enjoying your stay?"

Persephone spat down from her height, coming nowhere near hitting her enemy. "It's happening, isn't it? They're coming for you."

"Don't trouble your pretty head over it, my dear." Artemis reached the landing just even with the top of the world pillar, and ran her hand over a panel set in the wall. A bit of pressure at the opposite corners popped it open to reveal a concealed lever. With a smile, she caressed it fondly.

"What are you… No! Artemis you can't do this!

Stop!" Above her, Persephone struggled futilely at her bonds, the chains rattling as she snapped them taut time and again. "You can't do this!"

The huntress smiled to herself, murmuring, "You can't stop me." She pulled the lever.

And nothing happened. Startled, Artemis' gaze flew to the adamantine-tipped arrow, still suspended peacefully over the pillar. She yanked the lever back and forth a few more times, with no response, all the while a snarl grew on her face.

"I disabled that centuries ago." Heracles walked out of the overhanging gears, the catwalk barely swaying even under his considerable bulk. "It just wasn't safe."

"Traitor! Half-blood cur!" Artemis' hands curled into claws, and she could almost feel his flesh rending beneath her nails. She ached for it.

He had the audacity to smile faintly at her. "Odd that you should mention that… The black hound, Artemis. Who was he?" As he spoke, he continued the circle the suspended platforms around the pillar, making his way slowly closer.

It was an absurd question, given the circumstances. "How should I know? More importantly, why would I care?"

He ignored her questions, continuing on in his infuriatingly implacable voice. "You see, I believe I know who he was. And if I am correct, then you care a great deal. There was only one person in the world you would have hated that much. He wasn't worthy of death. Instead you kept him with you the only way you could."

Vague unease flitted through her consciousness. She had memories of an enormous black hound… "I don't know what…"

The massive warrior advanced across the last platform, nonchalant as a summer stroll. "And in your madness, you can't even remember who you punished, or why. There's a sad sort of irony there."

The black hound…yes, there was one in the kennels. Always one. Larger than the others. Smarter. Once upon a time, she would lead the Hunt herself, the ebon hound at her side. Didn't she? Half-formed memories warred and collided inside her head, confusing the black hound with the image of a raven-haired man with amber eyes. Who…?

"Where is it now? The hound."

"Safe." Heracles stopped on the walkway in front of her, broad frame filling the entire path. "You can't harm him anymore."

She sneered. "You swore to serve me."

"I swore to keep you from all harm. I've never broken my oath." He nodded solemnly. "So long as I live, no one will hurt you again. But I will *not* help you harm others. Or allow you to do the unthinkable." He gestured toward the world pillar, the monolith spinning serenely.

"I will kill you for your treachery." Her hands clenched at her sides, she took a threatening step forward.

He didn't move. "As you wish."

With a cry of rage, she threw herself at him.

~*!*~

After some hurried conversations both in the air and on the ground — and fervent assurances that steering the airship was not so different from driving a borer — a plan was put into motion.

That was how Geoff found his face encased behind glass and metal, breathing through the cumbersome gas-mask as the airship slowly motored its way through the thick smog, headed for the presumably clear sky above.

He could barely see the men on either side of him, so dense was the pollution, and he could feel the stinging against his skin, like the rain that fell to the ground. *The very air is poison. It's a wonder any of us have survived this long.*

Somewhere behind him, Jon and two others were manning the controls of the ship, maneuvering it above the corrosive clouds as fast as they could, to make an unseen approach on Olympus Tower.

"Do you really think this will work?"

"If a lightning bolt blasts us from the sky, we'll know it didn't." Jon winked at him, and Geoff had to wonder if perhaps his power had broken his friend's mind. "Have a bit of faith, Geoff. Hope, remember?"

The young man held tight to the railing and tried to have hope. His own breath was trapped inside the mask, echoing in his ears, a hollow desperate sound, and the air tasted of rusted metal and sweaty leather. Even if the smog had cleared, his peripheral vision was impaired by the protective goggles they'd forced on him, leaving him with only a long tunnel of sight, trying vainly to pierce the clouds. He took a few deep breaths, trying to fight back the unexpected claustrophobia.

To his right, he heard something snap, and felt the breeze through his hair as a popped rivet came dangerously close to puncturing his skull.

The man next to him yelled a warning, garbled inside the mask, but it was clear that the ropes that held the ponderous balloon were succumbing to the smog.

Hurry, Jon. Geoff had horrible visions of the gas-filled bag floating serenely away in the sky while the wood and metal hull plummeted into the city below, taking all hands with it.

The deck vibrated as the impromptu pilots increased the power, and suddenly, they were through. The upper edge of the smog bank fell away beneath them, and they were beneath the clear night sky for the first time in living memory.

Geoff didn't even wait for the all-clear. He yanked the gas-mask off and frantically gulped the fresh air.

"Gods and spirits…look…" The awed whispers forced his eyes up, and he moved to the railing to see what had caught the other men's attention.

The black sky spread out above them in all directions, flecked with white stars like a spill of diamonds. Geoff tried to count them and quickly gave up. It was just too overwhelming. *How very small we all must seem.* Below them, the pall of thick smoke concealed Elysia within her walls, and the night hid whatever might lie beyond. At the horizon, a fingernail sliver of moon hovered.

"Get a good look." Jon appeared at his elbow. "If we do this, this will be the last moon anyone sees."

"Regrets?"

The mechanic shook his head. "Not yet. Ask me again in a few years." He turned to look at his friend. "You?"

Geoff had no answer. "It's too late to stop now, regardless. The gears are in motion."

"True enough."

The bow of the airship came around, adjusting for the faintest of breezes. "Aren't you supposed to be steering this thing?"

Jon chuckled. "Fons is doing admirably. I'll get back on the levers when we're close to docking."

Geoff pulled his eyes away from the glorious stars above and looked around the deck. To a man, every person aboard had come from the Factory. Young Stan had made the climb up the ropes, broken wrist and all. Fons was at the helm. Others had made it clear that they considered this part of the rebellion their own duty, and they'd let no one else take it from them.

"What if we're wrong, Jon?" He kept his voice down, not wanting the other men to lose heart.

The big man leaned his elbows on the railing, eyes on the distant horizon. "I've thought on that. And the way I figure it is this. We're not doing this for Hades. We're doing it for us. For all of us. For all the people we love, down there on the ground. I mean, look out there, Geoff." He swept his hand out, presenting the world. "Do you know what's out there beyond the Wall? I don't. But I by the Gods want to. We're not meant to live penned up in this filthy hole. I think, if we're to survive as a race, we'll find the way out there."

Geoff couldn't help but smile. "I didn't know you were such a dreamer."

Jon turned to look at him, eyes serious. "I think you showed me the way." Nodding, he stood straight and clapped a hand to Geoff's shoulder. "I think, in the end, we'll need you as much as anything else that's coming. Be careful when we get to the tower, Geoff."

He could only nod, and Jon went back to the controls.

"If I am part of Apollo, why hasn't the sun returned?"
Hades smirked faintly. "Did you ask it to?"
That secret Geoff had told no one. His eyes

found the eastern horizon, opposite the dying moon. What would it be like, he wondered, to see the faintest spark of color there, the first glimmers of light? It could be spectacular. Or disastrous. They were a world built on darkness. Could they survive the return of the light?

That's a decision for later. Let's survive the night first.

It was hard to discern their location high above the smog bank. Even the elegant spire of Olympus Tower was lost somewhere in the clouds. Reluctant as they all were, it was decided that they would have to descend again for their final approach.

"Let's hope the folk on the ground have her undivided attention, or this will be the shortest offensive in history."

With cumbersome gas-masks affixed to their heads again, the airship began its descent.

They broke through the smog to the tune of the dynamo engine's wheezing protests. The entire deck shuddered, resisting the pilots who fought to make the damaged vessel obey. Jon's arms bulged as he forced the levers into place, aiming toward the brightly shining clock tower. They'd come out nearly where Jon and the others had planned, and if the ship would just hold together for a few more moments, they'd be able to anchor to the tower itself.

"Are you sure there's an entrance up here?" Geoff asked once he yanked his mask off again.

Fons answered in place of Jon, who was fighting to bring the ship to heel. "We've all seen the workmen up here repairing things. They didn't climb up the outside."

Geoff might have said more, but someone yelled "Brace yourselves!" He barely had time to make a grab for the portside railing.

Olympus Tower loomed suddenly large, and the entire ship groaned and screeched as the untrained pilots scraped it down the wrought-iron-railed walkway. With a scream of tortured metal, a good section of railing was ripped away, bashing down the length of the tower to smash on the ground below. The ship shuddered to a halt and the dynamos whined plaintively as they were powered down.

"Lost Lord of Tartarus! She knows we're coming now for sure, boys!" That earned a general laugh, but Geoff could hear the tension underneath. The chance to back out was long past.

They lashed the airship to the top of the tower as quickly as they could, but even as they began to file onto the damaged catwalk, the entire building shook and every man had to grab for something stable.

"Didn't think we hit it that hard," Jon murmured, and the rebels cast worried looks amongst themselves. Having Olympus Tower fall on their heads was not a pleasant thought. "Better give me that bow, Geoff. We may not have time to get ready, once we're inside."

Geoff handed over the precious weapon, and felt suddenly shaken without the strong wood to support him. Or, it could have been the tower itself; it continued to tremble like a frightened child as the men clambered onto the catwalk in search of an entrance.

They were perfect targets, silhouetted against the glowing face of the tower clock, had anyone bothered to look up. But even from their very great height, Geoff could see the battle raging in the square below. The rebels were pushing inexorably forward, and there was no doubt that there were more people down there than had left Shameless Row. Their makeshift army was growing.

The clock shook again, and one of the massive iron hands slid one notch downward. Another ten minutes, and the hand would sweep them right off the walkway. *Oh hurry...*

"Here!" One of the veterans, a man named Aster, pried at an almost invisible seam in the clock face. "There's no handle from the outside."

"Then we make one."

There was some careful shuffling as men with picks clambered past their comrades on the single-file catwalk. At Jon's nod, they laid into the door. These were men accustomed to breaking solid rock with only their own strength. The door, made of flimsier stuff, crumpled almost immediately. They wrenched the mangled metal out of the way, tossing it off the side. As if in retaliation, another tremor shook the tower, threatening to pitch them over the rail, too.

"Inside. Keep your eyes open and move quick."

One by one, they disappeared through the doorway, following Jon. Geoff was the last to leave the rickety walkway, leaning heavily on his single crutch.

The source of the tower's increasingly violent tremors became clear as they entered the clock room. What once must have been an intricate network of walkways and scaffolding now hung in disarray, entire sections hanging drunkenly from one or two bolts. The floor, at least two stories below them, was littered with the remains of the catwalks, twisted metal and shattered wood providing a dangerous nest for any who fell.

The catwalk jerked beneath their feet, knocking most of them to their knees.

"Darkest night, look!" Young Stan nearly upended himself over the railing to point at something beneath them. The catwalk swayed dangerously as they all leaned to see.

At first glance, it appeared to be a man and a woman, caught in ardent embrace. Pressed against the wall of the tower, they seemed oblivious to the destruction around them, bodies pressed tight to each other. Only when the woman leaned back did they see the blood, flecking her pale skin, trickling from cuts on his face. A face Geoff knew too well.

"Heracles…" Even as he whispered the name, the woman – Artemis, he knew her now – wrenched her hands free from the big warriors grip and attacked him again. The pair lurched off the wall and into the debris, slamming hard into the great silver pillar in the middle of the room.

"Lookit…he ain't even fighting back…"

Artemis savaged the target of her ire, nails rending as surely as claws, drawing blood with every swipe, and yet Heracles only defended himself in the most perfunctory way, and never once struck back. The goddess didn't have a single mark upon her.

As they watched in horrified fascination, the huntress fastened her hands about the warrior's massive throat and began to squeeze, screaming out her rage. All too quickly, Heracles' face turned dark, body starved for the air she was denying him.

Help him… "Help him." The men looked at Geoff like he'd lost his mind, but he fixed his eyes on Jon. They'd follow Jon. "He saved my life, please help him." There was no need to tap into that coil of power in his chest. The mechanic simply nodded.

"Find that arrow, Geoff."

A tall order to say the least. He wasn't even sure where to start looking.

The invaders crept gingerly down the half-fallen

stairs, Jon carrying the bow on his back to free his hands. Artemis, intent on throttling her one-time bodyguard, seemed oblivious to her impending danger as they picked their way over the mangled catwalks.

Even knowing he should be following them, should be going to search the tower for the one tiny thing that could give them an advantage, Geoff could not tear his eyes away from the scene below.

The men approached from behind, picks and pipes held ready. Jon hefted a borrowed weapon, shifting his weight back in preparation for the forward strike. Geoff's breath caught in his throat, a part of him still wanting to yell "No!" even as the pick flew forward.

Impossibly fast, the goddess whirled, dropping her near-unconscious victim and catching the strike against the palm of her hand. Everything froze for a horrifying moment, and Artemis smiled. There was nothing even remotely human in her eyes. They were the cold, dead eyes of a predator, the likes of which the world had not seen in more generations than it could count.

She tilted her head to the side, eyeing Jon up and down like so much meat. "You have something that belongs to me."

She was going to kill him. Geoff could feel it deep in his stomach, sense the movement that had only birthed itself in Artemis' mind. The muscles in her arm tensed, beginning at her shoulder and moving down into her fingers. Her weight shifted to the balls of her feet, and her knees flexed. All of those things could have taken no more than a split second, but Geoff saw them clearly.

And he used the only weapon he had. *STOP HER!* There was no gentle uncoiling this time. His power burst forth, slamming into the men below and staggering even the goddess herself. His own head felt like it was going to fly apart from the sheer force of it, his silent scream deafening him for a few moments.

They sprang into action before the dazed goddess could recover herself, weapons flying from all directions. With a scream of rage, she threw Jon aside negligently, the big man landing in a tangle of metal and splintered wood. Geoff couldn't even see if the bow remained intact.

"You there! Boy!" The voice startled him, croaking from above, and he tore his eyes away from the vicious battle below.

There was a woman on one of the platforms now hanging precariously from the ceiling. She was blond, and probably quite lovely under other circumstances. Now, her hair hung in matted tangles around her wan face, her skin drawn tight over her cheekbones. Her lips were split and bleeding, and there was a desperate fever to her blue eyes. "You! You are the one!" She clutched the bars of the railing, and Geoff could see the manacles that held her fast, chains attached even higher in the rafters than he could see.

If ever there was a person to be called "the one", he supposed it was him. He nodded, and she smiled ferally. It was disturbingly like Artemis' own grin. "Get up here! What you seek is within reach!" He must have given a confused look, because she jerked against her chains again. "The arrow, fool! Up here!"

"Up here" was a great deal more difficult in practice. The stairs circling the inner wall of the tower had been rattled loose of their moorings in the struggle between Artemis and Heracles, and the current battle below wasn't making anything easier.

Geoff picked his way up the rickety walkways, clinging to his crutch with one hand and the railing with the other. The woman's section of the catwalk was hanging free, a good three-foot gap separating it from the stairs. "Come on! Jump!" she urged. "Hurry!"

He swallowed hard, took a couple of half-running steps, and leaped. The landing hurt, the rough wood skinning already tortured knees and hands, but he didn't have time to even register it. The imprisoned woman was pulling him to his feet already, pointing just above their heads. "There! You can almost reach it from the rail."

"Oh bugger." He could see the slender shaft of wood handing suspended just out of arm's reach. Directly below was the flat top of the pillar, still spinning its tranquil silver circles in the midst of all the chaos.

"Go on! Climb!" The woman pressed him on until she reached the ends of her own restraints.

The platform swayed as he climbed into the tiny rail, barely more than two fingers-width of surface for him to perch on. He held to the suspending rod with one hand as he leaned far out, but could only brush the blackened arrow head with his fingertips. Even that small sensation sent an unpleasant tingle through his flesh. *Poisonous to me too, apparently.*

It was also firmly out of his reach. After a moment's thought, he used his crutch, trying to wind the arrow's cord around the length. Twice it slipped free, and each time Geoff edged out further to try again, spurred on by the blond woman's frantic encouragement.

"Yes, that's it! A bit further…there you are…"

The cord wound around the crutch in three neat coils, and Geoff took a deep breath, offering a prayer to anyone who might happen to be listening. With a sharp tug, the line snapped.

At the same moment, the tower gave a massive shrug, and the platform on which he teetered split neatly in half. The woman clung to her dangling section, spewing curses, and Geoff stared in horror as the line on the arrow came unwound and the delicate shafted dropped.

It clattered across the smooth pillar top and came to rest, balanced at the edge of the center hole.

"Get it! If that falls in there, we are all dead! Grab it you fool!" Even scrambling to keep herself on the crumbling platform, the woman still shrieked orders.

There was no easy way off the swinging remnant of catwalk. Far below, Geoff could see the men still battling with the enraged goddess. She tossed them around like toys, cackling her glee. Too many were down. Too many were not getting up. And the next blow might be the one that jarred the arrow on its way downward. He had no choice.

He let go before he could truly think about what he was doing, dropping the one story height to the top of the metal column. His right knee gave with a sick pop as he landed, sending bright streamers of pain through his vision. Swallowing the gorge that rose in his throat, he slapped a hand over the thin arrow shaft, pinning it in place. *Safe.*

Those below were not so safe. Jon and Young Stan were heading the assault now, but there were only four others aiding them. Jon had dropped the bow at his feet, but at least he still had it. Artemis seemed to be everywhere at once, parrying multiple attacks, lashing out with vicious blows between. At the base of the pillar, Heracles had once again struggled to his feet but remained hunched over in pain.

"Jon!" There was no time for subtlety. If she heard him, so be it. The mechanic's gaze darted about the room, looking for the voice yelling his name. "Jon, up here!" Geoff waved the arrow to get his attention, saw the moment Jon realized what he had.

Artemis realized it too. With a bestial howl, she made a dive for the base of the pillar, clawing at the mirrored surface in her efforts to reach Geoff. Without warning, Heracles barreled into her again, sending them both sprawling into the wreckage.

"Here! Throw it here, Geoff!" Jon held out his hand.

An arrow was not meant to be tossed like a spear, but the injured man did his best. It arced limply through the air, nearly fumbling from Jon's fingertips at the end. The big man's face was grim beneath the dirt and blood as he fitted the shaft against the bowstring.

Even so far above them, Geoff could hear the wood creaking as Jon drew the weapon, taking aim at the trashing forms of Artemis and her bodyguard. And lying atop the pillar, Geoff could do nothing but watch.

There came the moment where Artemis reared up, back to the humans. Heracles held her hands trapped, muscles straining to keep her from clawing his eyes out. And Jon released the string.

It happened so fast. The arrow streaked across the room toward Artemis' unprotected back. Heracles' eyes went wide, seeing the danger. With a great heave, he threw the goddess aside, rising to take her place. There was a wet thud as the arrow found a home deep in the warrior's chest. The force of it knocked him off his feet, taking Artemis to the ground with him.

No one moved. No one so much as breathed.

From his height, Geoff could see the look of startlement on Heracles' face and the creeping edge of black corruption that appeared at the edge of his shirt, moving up his neck like insidious black vines.

Artemis fought her way out from underneath the fallen warrior, only to stare horrified as he fought for wet gurgling breaths in front of her. "Heracles…" He grabbed her by the wrist, dragging her to her knees beside him, blood trickling from the corner of his mouth as he tried to say something.

The goddess smoothed his hair almost tenderly, leaning down to better hear him.

The demigod's hoarse whisper carried to Geoff's ears. "Until my death…"

In a flurry of movement, Heracles' free hand came up, capturing a handful of Artemis' hair, yanking her head down to press her lips against his. Artemis jerked in surprise, but could not escape the dying warrior's grasp, even when the dark poison clouded his face, moving across his lips and onto hers. Her struggles grew more frantic then, but Heracles' last act was to hold fast, and she was locked in the poisonous kiss.

The corruption spread over her pale cheeks, down her slender throat, blackness claiming her inch by painful inch. Her arms turned black down to the tips of her fingers which split like ripe fruit. At the last, she screamed, thrashing violently, her feet drumming panicked tattoos against the marble floor. The scream died away to a strangled moan, thick with noxious fluid, and then they were both still.

Was that it? Was there no more to the death of a goddess? Geoff stared in sick horror as the bodies rotted away before their very eyes, putrefying and dissolving into viscous puddles. Even their clothes succumbed, leaving behind only bits of metal here and there, the jewelry and fripperies of a now-dead era.

Jon broke the silence first. "Stan, check the wounded, see what can be done. Fons, how's the bleeding?"

Slowly, the last remnants of the rebel party began to stir, to see who was still amongst the living. Geoff rested his head against the silver pillar, noting that it seemed to echo with the throbbing of his broken knee.

"You there! The big man on the floor!" The blond woman yelled down to Jon, and Geoff turned his head minutely to watch. He'd all but forgotten about her, but there she still dangled, half supported by the shattered catwalk, and half suspended from her own manacles. "For the love of all that is decent, get me down!"

Down. Yes, down would be good. But until they figured out how to fetch Geoff from atop his perch, he thought he would just rest his eyes. Just for a few minutes.

Chapter 24

Geoff had a vague memory of being removed from the top of the world pillar, supported by someone's strong arms. They could have dropped him into the Factory slag pits after that, and he wouldn't have cared. He was so very tired, and the pain in his knees had resolved itself into a high-pitched whine in his ears, drowning out all else.

When he woke, he was in a bed large enough that he could stretch his arms out on both sides and still not reach the edges. The comforter over him was gold satin, as was the strange shirt he found himself wearing. The novelty of that lasted only until he realized someone must have undressed him while he was unconscious, and then embarrassment took over.

The agony in his knees seemed to have settled into its customary ache, and he decided that wherever he was, it wasn't where he wanted to be. He practically swam his way to the edge of the expansive bed and started to get up.

"Oh good, you're awake!"

The female voice called out at the same time that he realized he had no pants. Geoff scrambled to get back beneath the sheets.

The blond woman from the clock tower appeared, carrying a covered tray. "I thought you might be hungry." She looked better. Her tattered gown had been exchanged for something in a vibrant green, and her hair had been pinned up in neat whorls atop her head. She was still pale, showing signs of her imprisonment, but on the whole, she looked lovely.

Setting the tray on the table beside the bed, she seated herself in a plush chair next to it. "I wasn't certain what you'd like, so I brought a bit of everything."

The smell set off a humiliatingly loud growl in his stomach, reminding him just how long it had been since he'd had anything of substance. *The bread on the River Styx.* "How long did I sleep?"

"Barely four hours, once they got you down. It's just past First Light now." She rubbed her own wrists, still bruised from her manacles. "They had to fetch Hephaestus himself to free me."

"He…is he angry? With us, I mean. For Artemis." They'd killed her. Dark and light, they'd killed the goddess.

The blond woman chuckled softly. "I hardly think so. There was no love lost there. He's promised to stay on, run the Factory until he's no longer needed. Or until the sickness takes him."

Geoff rubbed his fingertips together, feeling the smooth skin where he'd touched the arrowhead, even briefly. The normal ridges of his prints had been seared right off. "What happened to the arrow?"

"Sealed away for the moment. Your Jon has a talent for thinking under pressure. He'll make a good leader." She pressed a cup of hot tea into his hands. "Eat. Drink. You need to replenish yourself."

Obediently, he sipped at the cup to give himself time to think, and found that he was indeed parched. Jon, as a leader… What had been happening while he slept? He opened his mouth to ask, and found himself the target of a glare.

"I mean it. Eat. I will talk, and you will learn what has taken place in a few short hours."   She rose, walking to the windows to look out over Elysia.

Since she wasn't looking, he grabbed one of the meatrolls of the tray and stuffed it into his mouth whole. It was possibly the best thing he'd ever eaten. Much better than anything they'd ever had at the Market, even if he hadn't been starving.

"Your…army has fortified positions within the tower. All of the Hunt has either been exterminated, or is being pursued even now. Most of them simply lay down and stopped fighting upon her death.

"Word has already started to spread through the upper wards. People know Artemis is dead. They're drifting into the square in small groups, but your Jon has set up a secure perimeter and questions are being handled by someone named Fons. So far, the wealthier part of the populace seems a bit numb. Those from the lower wards, they're celebrating or being drafted into service. There will be some sort of government in place shortly, or I miss my guess."

Geoff allowed himself to savor a flaky pastry, flavored with some sort of rich jelly. "All this in four hours?"

She cast a small smile over her shoulder. "It took them nearly two to get you and I down. So, six hours. But yes, your Jon moves quickly, and the others seem to follow him easily. He's even assigned you a guard detail. He seems to think you're important."

He nearly choked on his tea. "I…he…what? No…I'm not."

That earned him a laugh. He got the feeling it was the first time she'd laughed in a very long time. "I beg to differ. I am quite aware of what you are. Anyone would be, after the display you put on. We have waited a very long time for someone like you."

Geoff nibbled at his breakfast, watching her thoughtfully. "You're Persephone, aren't you?" She inclined her head with a small smile. "I've met your husband."

"I hope to be seeing him very soon myself."

"I'm surprised you've not gone already."

"Well, there was the small matter of me being chained in the tower." Chuckling, she returned to his bedside. "And then I thought I'd see what I could do for the wounded. Including you."

"You fixed my knees?"

She frowned. "As best I could. Unfortunately, there is simply a flaw in their making. They'll never be whole, I'm afraid. I am sorry."

"Don't be. I'm not." Hadn't he spent his whole life proving that there was nothing he couldn't do, whole legs or no?

She smiled, patting his shoulder. "Do you feel up to a bit of an excursion? Mother would very much like to see you."

The thought of the Lady Demeter brought a smile to his own face. "I would like to see her, as well." The feel of satin against his legs reminded him of his pants-less condition, and he felt color come to his face. "If you'll excuse me while I dress?"

"Of course. There is clothing in the wardrobe that should fit."

A short bit later, Geoff was dressed, albeit in finer clothing than he had ever owned himself. The black trousers were of fine fabric, and his shirt was no doubt silk. He'd managed to find a vest that had very little extravagant embroidery, but even then there was a subtle weave within the deep gold fabric itself that gave it a rich air. He felt like an imposter, pretending to be more than he was. Persephone nodded her approval when she saw him.

"Well, you're a bit broader in the shoulders than I realized, but the fit is better than I'd hoped."

Though she offered him a wheeled chair, he opted to walk with the single crutch they'd recovered from the clock tower's wreckage. The moment he stepped outside the door, two men in the hallway straightened and thumped their fists over their hearts in a kind of salute.

Geoff had never seen either of them before in his life, and gave Persephone a questioning – and uncomfortable – look.

She chuckled, linking her arm through his free one. "They take their duties very seriously. Be gracious."

It was hard to be gracious when all he wanted to do was crawl into a mineshaft and hide. As the small party proceeded downward through the tower, Geoff received quite a few of the odd salutes from total strangers. Some of them were obviously servants in the tower itself, uniforms neatly pressed. Others had seen fighting below, and were bandaged and hobbling. All of them smiled to see him pass.

"Do they all know?"

Persephone squeezed his arm, in what he thought was supposed to be a comforting gesture. "They know that you were with the group in the tower. The liberators, they're being called. Only five survived, counting you."

The thought made him want to squirm. He didn't want to be anyone's hero.

The moist air in the Greenery was not nearly the surprise it had been at his first visit, and he took a moment to simply breathe deep. He could sense the water all about him, filling the pipes, raining down on the hungry plants, coursing through the green veins. How had he missed all of that before?

They'd only gone a few steps before the drones appeared, chattering and scampering about joyfully. "Say she come! Happy happy she! Happy happy we!" They were almost childlike in their celebration, each of them pausing in their capering to touch Geoff's hands, his arms, gently urging him into the depths of the immense greenhouse.

Demeter's throne had been moved into the spinning room, a place where millions of caterpillars incessantly produced the threads of fine silk that made up Geoff's shirt. A few gossamer strands had drifted into her hair, giving her a silvery halo over her purple-black tresses. The guards took places at the doorway, careful not to intrude.

Persephone released Geoff's arm, allowing him to approach and offer a bow to the silent goddess. "Lady Demeter. I am glad to see you well."

"Say she, happiest of days." A drone appeared at his elbow, apparently the chosen translator. "Say she, free she. Free we."

"Of course you are. You are welcome to stay here as long as you want, of course, but we would never force you." Geoff felt comfortable making that promise without consulting anyone else. If they didn't like it, they could go stick their head in the gears.

"Say she, stay. Teach. Much to give."

"We'll need it, my lady. And we thank you." He bowed again, growing more accustomed to the gesture every time he made it.

"Say she, gift in return?"

"Anything. Darkness, there isn't enough we could give you." He could have been mistaken, but he thought a faint smile curved the alabaster woman's lips.

Another drone appeared, leading the biggest hound Geoff had ever seen. The creature was black as night and day, and walked with the slightest of limps. Geoff froze, waiting for it to spring at him, but it only watched the small gathering with a weary stoop to its massive shoulders.

"Say she, care for him. Say she, mistreated too long."

Geoff gave Persephone an alarmed look. "The Hunt was set on my scent. Won't he just attack?"

The blond goddess knelt at the dark hound's flank, running her hands over the ebony fur. "He is not like the others. And he has suffered more than any of us, these long, bleak years. He will be a protector for you, invulnerable and immortal. Until the end of your days, you will be safe, and your children after you."

"Immortal?"

Persephone rested her head on the dog's shoulder, the creature leaning into her with an almost sad sigh. "Once, he was the god Ares, the proudest warrior of us all. Once, we might have restored him to his true form. But our strength fades, and I fear these centuries may have broken his mind. Best to leave him with someone who will care for him, who will offer him kindness." Her gaze found Geoff's face, pleading. "You would do that, wouldn't you?"

He couldn't kneel, not without serious difficulty, so he merely bent, offering his hand to the wide muzzle. The dog sniffed his palm, and Geoff tensed, waiting to feel those white fangs sink into his hand. Instead, the wide pink tongue gave him one swipe, and the tail wagged once, feebly. Geoff nodded. "He's welcome for as long as he's willing to stay."

The drones set up a pleased chatter, and Geoff knew he saw Demeter smile that time, no matter how briefly.

"Gah, what's all this noise? Like a flock of magpies in here." The black hound bristled, moving to press against Geoff's leg protectively as someone walked from the clutter of web-strewn frames.

The Lord of Tartarus had chosen his brunet form, beard and hair neatly groomed. Even his clothing had settled into dark trousers and a deep red shirt.

"Hades!" Persephone threw herself into her husband's arms, and he plucked her off her feet to hold her close.

Geoff blushed, looking away from the tender reunion, trying not to hear the murmured endearments that had waited millennia to be exchanged.

"I would have been here sooner, my heart, but there was a wall that wanted taking down."

Persephone laughed. "What is a small delay when we have eternity before us?"

Geoff busied himself with petting the hound before he remembered just who resided inside that furry body. The dog leaned harder against him, almost enough to knock him over, inviting more attentions with a contented noise in his throat. Apparently, he liked it.

"How can I ever repay you for this?" When Hades spoke to him, he finally turned around. The dark god held his wife in his arms, her head cradled against his shoulder.

Geoff shrugged. "I've only done what you

created me to do, yes?"

Hades shook his head. "No. You are your own man, Geoffroi of the muses. At any time, you could have chosen a different path, and so I must say thank you. What may I give you in return for restoring my beloved to me?"

Geoff sighed wearily, leaning on his single crutch. "I just want to go home. That is all I have wanted since the moment they snatched me from Deeptown. Please, just…let me go home."

"Excuse me, sir?" One of the guards had entered, giving Hades and the ebon hound equally startled looks, but returning his gaze to Geoff. He thumped his fist over his heart again, much to Geoff's embarrassment. "There is a woman at the front perimeter asking to see you, sir."

"A woman?" Only one woman would ever ask for him, but it was almost too much to hope.

"Yes sir. She is most insistent. She gave her name as Lia."

Lia! For two seconds, his heart forgot to beat.

Behind him, Hades chuckled softly. "And sometimes, home comes to you."

Geoff found her outside on the steps of the tower, several of the armed rebels keeping her behind the secured barrier. Or perhaps they were merely keeping Keras back, the shifty trader's reputation preceding him. "It's all right, let them in." To Geoff's great surprise, the guards parted on his order, saluting smartly.

Keras gave them a sneer as he passed, jerking the brim of his new hat fiercely. "See there? Told you we were on the list." The disguised god stuck his beaked nose in the air and marched up the stairs. Lia, on the other hand, hesitated, her head tilted in bewilderment.

"I brought her for you, Geoffroi! Thought you might be needing some of the comforts of home." Keras gave him a lecherous, snaggle-toothed grin, until the black hound growled softly. Then, he took one cautious step back. "Interesting friends you keep."

"I thought you were supposed to stay in Tartarus."

He snorted. "They haven't built a Hell yet that can hold me. Though I give it another hour before himself sends Raffa to fetch me. And what a grand chase that'll be!" His eyes positively sparkled beneath the brim of his fedora.

"Come see us, when you can. Please?" That seemed right. The wards just wouldn't be the same without the plucky shyster. "And tell Raffa, too."

"Done and done." Keras glanced over his shoulder and chuckled to himself. "You tend to your girl. It's been a long night for everyone." Whistling a jaunty tune, the god sauntered off, wiggling his fingers at the guards by way of farewell.

Geoff's eyes found Lia's then, where she stood on the stairs, and he offered his hand. Her cheeks were flushed, a look Geoff had come to know as having her dander up. Obviously, the guards had been given the sharp side of her tongue as she waited.

Still, she approached hesitantly, her eyes moving over his grand new clothes and the black hound at his heel in puzzlement. "Geoff? What is happening here? Keras told me…impossible things. And did you know he has a car?"

For long moments, he couldn't answer her. He could only drink in the sight of her, a starving man viewing a feast. She wore the pale yellow dress he loved so much, nothing more than a simple shift that clung to her slender frame. Her hair was pulled up atop her head, tendrils caressing her cheeks and neck. She looked like a mote of long lost sunlight, drifting toward him. "I was so sure I wouldn't see you again." The nightmare of the past weeks seemed distant, even with the evidence of their revolution all around him.

She tilted her head to the side, frowning. "They're saying such strange things about you, Geoff. Is it true? Is she dead?"

"Come here." He leaned on his single crutch, holding his free arm out to her. She came to him slowly, and her reluctance hurt him just a bit. "Please, Lia. Please don't be afraid. I'll just die if you're afraid of me now."

She hesitated just a moment more, then seemed to reach some decision, stepping into his arms. He gathered her close, burying his face in her pale hair, murmuring for her ears alone, "It doesn't matter. None of it matters. What comes from this moment on is all that is important."

Lia leaned back to look into his eyes, and he tried to offer her an encouraging smile. Her own gaze was concerned, and her fingers traced the smooth line of his jaw. "Are *you* all right? That's important."

"I am now." He allowed himself to run his fingers through her beautiful hair, freeing the loose knot so that it spilled over her shoulders. "Marry me."

Lia burst out laughing, shaking her head in disbelief. "*Now* you ask me, you great idiot?"

"I have nothing if not impeccable timing."

"Yes. Of course it's yes. Idiot."

Despite the fact that she had assured him of her answer years ago, he still felt a dizzying wave of relief course through him. Cupping the back of her head, he drew her close and pressed his lips to hers. She melted into the kiss without hesitation, twining her arms around his neck almost fiercely. Geoff dropped his crutch to wrap his other arm around her, and it no longer mattered which of them was supporting the other.

Warm droplets of rain fell down around them, spattering lightly against their faces, their hair, plastering their clothes to their skin. They didn't notice. The unusual shower covered all of Elysia, bathing the city in clear, pure water until it ran in rivers through the cobblestone streets.

And it was a long time before anyone asked the couple to move.

www.ingramcontent.com/pod-product-compliance
Lightning Source LLC
Chambersburg PA
CBHW061016120726
47910CB00006B/1978